THE BROKE

Book One

*Dear Lou,
Thanks, + happy reading
Pete*

Original copyright © 2017 P. J. Blakey-Novis

This edition copyright 2019 P. J. Blakey-Novis

All rights reserved.

ISBN: 1544180993

ISBN-13: 978-1544180991

DISCLAIMER: "This is a work of fiction. Names, characters, places and incidents are products of the author's imagination and are used fictitiously. Any resemblance to actual events, locales or persons, living or dead, is entirely coincidental."

For my Leanne, for believing in my ability, for pushing me to write more and for the endless cups of tea.

ABOUT THE AUTHOR

This is the debut novel from author P.J. Blakey-Novis. Peter lives with his wife and four children in a small town in Sussex, England. As well as being a keen cook and wine enthusiast, Peter has been writing poetry and short stories for almost twenty years. It had always been an ambition to complete a novel and, after many long days hunched over his desk, this has become a reality. An excitement for literature and storytelling has led to Peter now having released a follow-up to The Broken Doll, with a third on the way. P.J. has also released four collections of short horror stories, a horror novella, and a children's book to date.

KEEP UP TO DATE!

More information about the author can be found on his website as well as social media profiles listed below. You can also subscribe to the email mailing list via the website for exciting news about future releases, as well as accessing short stories direct to your mailbox! If you have any comments or would like to just get in touch feel free to email directly at the address below. Happy reading!

Twitter: www.twitter.com/pjbn_author
Facebook: www.facebook.com/pjbnauthor
Instagram: www.instagram.com/pjbn_author
Web: www.redcapepublishing.com/our-authors
Email: redcapepublishing@outlook.com

The Broken Doll: Book One

ONE

Ella was startled by the front door of their one-bedroom, hilltop home opening. She checked the clock on the oven; it was only six-fifteen. Lee never usually arrived home until six-thirty. *Shit,* she thought, in a panic. Dinner wasn't ready, and she knew full-well he wouldn't be happy. Ella took a spoon and sampled a piece of carrot to find that it was still hard. She headed to the living room and found her bulky, slightly balding husband sat in the armchair, the television displaying some game show involving people falling from things, like a comedy version of a medieval gauntlet.

"You're early, honey," Ella said, as pleasantly as she could manage.

"Finished ahead of time. Where's dinner then?" he demanded, giving her a look, which made her nervous. She cautiously informed him that it would be ready in a few moments, at six-thirty, when she had been expecting him. Ella felt that this had come across as a reasonable response, but Lee felt otherwise.

"So, it's my fault?!" His voice began to rise, and he sat up. "I get home ten minutes early from working fucking hard, and that means that you can't even manage to have made dinner? What the fuck do you do all day?! You're useless, you know that? Your job is to keep the house tidy, feed me, and keep me satisfied. You've failed on the first two so far. We'll see how well you do on the third later."

Ella was used to being spoken to in this way. However, that didn't make it any less hurtful. She had spent the morning tidying the house (which never had the chance to get particularly messy), and then spent the afternoon reading until it was time to prepare dinner, ensuring that it would be cooked at the precise time Lee returned. Of course, him being home early would somehow be her fault, but she could not think of anything to say except for 'sorry'.

The Broken Doll: Book One

"I'm sorry baby. Dinner should be ready now. I'll go and bring it to you."

"Don't let it happen again," Lee shouted to her as she headed to the kitchen, then Ella made a mistake. She muttered. It was along the lines of 'well if you'd called to say you'd be early...'. Ella picked up a pan from the hob and turned to drain the vegetables in the sink. As she turned, Lee was standing there, his huge frame looming over her.

"What the fuck did you just say?" his face red, hands shaking with anger.

"Nothing baby. I'm just dishing up your dinner," Ella replied, voice trembling as she began to pour the contents of the pan into the colander. Then there was a searing pain up her right side. The kind of real pain you get when someone twice your size punches you in the kidney. Ella tried to remain standing and keep control of herself, despite the agony and her streaming eyes.

"All I had said was that if you can let me know if you'll be early, I can make sure dinner is ready," she managed, tearfully.

Ella turned to face Lee. His face was full of rage. *Maybe tonight he'll kill me,* Ella thought. This thought did not bring fear with it, or sadness, or relief either. It was more an indifference, as though dying or living this way were the only two options, and it didn't matter which one was forced upon her. The next few minutes were going to hurt, she knew this. It had been a while since he'd done any more than shove her and shout, but she knew all too well it would be only a matter of time. Lee slapped her across the face, hard enough to knock her small frame to the ground.

He screamed at her as she cowered on the kitchen floor, "This is my fucking house! How dare you tell me I need to let you know when I'll be home. I can come and go as I please; you must be hiding something.

The Broken Doll: Book One

What are you scared that I'll walk in on? You're fucking someone aren't you? Dirty whore!"

Ella sat, leaning against a kitchen cupboard, sobbing. "I'm not. I love you. I'm sorry."

Lee crouched down to Ella's level, his face pressed against hers.

"You know that if I find out you've been a slut, I'll kill you," he told her with a whisper.

Ella nodded, without making eye contact with this animal she had married. "I promise you, I have never betrayed you, and I never would."

"Well, you'd better fucking not! Now bring me the bloody dinner and stop moping about, you should be happy your husband's home!" Ella began to get herself up, but Lee gave her a kick to the ribs (without his work boots on, thankfully) and then sat back in his chair. Ella concentrated on not crying and got herself some codeine tablets to take the edge off. Both of her sides were in a lot of pain from the kick and the punch, and she could feel her left eye starting to swell from the slap. Gradually, she got the meal together and brought it to Lee. He rarely complained about the food and, other than telling her to go back and get some salt, he tucked in and stared at the television. *I guess I live to see another day,* Ella thought, as she tried to get comfortable on the sofa. *At least I might get to the end of my book.* Whatever this was on the television was mind-numbing, but Ella wasn't allowed to do anything else yet; she had to have 'time together' when Lee returned home from work. Once, she had tried to read whilst he watched a program but the sound of turning pages had irritated him, and she couldn't handle any more bruises, at least until these had gone. Ella's mind wandered; she thought of the garden and how, now that spring was almost here, it would be nice to make it more presentable, to have somewhere to read during the summer. She then wondered if she'd survive until summer but didn't dwell on it, her life was no longer her own to control; it hadn't been for the last six years, anyway. She wondered what lives were like for other twenty-four-year-olds, some still partying every night, some with children and jobs. She thought about how quickly, and completely, she had fallen for Lee, and now could see it for what it was; an eighteen-year-old girl having a crush on an older 'bad boy' who had a car and some money. *My God, if only I could go back in time and warn myself. Although I'm sure I wouldn't have listened.* Ella's thoughts drifted back to the garden as she planned what she would like to plant.

"Tea?" Natasha asked her husband.

"Go on then," he replied. Seb and Natasha busily moved around their kitchen; she set the table for dinner, whilst he concentrated his efforts on the various pots bubbling away on the hob. It was a noisy environment but not in a bad way. The radio was on, a weak attempt to drown out the sounds of their three offspring stomping through the house.

"I think they are playing with the Nerf guns," Seb commented.

"Sounds more like they're pretending to be elephants," Natasha replied.

"Roll on bedtime!" they declared in unison. They were both well practiced in organization and routine, something they firmly believed to be important for children. Some told them that they were too strict, but they preferred to think of it as ensuring the children didn't grow up to become little arseholes.

"Time for a ciggie before dinner?" Natasha asked.

"Of course, I'll just turn the hobs down," Seb replied. After a quick cigarette, Seb mashed the potatoes and plated it up with a pork chop each and a pile of greens for all but one.

"I'll stick some beans in the microwave for Mr. Fussy Knickers," Seb muttered, half to himself. Their eldest, Steven, was ten and appeared to be terrified of vegetables and any meat which wasn't chicken. The pork chops would be an experiment.

"DINNER!" shouted Natasha. After a half-second pause came a stampede down to the kitchen (which lies at a level below ground), and the three children came barging through with flailing elbows to take their seats.

Seb and Natasha absolutely loved the idea of dinner at a dining table, all together, as a family. Which is why they did exactly that, virtually every day. The reality of it was a little less idyllic, featuring a tirade of commands from the parents, including 'elbows off the table', 'use your cutlery', and 'don't talk with your mouth full'. All the words the parents uttered went completely unheard, and the three mini versions of themselves tucked into dinner whilst spraying ketchup everywhere, eating pork chops with their hands and explaining how homework is boring whilst flicking beans at each other.

"What's for pudding?" Steven enquired, tactically. He asked every time, as this information allowed him to weigh up whether it was worth finishing his dinner for. No pudding if you can't eat dinner.

"There's some chocolate cake, or ice cream," Natasha told him. Steven picked at the pork, studying it intensely.

"It's chicken," Seb informed him, rather hopefully, whilst trying not to get annoyed by the fussiness.

"It's a funny colour," Steven pointed out. "I'm full anyway." He was obviously not, but it's fine; he knows that there won't be anything later if he gets hungry. Eventually, the younger two children finish their dinners and ice cream, head off to clean teeth and

The Broken Doll: Book One

faces, and then get their pyjamas on. Steven made his way to his room and his beloved Xbox.

Natasha began to clear away, putting pans and cutlery into the dishwasher. Seb watched lovingly as Natasha began washing up the items unsuitable for the machine, thinking back to when they were first together, when he would grab her at the sink, and they'd end up having sex on the work top. She still looked gorgeous and he genuinely considered himself lucky to have her. He walked up behind her and squeezed her bottom.

"Bit rude," Natasha said, playfully.

"I can be a lot ruder than that my love," Seb replied. "Maybe I can demonstrate later once the little angels are asleep?"

"That's very sweet darling. I'll think about it. That's not a yes, just to clarify! It's a maybe."

"I'll make another ciggie," Seb offered, a little deflated. After their cigarette and clearing up from dinner, Natasha poured them both a gin and tonic, something which was turning into an almost daily habit.

"We'll have this and then tackle stories and bedtime," she informed her husband. "What are you doing tomorrow? Seb was self-employed and worked mostly from home, trading online in used items which he kept in a lock-up a few roads away. Although his profession sounded 'a bit Del-Boy', he had developed a talent for finding bargains, delivering most items himself and turning a good profit on most weeks.

"I'll take the dog out in the morning once they've gone to school; it's meant to be sunny tomorrow. Then I need to be at the lock-up as I've got two Chesterfield sofas coming between eleven and one. Not much other than that. What about you?" Seb asked.

"I can do the school run if you'd like? I'm going for a coffee with Jo straight from the school. I need to pick up some bits from the town then I'll be home before lunch, so we should have the afternoon together."

The gin tasted amazing but was interrupted by cries of "he shot me in the eye" coming from the living room.

"Sounds like bedtime," Seb suggested.

"FIVE MINUTES!" Natasha shouted in the direction of the living room. No response came from the children, of course, and Seb and Natasha took the opportunity to squeeze in another gin and tonic before having to read any stories about talking fire engines, or fairies with wardrobe disasters.

What's he up to now? wondered Ella. Lee had received a text message and then disappeared into the bedroom without saying anything. A moment of dread passed over Ella as she thought, perhaps, he was getting undressed and was going to summon her to bed. She used to love sex, but it had become an obligation, and needless to say that it was completely aimed at satisfying Lee. She no longer remembered the last orgasm she had had that wasn't when she was alone, imagining a stranger's tongue inside her (something Lee would never do but, of course, he expected her to go down on him). She began to feel sick. She was bruised on her sides and back; one eye was swollen, and the other puffy from crying. The last thing she wanted now was that ogre hopping on with his big hands and smaller-than-average member.

Lee emerged from their bedroom in jeans and a shirt; the smell of cologne was noticeable from across the room.

"I'm going down the King's Head," he told her. *Oh, thank God!* Ella thought.

"OK baby, love you," was all she could think to say, for fear of saying the wrong thing. Then he was gone, just like that, no 'I love you' in return, no peck on the cheek, not even a 'goodbye'.

For a while, Ella just sat on the sofa, too exhausted and bruised to move. She really didn't know how to feel. He was out again. A large part of her, understandably, wanted to be as far away from him as possible. Nevertheless, he was her husband, and she wanted their marriage to be a good one. She wondered whether he was really going to the King's Head and who he was meeting. It had been months since they had been out together; he never asked her to come with him anymore. She felt a pang of jealousy as she considered that he might be meeting another woman. *Maybe he's having an affair?* she thought. *Do I really care if he is? It keeps him out of the house, and if he's screwing her, then it's one less job for me to have to do.* Ella couldn't think about it properly. She had never believed that you could truly love and hate the same person at the same time, but it seemed that she may have been wrong. Ella got herself up from the sofa (with a lot of groaning) and went to the bathroom to inspect her injuries. Her face didn't look as bad as it felt, slightly swollen and red, but not bruised. She lifted off her dress and stood in front of the bathroom mirror in her bra and knickers. Her back looked red, and there was some bruising to her side from the kick. *Not as bad as some of the times before,* she thought. Ella fancied a hot bath but was too tired and sore, so decided to go and read while she had the opportunity.

In the kitchen, a room which Lee wasn't very well accustomed as he viewed it as 'the woman's room', Ella reached to the back of a cupboard full of what would be best described as junk. The sort of things all kitchens accumulate but rarely need; garlic crusher, broken tin opener, pastry cutters, and old Tupperware boxes. In one of these Tupperware boxes, hidden down the back of the cupboard's shelf, were Ella's tobacco and rolling papers. A small pouch would last her a week, a luxury she managed to skim off the top when she did the weekly food shopping. Thankfully, Lee never checked the receipts, and she never kept any more money for herself, so he never became suspicious. Lee would not allow Ella to smoke cigarettes or drink alcohol, and any drugs were a big no-go. These were 'unladylike', and therefore these rules only applied to her, and not him.

Over the last couple of years, Ella and Lee's marriage had changed. She looked back and could see that, even from the outset, he had had control of her. This hadn't been a problem at the time as she was younger, and it was nice to be taken care of, provided for, and so forth. She had hardly noticed that she had gradually lost contact with the few friends she still had after leaving school, and she didn't take much persuasion to reduce visits to her mother's. 'Mother' was a loose term in this case; she hadn't been particularly horrible or abusive but was just simply not interested. Ella had been free to do as she pleased from a young age and was virtually fending for herself by the age of ten. Through Ella's teenage years, her mother showed no interest in her schooling or personal life, but was civil, as if accepting a financial burden that would, no doubt, soon move out. Ella had never worked; all the dreams of years ago about teaching or writing quickly vanished as Lee was a traditional breadwinner and Ella's role within the marriage was the somewhat outdated ideal of a 1950's housewife, to be seen and not heard. So, Ella contented herself with keeping their small home up to a good standard and reading a lot of books, spanning many genres. She daydreamed about writing her own stories but only managed short tales. In the beginning, these were romantic tales, and later, more depressing in nature. As it is so often the case in a relationship where one partner is hugely dominant, the level of control reached a point where Ella had little access to money, had no contact with family or friends, and rarely left the house. Lee's drinking became more frequent, usually when he'd been on a stressful job, and this made him aggressive. Minor issues became huge as he looked for reasons to argue. Ella quarrelled back, and this led to pushing, escalating to full-blown violence.

Ella remembered the first time he'd hit her. He'd been drunk when he had come home, and Ella wasn't in. It was the middle of summer and an especially warm day, so she had visited the library, borrowing a book by one of her favourite authors, the kind of book that takes ten years to write and is a masterpiece in its own right. This was early afternoon and she had decided to take a detour to sit by the river on her way home, planning to read the first chapter. This turned into her reading the first half of the book and then rushing home in a panic about preparing dinner on time. She was too late, of course, and Lee went ballistic. He had accused her of having an affair, not showing him respect, being a terrible wife, and so she told him to "stop being such a dick!" Then he hit her, hard, in the face, and walked out. She cried for hours, immediately scared of this man, and with no-one to talk to about it. The relationship had steadily worsened from that day and now there was barely a thread. As much as Ella didn't want to give up on the marriage, there was nothing worth saving either, although she could see no escape from it except death, and it didn't really matter whether that was hers or his.

She rolled the cigarette and went out to the garden. She felt a tingle of excitement as she lit it, knowing that it was an act of rebellion, but at the same time she was certain Lee wouldn't be back until the pub closed.

Natasha clicked the kettle on and looked at her watch. It was not quite seven-thirty, pretty good going to have all three children in bed; two busy snoring and dribbling, one reading yet another Dr Seuss book. Their daughter, May, was six and would happily spend all her time alone, reading. Bedtime had always been difficult with her, however, and it was now routine that they say goodnight and let her sit in bed with a book until she falls asleep. Seb made his way down to the kitchen.

"Now what?" he asked, "TV?"

"I don't mind darling," Natasha replied. "What do you fancy?"

"I'd go for another gin and tonic, something short on the telly, then take your clothes off on the sofa," Seb replied, trying to sound both seductive and demanding, whilst trying not to convey any hint of begging or desperation.

"You, Mr. Briggs, are a very naughty man. The sofa is too squeaky, but the gin and TV sounds good."

"Fine... you can be naked when we go upstairs then my love," Seb suggested, trying to hide his disappointment after having envisaged turning his wife around on the sofa and taking her from behind, thus getting himself a little excited.

"Just sleep tonight baby, I love you," Natasha hoped that this wouldn't cause Seb to get moody, but they had been at it most days for the last couple of weeks and he had no cause for complaint. "So, gin?" she asked.

"If you want," Seb mumbled and headed up to the living room. *Men!* Natasha thought to herself. *Guess I'll make the gin then!*

After almost an hour of some awful television show where rich tossers bang on about wanting to build mansions in the countryside, thereby destroying the views and local ecosystems in order to create a 'dynamic space' (whatever the fuck that is), and two large gin and tonics, Seb was fairly sure that he wouldn't be getting any action that night. He tried to snap himself out of his growing bad mood.

"Think I might go for a run," he announced.

The Broken Doll: Book One

"Now?" she asked, a little surprised. He would go for runs some evenings, but never after dinner and having had a drink. She could tell he had been a bit off since telling him there was no entry tonight, so maybe it was for the best.

"OK baby, you look hot in your running gear. I love you."

"Love you too," Seb told her. *If I looked that hot in the running clothes, surely she'd want me,* he thought to himself, a little sulkily.

Seb made another ciggie, thinking that smoking was such a stupid idea, especially when trying to increase one's fitness. He smoked it anyway, and then went to get changed. Once he was in his tight running shorts, top, comfy trainers, and had his phone and headphones set up, he said goodbye.

"I won't be long," he said, a little too loudly over the music already playing in his ears.

It was dark, and the streets were virtually empty. Seb made his way along his road and then turned left, downhill towards the river. It was a good spot, flat and paved, with pleasant views of the boats stretching along to the beach and cliffs. He jogged along for only about five minutes and then sat down. He was out of breath already and felt heavy. *This is why I don't run after a meal,* he thought to himself. *I should probably go back.* The thought of staring at the TV in silence wasn't very appealing, and it was a nice evening, so he decided to walk for a while. His mind drifted on to work, the things he needed to get done in the morning, and the usual mundane thoughts that float about at the end of each day. His life was in a routine. He knew what each day was going to consist of and, mostly, he liked that fact. He loved his job, his wife, and his children. He began to think about how lucky he was, and his mood began to brighten. He changed the music to something a bit more uplifting and happily strolled further along the river, past the lifeboat station, past the little row of shops and restaurants, and along towards the beach. He wondered again about turning back, but he was enjoying being out, alone, with music on and lost in his thoughts. He was blissfully unaware that very soon a chance encounter would completely change his life, affecting everything, and everyone, who mattered to him.

TWO

The sea looked calm from high up on the cliff-tops. Ella had fallen in love with the house as soon as she had set eyes upon it, a little run down and small, but they didn't need much room. The garden was almost as big as the house and the views, well they were incredible. The edge of the garden was no more than one hundred feet from the cliff edge, affording them views over the English Channel and along the south coast for miles to both east and west. From her small garden bench, Ella could see the ferry slowly pulling in and out of the mouth of the river, she could see the concrete arm, outstretched to the west of the sandy beach, a red and white lighthouse standing proudly at the end of it. Further down the cliff-top, to the east, maybe a ten-minute stroll away, was an old fort. The fort had been a key defence during the world wars and was now a tourist attraction. She had only visited it once, on a school trip when she was about fourteen, and it had seemed dull at the time, but now she felt that it would be a wonderful way to pass a day, exploring the tunnels and educating herself a little.

Of course, being England, the weather was usually on the grey side at least, and largely wet regardless of the season. Living in a run-down (for want of a better word) shack on a hilltop during high winds and rain wasn't pleasant, but the feelings that a sunny day would arouse in her made it worthwhile. Lee didn't like the house when they first saw it, and she blames the weather for this. It was blowing a gale that day, and the sash windows were taking a battering. The garden was overgrown and the interior, although in reasonable condition, was hideously decorated. Whoever thought brown wallpaper and orange carpets were acceptable past the 1970s must have been insane. Ella had had little say about their choice of home as she had nothing to contribute financially, the deposit for the mortgage

The Broken Doll: Book One

and the income that the lender looked at were Lee's, something he would remind her of frequently. In actual fact, the deposit was from his parents who didn't seem to care which house he lived in as long as it wasn't theirs, plus Ella and Lee were soon to be married and couldn't very well be living with anyone else. Fortunately for Ella, this was the only place that they could afford so it was agreed upon, and they had moved in.

Lee worked for himself carrying out a range of tasks, based on property renovations and repairs. This proved useful in the beginning, and he had taken up the orange carpets and replaced them with a more tasteful light blue, as well as stripping the wallpaper. These were the only jobs he had carried out in their home, leaving the decorating to Ella. His reasoning being that he does 'that sort of thing all day and didn't want to be doing it when he got home'. *When you get home, you just want to be served dinner before you bugger off to the pub,* Ella had thought, but not dared to say. Fixing up the house gave her a project to do herself, to fill her days as well as giving her access to some money for paints and so forth. Now she was proud of her home; the carpets and furniture were perfectly acceptable, the walls still looked as though they had not long been painted, and everything was cleaner than the average house. She was desperate for a new kitchen as they had never got around to, or been able to afford to, replace the original one. The oven was ancient; it had a broken light and sounded like a plane taking off when you turned it on. The cupboard doors were a bit wonky, and one would swing open on its own. The linoleum was torn in one corner. Nevertheless, it was home, and she could make do. One day, she would approach the subject of fixing it up with Lee. Maybe one day Lee would again be the man she fell for in the beginning, at least she could dream.

Her real pride came from the garden and what she had created in it. It was such a shame she hadn't taken before-and-after pictures. From an overgrown mess, just about penned in by a small, stone wall, containing only a very dilapidated greenhouse, she fashioned her own Garden of Eden. The first thing to go had been the remnants of the greenhouse, which Lee had taken a week to dispose of for her. Then she began pulling up the bushes and weeds, filling garden sack after garden sack with leaves, twigs, and prickles. Her hands were raw and bleeding, but the transformation was becoming clear, and she was thoroughly enjoying herself. Once she had cleared the garden down to bare grass, she had walked back and forth to the beach to fetch stones. This was exhausting, much more so on the way back up. With the stones, she divided the garden into areas for planting, and asked Lee for his credit card to go flower shopping. He had said no, deeming it unnecessary. Even so, she nagged him, and they were still in the early stages of the relationship when he was generally pleasant to her. After an evening that she had been particularly seductive, he relented and the next day she went wild at the home and garden shop. She bought shrubs that would survive the weather. She bought a crazy number of pansies to add colour along the stone borders. She splashed out on a bench (*There is no point having a lovely garden with nowhere to sit*, she reasoned), she added a plastic greenhouse to grow seedlings (an error as this didn't make it through the tiniest breeze), and she got Bob. Bob was a gnome. He was fishing, and it seemed appropriate with the sea views.

I can't get into this Bob, Ella thought as she sat on the bench, struggling through the first chapter of a supposed classic piece of literature. *I can't tell if I'm simply not clever enough for it, or it's just not actually that good.* She put the book down on the bench beside her as she finished her cigarette, gazing out across the cliff-tops which were darkening with the dusk, watching as the shadow of a man half-walked and half-jogged along the path towards her garden. She sat quietly and rolled herself another while she had the chance.

Seb had reached the beach which was almost deserted, apart from a few guys' fishing and drinking beer, and a souped-up Ford Fiesta in the car park, some awful garage music blaring from it, the passenger window down with pungent weed smoke billowing out of it. This was as far as he could go, only water now and then France. He turned to begin the walk home and checked his phone. There was a text message from Natasha. It read 'Hope you're OK honey. I'm heading to bed, see you in the morning xxx.' *Guess I don't need to rush home then,* Seb thought. The message had been sent fifteen minutes ago. *I'd better reply.* He replied with 'Love you, won't be much longer xxx.' Heading back from the beach he passed the turning for the fort, next to which was a path which led through some woodland up to the cliff-top. He paused and considered a route. He could head up to the cliff-top, around past the school and back to his house, probably no more than a thirty-minute walk.

The path through the woods was muddy from the rain which had poured down a couple of days ago, the trees sheltering it from the sun and delaying the drying process. Although the evening was still in half-light, in the wooded area it was really dark, so much so that it caught Seb by surprise. He almost fell over a tree root and decided that he should turn on the torch on his phone. Now able to see, it only took a few minutes to reach the top, and he stopped to admire the view. The sea looked calm; a few ships were dotted about on the horizon, just shadows with flickering red lights. Seb followed the path as it wound along, in some places very near to the cliff edge. He felt alone up there; all was silent and growing darker.

Seb startled a little as a rabbit ran across the path in front of him, its white tail bobbing as it

The Broken Doll: Book One

darted into a tiny hole in the ground. He turned his phone's torch back on for fear of twisting his ankle in a rabbit hole. His mind turned to Natasha; she had not replied to his message. *Perhaps she's already asleep,* he wondered, *or is she annoyed?* He began to wonder whether him going out like that had upset her, but he didn't like the mood he got in when she denied his advances. It was perfectly reasonable for her not to want sex every now and again, and he was pretty certain they had a lot more than any of their friends. Nevertheless, maybe she was right, perhaps he was an addict. He thought about the cravings, how they were similar to the times he had tried to quit smoking and, many years ago, giving up his drug addiction. When they had sex each day (sometimes two or three times in a day, even this far into their relationship) he was happy. If he couldn't have any, even on nights when he was exhausted and couldn't really be bothered himself, he felt irritable and found it hard to sleep. This was the case for the initial two or three nights, then it became easier, just like the first few days without smoking are the hardest. He didn't want it to be a problem, and he could easily see that the issue was with him; he was very fortunate to have such a sexual wife.

It was as he was having these thoughts that he noticed, just to his right, a small red dot. It was hard to tell what it was in the fading light, so he shone his phone in that direction only to realize that it was a woman with a cigarette. She flinched from the glare of the light and, as she turned her head from the beam, Seb could see that her face was swollen and beginning to bruise around the eye.

"Sorry," Seb called out. "I hadn't noticed you there." There was no reply. He took a few steps further along the path then paused. "Are you alright?" he asked the woman. There was still no answer. He kept his light pointing toward the ground in front of him and slowly approached the small stone wall, gradually raising it to illuminate the garden. He'd been past many times and had noticed what a lovely place it looked, often thinking how great it must be to have these views on sunny days.

The light from Seb's phone finally reached Ella, slowly working its way up from her bare feet, her rather attractive legs, and across her pretty green dress. She was holding the end of the cigarette, now burnt down to virtually nothing, and scurried over to the wall at the side of the garden to throw it away. Ordinarily, she would have gone to the far end of the garden, but this man was standing there, and she did not want to talk to him, somewhat due to embarrassment over the state of her face, partly through fear that someone would see and then Lee would find out. The last thing she needed was to be seen talking with another man on the same day that Lee had accused her of being unfaithful. Ella hurried back to the bench to grab her book and went inside, locking the door behind her.

It was difficult to make out the man's appearance in the half-light, but he looked fairly athletic, dressed in something tight, so she assumed he was out for a run. She watched from the kitchen window with the light off as he hesitantly moved on, continuing on the path in his original direction. As soon as he was out of sight Ella made her way to the sofa, sprawling out as comfortably as she could manage, trying to avoid putting pressure on any of her new bruises. After another failed attempt to finish the first chapter of the book, her mind wandered onto the stranger at the wall. From as much as she could tell in the poor evening light, he looked a little older than her, maybe mid-thirties at the most. His figure had been attractive, although she hadn't been able to make out any facial features. She replayed the contact in her head, but this time fantasized about talking to him, telling him about her face, and the details of what had happened. *What would he have said? Would he have called the police? Would he have done something himself or just not wanted to get involved?* Whatever the outcome would have been, Ella couldn't see any way that it would have been a happy result. She tried to push him from her mind and forced herself to keep reading, but the words were hardly sinking in and the pages seemed to take forever to complete. As she had nothing but time, she saw no reason not to keep at it.

Seb continued his walk, a little slower than before, whilst trying to process the situation he had just encountered. A logical man, Seb considered the facts. A woman (a notably pretty one, at that) was sat in (presumably) her own garden with a cigarette. She had grabbed a book on her way back in the house, so it was reasonable to assume she had been relaxing outside on a nice evening reading. Nothing strange so far. What was odd were the marks on her face and her reaction to being spoken to. OK, it was none of his business what had happened to her, and it made sense that she may not want to tell a stranger, but she was clearly hurt. *It's a normal human reaction to check on the well-being of others in a case like this,* he thought. *It's not like I was chatting her up, I'd only spoken a few words.* The injuries to the woman's face were quite clearly inflicted by another person, most likely a man. She seemed frightened, and Seb couldn't decide if this was a fear of men in general or of someone getting the wrong idea about her speaking to him.

His walk home was starting to feel like a long way, and he was lost in his thoughts about this mysterious woman. After going over and over possible explanations, he decided that the only realistic scenario was that she was being knocked about by her boyfriend or husband. Or maybe her dad? Then came the big dilemma: what to do? He went over the options; Option 1, call the police and let them deal with it, Option 2, go and knock on the door and investigate it himself, Option 3, do nothing. There was also the consideration to make regarding why he had hit her. Not that Seb thought it justifiable at all, but maybe they were one of those couples who fight physically when they argue, and they both give it out equally. Or perhaps her ever-loving partner had found her screwing around and lost it, again not acceptable but understandable even so. Something gave Seb the feeling that these were unlikely; she had seemed genuinely scared, which didn't fit all too well with these theories.

Seb was almost home as he considered the implications of each course of action. Option 1 would either result in a police visit when the woman was home alone, and she may well deny any problem, or her partner may be there, and it could lead to her being at further risk from him. Option 2 essentially led to the same possible outcomes. And Option 3 just felt wrong. However, he knew he had to do something to help, if she needed it, and if she didn't, then at least he would know.

THREE

Seb arrived home, well over an hour since leaving. He was surprised to find Natasha still awake, flicking through one of the free food magazines you find at the tills of some supermarkets. The television was on in the background, some supposedly hilarious show featuring clips of people falling off things.

"Hello," Seb greeted his wife. "I thought you would be asleep by now; you didn't reply to my last text. I thought you were heading to bed?"

"Changed my mind," Natasha replied. She looked exhausted, and it felt a little odd that she was still awake. She chucked the magazine over to the coffee table, onto the heap of junk mail and art works the children had created at school and looked up at him. "I thought I'd wait for you. Where did you go?"

"Come up to the bathroom," Seb suggested, "I really need to get in a hot bath then I can tell you all about my adventure."

"Well that does sound interesting," Natasha replied. "I'll get a bath ready for you my love."

"Are you tired?" Seb asked.

"Very, but I missed you this evening and didn't know if you were in a grump when you went out?"

"No darling, just wanted to get outside for a bit, but I'm fine," Seb reassured her. Natasha began running a bath and took a seat on the lid of the toilet whilst Seb removed his trainers and socks, followed by his running clothes. He stood naked in front of her as she eyed his form; regular exercise was certainly making a difference. His belly was almost gone, and he now possessed a rather chiselled torso. His arms were becoming more muscular from weights in the gym a couple of times a week, and those legs! They had been impressive when they had first met, he was a keen walker, but the calves were now solid and there was muscle definition at the tops of his legs too.

The Broken Doll: Book One

"You look good," Natasha told him.

"Do I?" he replied. "I'm all sweaty."

As he walked over to the bath, she glanced at his cock as it hung down. For a penis, it was rather good looking, both width and length were impressive, and he was also circumcised which she found to be a real turn-on, having not experienced this with previous lovers. As he stepped into the very hot bath, she complimented him on his backside.

"Such a cute little bottom," she said. Seb slipped into the water and gave her a smile.

"Feel free to jump in if you like what you see," he said playfully.

"The bath isn't big enough I'm afraid. And I'm pretty sure I just said I'm really tired. Nevertheless, I love you and I honestly do still fancy you like mad. Once I've had a good sleep I'll be more in the mood. Maybe I'll let you pop it in me in the morning." That sounded great to Seb of course, but he wouldn't get too excited as they'd probably oversleep and be rushing around in the morning. It felt nice to be found attractive though, especially as he still found Natasha gorgeous with her curves, tattoos, and such a pretty face. He got very lucky with this one.

Seb lay in the bath, just his face visible over the bubbles. They looked at each other lovingly, both thankful that they had each other, and that they got on well, rarely arguing and, even then, only over trivial things.

"So, you had an adventure?" Natasha prompted. "Are you a secret crime fighter by night? Hope you haven't been out rescuing damsels in distress!" she teased.

"Funny you should say that," he replied. Her face changed slightly as a little pang of jealousy showed itself, suddenly imagining him rescuing a beautiful woman who was ever so grateful and seductive.

The Broken Doll: Book One

"Hmm? Go on."

"Well," Seb began, trying to tell it like an adventure story but consciously not wanting to make light of the situation he had come across.

"I left here on a mild, spring evening, there was little wind and the light was starting to fade." *I should just get to the point,* Seb thought. "Anyway, I jogged along the river, not even as far as the lifeboat house when I realized that jogging after food and gin wasn't a great idea, and I felt a stitch coming on, so I sat for a bit. Then I walked along towards the beach, went to the end of where you can walk to, and saw your text. I began to head back but thought you were going to bed so decided to walk up by the fort and over the cliffs, past the school and around the long way home."

"Sounds like a nice walk, I wouldn't call it an adventure though," Natasha said. "Where's the action then Mr. Superhero?"

"I met a woman," Seb said. "On the clifftop." Seb paused at this point. Natasha took a quick breath in and looked like she was preparing herself for bad news, a confession perhaps. Seb could see in his wife's face that she was a little concerned. He wondered why he had phrased it that way, perhaps he subconsciously took pleasure in making her a little jealous.

"Don't forget I'll remove that beautiful penis and pickle it if you've been a naughty boy, and don't think I'm joking," Natasha warned.

"I know darling. I wouldn't dare." Seb then looked serious. "But you know I wouldn't want to anyway. You really are all I need, forever."

"OK, well I hope so. What happened with this woman? Did you save her from falling off the cliff? Please tell me she was frighteningly ugly."

"Do you know the little house up there? About a ten or fifteen-minute walk along from the fort."

"I haven't been up there for ages darling. You're the one going out being all energetic! However, I know there are a few houses up there, yes."

"OK, well, there is a little one with its garden on the south side, overlooking the sea. It's surrounded by a small stone wall, nice garden. As I passed it, I noticed a woman sitting in the garden. Well, I hadn't noticed her at first. I accidentally shone my light in her direction."

"Accidentally?! You mean you were checking her out by torchlight, and she caught you? You're such a pervert!" Natasha said, smirking a little.

"I saw what was the lit end of a cigarette and shone my light that way, and it was a bit bright so it dazzled her, she turned her head and I saw that she was covered in bruises; someone had given her a real beating. I asked if she was alright, but she ran in the house."

"Then what did you do?" Natasha asked, wondering if he'd entered the house.

"I carried on walking home. She hadn't said a word to me, she looked scared. And now I feel like I should have done something. What do you think?"

"Well if she has been beaten up, then it's a job for the police. It's not your place to get involved really; you can't just knock on the door and save her. Plus, if someone with a temper lives there I doubt they'd be too keen on you showing up and, as much as I love you, you're not very scary looking."

"I did think about calling the police, but it could make things worse for her."

"Maybe, but it's either that or just keep out of it. There isn't anything else you can do. We don't know the situation, and I don't think we should get involved. If you are that worried, then call the police. If not, just forget about it. Also, please tell me she's hideous. It'll make me feel better." Natasha was trying to keep the conversation light and genuinely didn't want

Seb getting involved, partly for his own safety and to some extent, because she didn't want her husband out rescuing other women.

"She looked like Quasimodo with meth mouth," Seb told her. "Frighteningly ugly."

"Maybe that's why she'd been knocked about then," Natasha joked, a little inappropriately. "I'll let you get washed, and I'll go get into bed. Think about the police once you've slept on it."

With that she headed upstairs, Seb got washed, dried himself off, and climbed into bed. Natasha was out for the count as soon as her head hit the pillow, but her husband lay awake for a while longer, thinking about the mysterious woman and what he should do.

Ella was pleased with herself. She had persevered and not only completed chapter one but was now on to chapter four. She still had no idea what was happening in the book and had had to refer to a dictionary several times, but she was getting there. It was almost ten. She didn't know when to expect Lee home, but the pub kicked out at twelve so presumably around then. She had a quick scan of the house to check for any mess or other reasons that Lee would have a tantrum. He was going to be drunk, so everything needed to be in order. The living room was fine; she just puffed up the cushion of his chair. She didn't have the energy to run the hoover over but did manage to wash up a couple of bits in the sink and wipe the kitchen sides down. *With a bit of luck, he'll just stagger through the door and pass out,* she thought.

That small amount of effort around the house caused Ella's injuries to throb a lot more. *I must be due to have some more painkillers,* she told herself and headed back to the kitchen to grab some. She took two with a glass of water and put the kettle on. While the kettle was reaching temperature, she stared at the clock upon the kitchen wall, a rather expensive clock she had picked up years ago when she had bought the garden items. Lee hated it, perhaps because he wasn't as intelligent as Ella and the clock had no numbers. On the other hand, possibly, and quite reasonably, because it was a garish shade of lime green. He had often got confused as to which hour the hour-hand had just passed and now refused to look at it, favouring the clock on the oven for its digital simplicity.

As Ella stared at the clock, she wondered how long it would be before he returned. More importantly, she wondered if she had time for another cigarette without getting caught. She rarely chanced it past ten as she had nearly been busted at ten-fifteen one evening when Lee had returned earlier than usual following some kind of altercation at the pub, the details of which he was reluctant to divulge.

Ella considered texting him. That was about the limit of her mobile phone's functionality, aside from calls of course. It wasn't modern, there was no Internet access or app store. It was essentially a way for Lee to ensure she could be contacted and, to a certain extent, monitored. Lee had full access to the phone, which he checked regularly, paranoid about his wife contacting other men, his own insecurities worsening by the day. However, there was never anything untoward to be found. The only numbers in it were his and a few necessities such as doctor, dentist, library, etc. He had even checked that the numbers stored matched their names by calling each of them. There were rarely any numbers recently dialled, the library maybe every other week if Ella wanted a particular title, but that was all.

Ella was worried about texting him as he didn't like to be checked up on. *How can I word it to find out when he'll be home? It'll just make him suspicious, as if I'm doing something he won't like whilst he's not here. Which I am, but smoking isn't quite as bad as an affair. I don't know if he'd believe me if I said I missed him or,* even worse, wanted him to come to bed with me. And if he did believe that, he'll definitely expect some when he gets home. The thought of sex with her husband made Ella sad. It felt like another unpleasant chore that she had to endure and, particularly with her bruises, something she really wanted to avoid.

The kettle clicked off and she made a chamomile tea, dug out her secret smoking stash, and rolled a thin cigarette. It was now dark outside; a black darkness you only get in the countryside where there is little or no light pollution. Instead of sitting on the bench, she stood in the far corner of the garden to her right. From there she could see the road that led towards the house and would see the lights of a taxi, or a staggering drunk with his phone light on, if Lee were to arrive soon. She just hoped he wouldn't be able to see her stood there, as she was unable to tell how visible she was but guessed that she was fairly safe.

She finished her cigarette quickly and moved inside, tipping half of the tea into the sink and rinsing the mug. She felt hurried, as if she was about to be caught, so went into the bathroom to clean her teeth and rinse with mouthwash. She knew better than to spray a little perfume as Lee would want to know if it was for his benefit (back to the risk of having to have sex), or someone else's (back to the risk of a beating for an imaginary affair).

Ella got herself into bed, struggling to get comfortable. Her mind had flitted back and forth between the book she was struggling to understand and the stranger who had tried to talk to her. *What was it about him that kept him in her mind? Maybe it was a kindness in his voice, something that had been unfamiliar to her for some years.* She daydreamed about him coming back to check on her, fantasizing about having the courage to have a conversation with him. There was nothing sexual to her thoughts, the fantasy of having a pleasant human to talk to was exciting enough. Gradually, she drifted off to sleep, desperately hoping that Lee wouldn't wake her when he came in.

The next morning Seb was awoken by his alarm at six-fifteen. It was Friday, and he could now change it to his weekend alarm. The sun was already creeping through the gap between the curtains as he lay there. Natasha was still fast asleep, her back to him. He peeked under the covers to admire an area of her bottom, which was exposed beneath her nightgown. He remembered her suggestion for a bit of morning sex and considered making a move, but he decided against it as she was exhausted, and it was still early, her alarm not having yet gone off. He should wait, hoping that once she had slept in a while longer then she may be more likely to welcome to his advances. He got himself out of bed and went downstairs. There was silence throughout the house, all three children still sleeping. Seb stood in the kitchen in his slouch bottoms gazing out of the window. *I really must do something with that garden,* he thought, looking at the scruffy bushes and old trellises in need of repair or, more likely, replacement. Seb boiled the kettle but decided against a hot drink, instead tipping orange juice in the blender with a banana and a handful of strawberries. After he had virtually downed the smoothie, he crept back to his bedroom, careful not to disturb Natasha, and chucked on trainers, jeans, and a long-sleeved T-shirt. He grabbed the dog's lead from the peg near the front door and, at the sound of the metal chain lead rattling, Penguin, their chocolate Labrador puppy came bounding towards him.

May had named the dog. She had heard her parents mention that he was a chocolate Labrador and, whilst eating a Penguin chocolate bar, suggested they called the puppy that. It stuck; the boys didn't have anything better to offer, and Seb and Natasha liked the oddness of the name.

Seb and Penguin left the house, into the fresh morning air. It was colder than last night had been, the air still waiting to be warmed by the sun. Although the thought had not been a conscious one, Seb soon noticed that he was heading in the same direction that he had walked on the previous night. His mind returned to the woman he had seen. He wondered how her night had been, whether she was alright or if she had been hurt any more. He thought about Natasha, sleeping peacefully, and felt a little guilty. *Should I be going back past that house? Natasha had said not to get involved.* The route that he was taking, and had taken last night, was a walk which he had taken the dog on many times before. It was perfectly reasonable for him to be going that way again. Even so, it felt a little wrong, as if he had sneaked out while his wife slept, using the dog as an excuse to try to see the woman again. And maybe that is exactly what was happening.

Before he realized it, he had taken the turn-off by the fort and was heading up through the woods. It was almost seven; there were only a few people about, and they were mostly dog-walkers that greeted Seb with a nod or a cheery 'Morning!' He started wondering if he was being a bit stalkerish. She'd probably still be in bed anyway. When Seb reached the clearing on the edge of the wooded area, he sat on the grass with Penguin, looking out to sea.

Ella awoke as sunlight streamed in on to her face and noticed that she was alone in the bed. She had slept through and didn't remember hearing Lee arrive home. *He's probably passed out on the armchair,* she thought. She crept to the living room but there was no sign of him. It didn't take long to glance into the bathroom and kitchen and quickly understand that he didn't come home last night. It was unusual for him to stay out like this. Ella clicked on the kettle and grabbed some more painkillers. She went to the loo, checked her face and sides, which had turned a dark purple, and picked her phone up from the bedside cabinet. No messages or missed calls. *I should text him, in case he's in trouble. Perhaps he's been arrested. Or he's lying somewhere hurt. Or dead. Or he's been with a woman for the night.* Ella wasn't too bothered if Lee had been beaten up, it's no worse than what she goes through at his hands. If he was dead that wouldn't be all that tragic either. Of course, she'd be sad, and would grieve, but she'd be free. And she assumed she'd then own the house, plus Lee had a life insurance policy. *Hmm, it's unlikely but here's hoping.* Ella made a coffee and gazed out of the window at the sea, sparkling from the bright morning sunlight. It was going to be a beautiful day. *He did look like he was going on a date last night, I guess it's likely he's been with some tart and is still very much alive,* she thought, a little confused that the thought of him with another woman made her feel angry and sad, but the thought that he may be dead was nowhere near as painful.

    Seb got up and carried on along the path; he could see the little stone wall just ahead. As he approached it, he could take in the garden in daylight and the effort that had gone into making it look good. It reminded him again that he needed to work on their garden at home. Whilst he was stood there, glancing around at the bench and an odd looking, fishing gnome, he felt eyes on him. He looked toward the kitchen window and saw her, holding a mug and gazing out at him, her face swollen and bruised but still pretty. She wore a white nightdress, judging from the straps, but he could only see as far down as her chest. He gave a little wave, wondering if she recognized him. As soon as he had done it, he felt awkward, he was clearly looking at her through her window like some kind of peeping Tom who didn't even try to hide. She seemed to snap out of

The Broken Doll: Book One

her stare and suddenly wound down the blind and was now nowhere to be seen. *Shit!* thought Seb, *that wasn't very smooth.*

What is going on? Ella wondered. *Is that the guy from last night? Why is he standing there, looking through my window? He's handsome though, but he's acting kind of creepy.* She was pleased to see Seb standing there but was puzzled. She wasn't sure if he was actually staring at her or just being nosy, looking across the garden. Then he gave a little wave. Ella panicked, closing the blind and went to the sofa with her book. She had no intention of reading it yet. She was feeling lost and muddled, with no sign of her husband since yesterday and suddenly a handsome stranger waving at her in the early morning. *Today could be an interesting one,* she thought, enjoying the quiet of a morning alone, of not having to make Lee his breakfast before work. Ella sent him a text, just one line checking that he was OK and asking when he would be back. It would be another couple of hours before she received a reply, a brief 'I'm fine, home at 4 today.'

FOUR

Lee came through the door a little after 4pm. It was too early for dinner so Ella had just made sure things were tidy and hoped that there wouldn't be any arguing. In an odd way she missed him last night, still wondering where he'd been, although as he said he was fine she decided the most likely explanation was that he spent the night in another woman's bed. This hurt Ella, but she did not dare to ask him. She had never had any real reason to suspect him of cheating before, and as she wasn't a particularly jealous or paranoid person, she had at no time worried that he would. But, of course, if he had such little regard for her that he would be so controlling and aggressive, there was no reason that he would draw the line at an affair, or at least the occasional one-night stand.

He was humming a little tune when he came in which was very much out of character. He seemed happy but looked exhausted. *A busy night,* Ella thought. Naturally, she wanted to know where he had been but had to consider how to approach the subject without setting him off.

"Hi," she said, greeting him as sweetly as she could whilst still covered in the bruises he had left on her only the evening before. She moved towards him and gave him a peck on the cheek; her plan was to try to detect any suspicious smells. There wasn't the obvious 'other woman's perfume' but he no longer smelled of his own cologne and there was a new smell, an odour of men's toiletries but unfamiliar. He had an odour of cleanliness, recently showered perhaps, but not with his usual products.

"I'll make you a coffee," she told him as he sat down in the armchair. Whilst the kettle heated the water, Ella gazed again out of the window, deep in thought about her husband's actions. Out all night, coming home in a better mood than usual, smelling fresh. Ella had no doubt he'd been unfaithful last night, but he would deny it and accusing him came with a renewed chance of violence. Even if he did admit it, what could she do? He wouldn't let her leave him, and she doubted he'd ever leave her. The smell bothered her though. Lee was a creature of habit and always used the same shower gel; he had done for years. It was unlikely he had bought a different one, even if it was to keep at someone else's house (indicating regular, overnight visits, which wasn't the case). Which means either the woman was a colossal whore and kept men's toiletries to hand for the many men who pass through to use, or she was an actual whore, but this was quickly dismissed as, no matter how cheap she may be, Lee couldn't afford to stay all night. Whatever Lee had used to wash with had to belong to someone, a boyfriend or husband perhaps. *God, I hope he gets caught by a huge, jealous, ape of a man,* thought Ella, smirking little at the image of two shaved gorillas beating each other over a banana, which ran through her mind.

    The kettle clicked and she made two coffees, took one to Lee, who was now engrossed in the television and took the other one to the sofa.

    "I'll just have this," she told him, "and then I'll start getting dinner ready." The evening passed like hundreds before it; they ate in silence, he drank a few beers, and fell asleep in the chair. She went to bed. Mundane, repetitive, lonely.

    Sunday came, the day of rest, but Seb had things to do for work as he had been slack the day before, preoccupied by the woman he had seen. He sat at his dining table working on his laptop, trying to banish her from his mind. He had made a few bids online for some used items that he had hoped to resell as part of his business. He had a potential customer who owned a takeaway nearby and who was after some vintage-looking seating, hence Friday's delivery of the

Chesterfield settees. He bought them at an online auction, one in traditional green and one in a burgundy. Their condition was fairly good, and he reckoned he could make a bit on them, especially being sold to a business, as tax-deductible items. The takeaway owner would take both certainly, possibly making enough profit to buy a third for someone else. He had been struggling to concentrate all day, despite having the house to himself. The children were out with Natasha visiting Seb's in-laws for Sunday lunch. They'd been gone a few hours now after some debate about why he didn't want to go.

"I have a pile of work to do," Seb told his wife. "I've got to be at the lock-up tomorrow morning for the courier, and I need to make sure I can get these settees organized; we could make at least £500 off it. It's not that I don't want to come..."

'Hmm,' Natasha murmured, not convinced.

"Honestly babe, it's just work, and with you all being out, I can quickly whiz through it."

"Fine," she retorted, "but I'm telling Mum you would rather work than eat her cooking."

Shortly after this Natasha had gathered up the children and headed off, planning to return in time for baths and bed at the usual time; it was a school night, of course.

Ella kept popping into his mind still. He was embarrassed about being there yesterday morning, especially the little wave. He had a constant feeling of guilt but was unsure as to whether it was guilt from not doing something to help her or guilt because he wanted to see her, knowing that his wife would not approve.

I have to talk to her, even if it's just to be reassured she's fine and told to piss off, at least I would be able to forget about her. Hopefully. Seb wondered what the conversation would entail and whether it would even be possible, as she'd essentially fled from him twice in as many days; perhaps going past her again today would be bordering on harassment. *What the hell?* Seb thought, *one last wander past.* Penguin was asleep, and had been for a long walk that morning with the neighbour and their dog, so Seb decided to leave him behind and put on his running clothes. *Nothing suspicious about someone jogging along that path, and if she happens to be in the garden, then great, but if not, I'll just head home.*

Seb jogged along the same route as usual, along the river, past the shops, through the woods, and along the cliff-top to the small stone wall. And there she was, kneeling on the grass with a trowel in one hand. She wore another dress, short and summery. The damage to her face was partially covered by large sunglasses, and her feet were bare. She was digging about in the mud, pulling up the tiniest of weeds and chucking them, and loose leaves, into a bag. Seb felt nervous. His stomach was in knots, as if he was about to ask out the prettiest girl in school. He stood there for a moment, admiring this woman, and then let out a kind of half-cough; the sort used to get someone's attention.

Ella heard someone nearby and looked up to find the man, again, stood by her wall. He was dressed for running, dripping with sweat, and looked a little shy. *What on Earth is he doing here again?!* Ella thought, panicking slightly that she may have a stalker. *I need to go back in.* Ella stood up and began to move toward the door when he spoke.

"I'm Seb, Sebastian, er, I blinded you with my light the other evening. I wanted to see if you were OK?"

Ella looked at her watch; it was just a little after three. *Thank God Lee isn't here.* Lee was playing pool for the Sunday league at the pub and wouldn't be back until around six. Usually anyway, unless he decides to stay out again. Either way, it would be very unlikely for him to turn up this early in the day.

The Broken Doll: Book One

"Yes, I remember. I'm fine." Ella knelt back down to continue with the weeding, a little flushed, feeling as though she was perhaps being chatted up. *He's quite handsome,* she thought and smiled to herself.

"Sorry, but you don't look fine." Seb sounded, and was, genuinely concerned when he said this and suddenly, surprising both of them, Ella broke down into tears. Seb went over the wall and approached Ella, but she became distressed and yelled at him.

"Get out! You can't be in here; this is *my* garden!"

Seb quickly retreated to the other side of the wall. "Is there anything I can do to help?" he asked. "Who has hurt you?"

It became too much for Ella. She wasn't used to people talking to her; she tried her best to be invisible and blend into the background. Panic took over. She was in no way ready to tell anyone what Lee does to her and was terrified of being seen so she ran back into the house, locking the door behind her once again. Seb tried to decide whether to go to her front door but felt that would be over the top and continued his run, back towards home. Something was very wrong with that woman, and she clearly needed some help, but Seb understood his desire to help her was largely based on wanting to get to know her. He could not deny, especially to himself, how attracted he was feeling towards her.

Ella spent the rest of the afternoon hiding out in her house, occasionally checking through the blinds to see if there was any sign of this Sebastian. He'd gone, and she was so very confused. She was disappointed that he had gone, despite her telling him to. She was terrified to talk to him, partly for fear of Lee finding out and also because she hadn't spoken to another man, at least an actual conversation, for a long time. She was nervous around him in a way, which reminded her of when she first met Lee, a teenage girl

The Broken Doll: Book One

with a crush, and now a woman being shown some interest by a handsome stranger. *Of course, he may well only be concerned for my well-being, just a kind person,* Ella considered. *I can't imagine he thought I was attractive with my swollen face.*

From the kitchen came a beep, a signal that Ella had received a text message. It was from Lee; Ella would have been shocked if anyone else had her number. 'We're still playing. I'll be back at seven, do dinner for then.' *Right,* she thought, not even bothering to reply. Ella went to the bathroom and decided to run a hot and bubbly bath as she hadn't felt able to yesterday. Today, finally having the energy to do some work in the garden and hence getting muddy, Ella thought she would make the most of the time before His Highness returned from his hard day of drinking with his friends. Ella carefully removed her dress, avoiding touching her sides where the bruising was most delicate. She removed her underwear and stood naked, looking at herself in the mirror. *If I wasn't covered in bruises, and if I could get away with a bit of makeup, I'd still be quite attractive,* she thought, slightly disappointed that Lee no longer appreciated her figure and that it looked very unlikely anyone else would get the chance to see her without her clothes on.

She slipped into the hot bath and let out a little gasp as her bruises moved below the surface. Ella tried to sit herself up so that she could use the shower head to wash her hair, but it wasn't very successful, raising her arms to apply the shampoo was painful, and so she just managed to wet it. She squeezed some gel onto her hands and rubbed it over the parts of her which didn't hurt, or only hurt a little. Then she laid back, completely relaxed, and closed her eyes. Her thoughts were only of Sebastian, questions as to what his intentions were, but she could not come up with a satisfactory answer. Her mind moved onto the less puzzling, the more carnal. His figure was toned, not especially muscular but fit. She began to daydream, to fantasize. She imagined inviting him into the house, drinking tea and chatting. She imagined him asking to use the shower to freshen up from his run, and before she knew it, she was holding the shower head between her legs, her imagination going wild playing out scenes in which Sebastian was taking her from behind in the bathroom. She fantasized about being sat on him on the sofa, and as she pictured Sebastian kneeling before her, his tongue deep within her, she reached a momentous orgasm in the bath letting out a whimper and smiling from ear to ear.

Once Seb had returned home after his jog, he jumped into the shower, his mind reeling, still wondering what he should do. After a quick wash, he threw on some comfy clothes and went to his laptop. The right course of action, if one even existed, eluded Seb, and so he turned to Google for help. In the search bar he wrote *'how to help a victim of domestic violence'*. There were a huge number of hits, mostly with telephone numbers to confidential advice lines. He found one site, which listed actions that he could take, all of which seemed fairly obvious. Essentially, he should initiate a conversation with the victim, in private, reassuring her that he was there to help. *Well, I tried that, but I guess that I could give it another go,* he thought. The website listed a few useful numbers such as social services, The Domestic Violence Helpline, Victim Support, etc. Seb wrote these down on a sheet from Natasha's notepad and put them in his pocket.

All I can do is try to talk to her again and give her these numbers, and mine. Then it's up to her to ask for help. He checked the clock, almost 5pm. Natasha and the children should be home soon. Seb was getting hungry; he'd not eaten since breakfast, and the others would have had a roast already. He decided to text Natasha to find out their plans and whether she

The Broken Doll: Book One

would be hungry later. She usually replies almost immediately, but twenty minutes passed with nothing. Seb looked in the cupboard, then the fridge, after that back in the cupboard. He grabbed a cereal bar to keep him going until he heard from his wife.

As he was munching through it, the front door opened and Natasha came in, hands full of cotton tote bags. Seb went towards the front door to help and noticed she was alone, with no sign of any children.

"You've lost something," he said to her.

"Shit," she replied, playfully, "I must have forgotten them."

They moved the bags down to the kitchen, and Natasha explained that they contained 'gifts' from her parents. By gifts, she meant a few random items of crockery they had no longer wanted, some opened biscuits, and a couple of bottles of wine which her mother had passed on to her saying 'they know we don't drink white, so I don't understand why they bought it for us'.

"So, the children?" Seb inquired, a little puzzled about their absence on a school night.

"Staying with my parents for the whole night! I didn't ask, or even hint. Dad did his usual, making plans with the kids before talking to me, and invited them for a sleepover. I reminded him was Sunday, and they had to be at school tomorrow, that they would need lunch money and, more importantly, uniform. He now plans to drop them home after breakfast for us to get them ready and take them."

"Right, well it'll be a rush in the morning then. Not to mention an early start for them!" Seb complained.

"Don't moan, it'll be fine, let's just make the most of some alone time! Have you got everything done that you wanted to do?"

"Yes, I think so, I'm getting hungry. I'm assuming you've eaten?" Natasha had opened one of the bottles of white; it wasn't fridge temperature but had been in her parents' garage so was cold enough to enjoy. It was from Burgundy, at the cheaper end but still pleasant.

"We all had roast lamb. Except Steven, he had roast potatoes, Yorkshire puddings, and ketchup. I didn't have all that much though, so I thought we'd go out for something, if you want?"

"Can we stay in? Sorry, I'm just feeling a bit lazy. I could certainly manage a takeaway and some television."

"That's fine baby, sounds good. I'll let you choose, but don't order too much for me," Natasha told him. She finished her glass of wine and kissed her husband more passionately than he had expected. After a cigarette they went up to relax on the sofa, feeling a little lost with no children to put to bed. They chatted about their days, Natasha doing the most talking as usual. At her parents' house, they had played some board games, eaten, and watched part of a film that happened to be on. She was saying something about redecorating their hallway, but Seb wasn't paying much attention by this point. When asked about his day he told her about the Chesterfields, and how much they would make on them. He mentioned that he'd been for a jog but didn't go into detail. Natasha looked suspicious.

"Did you go past that woman's house again?" she asked.

"No," Seb lied. "I went up to the cliffs but around a different way." He immediately felt guilty and didn't know why he'd lied; he didn't do anything wrong. Even so, Natasha had clearly not been happy with him showing so much interest in the 'other woman', and it would reduce any tension between them this evening if she didn't know he had spoken to this person, or even just been past.

The Broken Doll: Book One

"You'd better not be fibbing Mr. Briggs," she said. Although playfully worded, Seb had no doubt she was serious.

"Chinese or pizza?" he asked, changing the subject as he reached for another glass of wine.

"Chinese definitely, I'm not hungry enough for pizza." An evening without children was a rare treat, and they were managing to relax, joking about with each other, watching hilariously awful horror films, and drinking wine. Their dinner had not taken long for them to devour, Natasha having a small amount of noodles with a couple of side dishes, and Seb had tried to ignore his hunger and also have a smaller-than-usual portion. This was, to some extent, because he was attempting to lose a bit of weight and increase his fitness levels, and partly because he didn't want to get too full in case Natasha was after some sex this evening.

Well, that was rather exciting, Ella thought as she dried herself, feeling as though she should feel guilty but didn't at all. *I haven't actually done anything wrong, and surely I'm entitled to an orgasm every now and again; it's not as if Lee will even bother trying to sort me out.*

She made her way to the bedroom, towel wrapped around her, and noticed the time. It was a little after six already. *Time for my slave duties,* she thought as she contemplated what to make for dinner. *Poison would be nice.* Ella got herself into some comfortable pyjamas and raided the cupboards in search of something quick to cook which Lee wouldn't have any complaints with. She found a jar of tikka sauce and some rice, but there was no meat left, only vegetables. *Vegetable curry then,* she decided, hoping Lee would be OK with that. *He's had it before and liked it, so with a bit of luck he will have had so much to drink today that he won't notice that there's no meat.*

The Broken Doll: Book One

As Ella began cooking the meal, she thought of Sebastian, her body still tingling from her self-pleasuring, and she wondered if she'd see him again. She knew full well that if she did, she must not speak to him, that he must remain a fantasy only. There was no other choice; an affair was too dangerous as was a one-off liaison, even talking to him carried a risk. *The fantasy was incredible so why spoil that? He might be terrible in bed,* she pondered, although she strongly doubted it.

Around seven, as he'd planned, Lee returned home. He was drunk of course, having spent hours in the pub, but his team had won the pool tournament, so he was in a fairly good mood. He came in and rather than immediately falling into his armchair, he approached Ella and gave her a peck on the cheek, simultaneously having a little grope of her bottom.

"We're OK, aren't we?" Lee asked, "I mean, I know sometimes I'm not great to you, but I do look after you, and it's not too much to expect you to do what I say really, is it?"

"We're fine baby," Ella replied "Sit down, and I'll get dinner." *He must be pissed, that was almost an apology. Maybe he feels guilty? He should do; he has plenty to feel bad about.* However, Lee had no more to say on the matter; he ate, demanded a beer, and fell asleep before he'd finished drinking it. Ella got her book and slippers, planning to sit on the bench outside but changed her mind. *What if Sebastian came past again?* She decided it was too risky and got into bed to read, but, as soon as she started, she could feel her eyelids becoming heavy. *That orgasm must have taken it out of me,* she thought, happily, drifting off with a contented look on her face.

Natasha was drunk. They finished the two bottles that they'd been given and wanted more. There

The Broken Doll: Book One

was enough gin for one large one each so Seb poured these whilst Natasha made a cigarette.

"Are you sure you didn't go near that house?" she asked Seb, slurring a little, sounding as though she was picking a fight. She did this sometimes and Seb had learned to ignore it most of the time, knowing that he would always be the one to apologize after a fight regardless of who was at fault.

"I am definitely one hundred percent sure that I did not go near that house today. Furthermore, you look very sexy," Seb replied, trying to turn the conversation to something more pleasant.

"I do not!" Natasha exclaimed, "I'm all wobbly. It is nice that you find me sexy after all these years though. I can be sexy when I try."

With that, Natasha groped at the front of Seb's trousers, immediately noticing some movement.

"I'm going to get into something more comfortable," she told him. When she came back down from the bedroom, she had certainly managed to pull-off the sexy look, although it was possibly not something comfier. Seb gazed at his wife as she approached him in a crimson and black corset, suspenders, and red high heels.

"Get your cock out then big boy!" Natasha demanded. Seb didn't hesitate. No sooner had he exposed it than his wife was kneeling before him, head bobbing as she took him fully into her mouth.

"Fucking hell!" Seb muttered, knowing that this wouldn't take long, but she stopped abruptly.

"Get downstairs!" she ordered, and Seb put himself away and went to the kitchen. Natasha bent herself over the dining table expectantly. Making love wouldn't be an accurate description of what followed. It would be better described as a drunken, dirty session. Seb put his tongue in her. He had her from behind holding her head down on the table. They had their hands, and tongues, all over each other. It was intense, more so than it had been for a while, and Seb managed to refrain from climaxing until Natasha had reached orgasm.

"Do it all over me!" she demanded, flinging off her corset for him to ejaculate on her breasts, in the style of most pornography. She sat in a chair while he stood in front of her, his hand working his cock quickly. It was taking longer than expected, perhaps the wine was having an effect. He closed his eyes and, unexpectedly, the woman from earlier popped into his mind. Her dress and her legs appeared clearly and, in that moment, before he could even consider what was happening, he came. Natasha moaned as she felt his semen spray onto her. Seb immediately felt awful for thinking of someone else, especially as his own wife had made so much of an effort this evening.

"That was great!" Natasha said. "Thank you."

"Oh, any time dear, whenever you want. You're so hot," Seb told her. She looked content and satisfied as she cleaned up and grabbed her dressing gown before having one last cigarette. They yawned in unison.

"Bedtime," Seb said.

"It certainly is. Jeez, it's almost midnight! I love you."

"I love you too baby," Seb replied, exhausted and drunk, ready to fall asleep.

FIVE

Last night was a close call. Ella didn't remember falling asleep so it must have been quick. She did remember Lee getting into bed in the early hours, after he had awoken in the armchair. He had stripped off and got into their bed, slipping his hand down the front of her pyjama bottoms. She woke to this but didn't move, hoping that he wasn't about to hop on. She could feel his erection against her leg, whilst he jabbed at her with his fat fingers. He must have still been pretty much asleep as he rolled on to his back and began tugging at himself. Ella remained silent; eyes closed, as if sleeping. Either he was too tired or still drunk, but she soon heard snoring. *He can't even get himself off,* she thought. *So, there's next to no chance that he could sort me out, even if he wanted to.*

When the morning came, they were both tired, much more so than usual, and struggled to get up. The alarm went off at 6.30am. Lee hit snooze every twenty minutes until suddenly it was 7.30am. This resulted in Lee angrily rushing around, trying to get ready as he had a job to get to by 8am. Ella quickly went to the kitchen to make Lee a coffee to have while he got set, but there was no time for breakfast. She brought it to him as he was tying his shoelaces. He grabbed the mug and took a swig, burning his tongue in the process. In a rage, he threw the full coffee cup at the wall, smashing it and spraying thick, black coffee across the carpet and skirting board. He finished tying his shoes, told Ella to 'clear that shit up', and stormed out.

Yay, Ella thought, sarcastically. *Well at least I have something to do today then.* The monotony of her life was becoming unbearable. She looked out of her kitchen window, and the weather had changed. It was still dry, but the wind had gotten up; the sky was grey, and it felt much cooler. Ella hated the wind; it was cold and aggressive. It also seemed to cause some kind of damage to the house whenever it got up, whether it was a garden ornament or the cracking of a sash window, a drawback to living in such an exposed location.

Rain was another matter. In the winter it was shit, but this stemmed from the drop in temperature. Summer's rain was magnificent though. There was something beautifully liberating and almost sexual about getting soaked through on a warm day in a thin summer dress. At least, that's how Ella saw it.

Ella discovered, rather unsurprisingly, that black coffee is a pain to clean up. She gathered her bucket full of hot, soapy water, a couple of cloths, a tea towel, and a multi-surface cleaning spray. They were out of actual carpet cleaner, so Ella wiped down the skirting first which came up clean without difficulty thanks to the gloss paint. She had to make do scrubbing the carpet with hot water. After she'd given it a good going over, her body aching from the chore as well as her bruising (which had hardly started to fade), she stopped for a break. Ella made herself a chamomile tea and dug out her secret tobacco stash. She hadn't even had chance to get dressed yet so just grabbed a dressing gown and opened the back door. It was colder than she expected, and the sea looked quite rough. There was not a soul to be seen from her garden; no dog-walkers, no ramblers, not even any boats out at sea. And no Sebastian. He hadn't entered her head so far that morning; after all, she had cleaning to do and had been busy being shouted at.

She rushed her cigarette. She was cold and nervous that Sebastian might appear. Nervous, and hopeful. *Suppose it's too cold for anyone to be up here today.* Ella went back to scrub the carpet, hoping that it would come up clean enough.

The day passed in the same way that they always did. Ella cleaned, read, drank tea, daydreamed. Sebastian fluttered through her mind every now and again. She wondered what Lee would be like when he came home. She tried to imagine her life in five years' time and saw no difference whatsoever.

Late afternoon, around five, Ella received a text. 'I'm going down the pub with Graham after work so won't need dinner.' No suggestion of when, or if, he'd be back. Ella took the opportunity to read a bit more, now finding her book easier to get through, although still rather dull. She made herself a sandwich as Lee was eating out. After two previous attempts to scrub the carpet Ella could still see a coffee stain, so she decided to keep busy and had another go. It was as she was on all fours, her rear towards the front door, that Lee turned up, much earlier than expected, drunk, and with Graham.

She had met Graham on two occasions before. He was a little older than Lee, probably not that bad looking but this was ruined by the fact that he was a prick. He was the sort of guy who honestly believed women should be honoured to sleep with him, as if he was some kind of god. He was sexist, racist, and a complete sleaze. The fact that Lee chose to hang around with him said a lot about Lee's character; after all, if you want to know what someone is really like, then just look at their friends. Ella was glad she was still in slouchy pyjamas. On both occasions that Graham had visited before, she had been wearing a dress. The first time was just for a few minutes, while Lee got changed before they went back out. Ella and Graham had chatted but the entire time his eyes hadn't even glanced at her face, finding something more interesting on her chest. The second time he stayed for drinks. This meant that Lee could show off his control over his wife, telling her that she was to wait in the kitchen and bring beers when summoned. *Better than having to listen to your conversations,* she'd thought at the time. That evening was spent reading in the kitchen with a chamomile tea, a shout for more beer coming through every twenty minutes or so. The first hour was fine. Then Lee had needed the loo, which Graham took to be his cue to come and talk to Ella. Again, his eyes didn't get to her face, but she could ignore that. Ignoring his hands was different. He had placed his hands on her hips, pressing against her as her back touched the work top. Ella moved to the side, and as she pulled away from him, he lifted her skirt and squeezed her bottom. From the kitchen, they both heard the chain flush and Graham grabbed two more beers, winked at Ella, and went back to sit with Lee.

"Where have you been?" Lee asked him.

"Went to grab another beer," Graham told him. "I did shout for some, but she must have been busy."

"Probably got her head in another stupid book, that woman's fucking useless," Lee said.

Ella was shaken; she had been afraid of what Graham was going to do. She had not known someone to dare act like that, especially when Lee was nearby. She didn't feel that she could tell Lee, so it was left at that, and she didn't see Graham for a few months after that evening.

Nevertheless, here he was, standing over her, checking her out. He had an open beer in one hand and a 12-bottle case under the other arm. Lee also had a beer in one hand and carried a plastic bag with some cans in it.

"I'm gonna put these in the fridge," Graham said as he staggered toward the kitchen. They had clearly had a lot to drink as they both looked like standing was a challenge. Lee gave Ella the plastic bag.

"Put these in the fridge as well, will ya?" he ordered. As Ella got to the kitchen, Graham was drunkenly trying to open the cardboard box containing his bottles.

"Go and sit down, Graham, I'll put them away," Ella told him, impatiently.

"You're a sweetie," he said, slapping her rear and heading back to the living room. Lee had put a sports highlights program on, and they sat, transfixed, like two chimps seeing fire for the first time.

Ella went and got her dressing gown, wanting as many layers as possible between her skin and Graham. As she passed behind the sofa, Graham looked at her in a way which gave her the creeps.

"Oi, beer wench!" Lee called out. They both giggled like schoolboys. Ella dutifully opened two beers and delivered them to the men.

"Grab yourself one too honey," Graham said. Ella was taken aback; Lee didn't allow her to drink. She looked to Lee for permission. *God forbid I make my own choices!* Ella thought.

"She doesn't drink," he said.

"Sure she could manage one, just to be sociable?" Graham suggested.

"Whatever," Lee said, "as long as she sits there quietly." Graham looked at Ella and patted the sofa next to him. It was the only space to sit in, but surely he wouldn't try to touch her with her husband sitting right by them. She was wrong.

Graham's hand was by his side, and his finger kept stroking her leg, ever so slightly. Lee was into the sports program and didn't notice anything.

"You've got a hot one here mate," Graham said to Lee.

"She used to be," Lee said. "It gets dull after years of fucking the same thing."

Ella fought back a tear. He was a nasty shit when he wanted to be.

"Well if you're bored with her feel free to send her my way, I'd give her a good seeing to."

Lee turned to Graham.

"You fucking what?!" he said. "That's my wife." Ella wanted to get up and away from the situation which looked like it may turn nasty. She didn't dare to

The Broken Doll: Book One

move though. Graham must have not noticed that Lee had taken exception to his comments.

"If you're up for it," Graham continued, "we could both have a go now. It could be fun, and I don't mind which end I have." Ella's heart was beating quickly, knowing this wouldn't end well. She was frightened that Lee would agree to this, agree to let someone rape his wife. However, he didn't. Instead, he swung his beer bottle at Graham's head, hitting it three times before it smashed. He was like a crazed animal, throwing punches and threatening to kill him. In only a matter of minutes Graham was on their floor, bleeding and swollen. Ella had to scream at Lee for him to stop before he killed him. Lee snapped out of his rage, grabbed Graham's arms and pulled him out the front door. He was still conscious and began to stagger away from the house.

Thank god, Ella thought. As violent as that had been, she was relieved that Lee had taken her side. So, she didn't see it coming when he punched her in the eye, directly onto the place he'd slapped her only a few days beforehand. She dropped to her knees, eyes' watering, waiting for the next punch. Her head was spinning, and she could make out Lee saying something, but it wasn't clear what. She heard the word 'whore' and knew that he blamed her for Graham's behaviour, regardless of how ridiculous that was. He started to go on at her about leading him on and how she would have loved it if they had both had her. He called her a 'filthy, little slut', keeping a tight grip on her hair with one hand and, with his other, pulled down his jeans and boxers.

"Open your mouth," he told her. She resisted as much as she could, trying to pull away, crying. He grabbed her face and pulled at her mouth with his hand, forcing it open just enough. Ella understood that she had no choice. He was too strong and maybe it would be better to get it over with. So, she doid what she was told, and he entered her mouth. He forced himself in hard, repeatedly, hurting her with each thrust. It felt like forever, but he finally stopped, unable to climax. His anger now fuelled by being dissatisfied, having seen filling her mouth with come against her will as a punishment for her.

"You used to be good at that," he told her. "Now you can't do anything right." His hand curled into a fist as he stood above her. *I'm going to die tonight,* she thought. Before Lee could lay into her with his fist, she scrambled to the kitchen, but he was too quick for her. He landed a couple of hard punches to her back, and she flopped to the floor, unable to move, waiting for him to kill her. She covered the back of her head with her hands and waited, but the next sound was a slamming door. She looked up, and he'd gone.

Seb was awoken by his alarm blaring like a siren. His head ached from the alcohol that he had consumed the night before, and his mouth was in dire need of water. He switched the alarm off and got up, went to the bathroom, and then downstairs to get water and painkillers. *I'm getting too old to drink,* he thought, quite happily remembering how naughtily his wife had behaved. *No kids!* he remembered, forgetting about the plans for the morning and their impending return at any time soon. Seb toyed with the idea of going back to bed regardless but decided against it. He had to be at his lock-up this morning and felt as though it may take him a few hours to get a clear head. Seb downed a second pint of water and grabbed some clothes from a pile of clean ones by the tumble dryer, moving towards the door to grab Penguin's lead. It looked miserable out, not raining yet but grey and gusty.

Penguin took Seb for a quick stroll around the block; the wind was icy, and neither of them liked it. After a speedy shower, Seb went to get dressed again and woke Natasha up.

The Broken Doll: Book One

"What time is it?" she asked, bleary eyed.

"Just gone seven," he replied, "What time are the kids coming back? They're eating at your parents' house, aren't they?"

"Yeah they will give them breakfast and drop them home. I told them by eight at the latest, then they'll have enough time to get changed."

Don't think I can deal with the in-laws and the children just yet, thought Seb and so, rather selfishly, he told his wife that he had a delivery due any time between 8 and 1 and that he needed to make some room at the lock-up.

"Sorry baby," he told her. "I really wish I didn't have to go yet."

Natasha didn't seem concerned or annoyed, maybe feeling a little sorry for Seb that he had to go off to work already.

"OK darling, have a good day, stay in touch."

"I will. Love you"

"Love you too."

Seb grabbed his car keys and wallet and drove down towards the lock-up. He parked in his space, between the bright white Range Rover which was often there, the pimp-mobile as he called it, the owner of which he'd never seen, and the not very seaworthy rowing boat, the owner of which also had a lock-up but no car and hence made good use of his parking space by dumping the rotting shipwreck there. Seb let himself in and slowly shifted a few items about; namely the two storage boxes of records he'd grabbed out of a charity shop, a garish chaise longue with silver-painted frame and Union Jack fabric, and a couple of art-decor lamps which may well have been much more recently made but were, at least, stylish in their own right.

Seb glanced toward the clock on the wall which read 7.20am. *Hmm, got a while to go,* he thought.

The Broken Doll: Book One

Seb rolled a cigarette and wandered over the road to the food trailer for a coffee. He had a kettle and all the necessary components in the lock-up to make a hot drink, but they had a proper coffee machine there and he could say hello to Daryl, who owned it.

"Morning Daryl," Seb said in a jolly tone as he approached.

"Seb," Daryl replied. "How's things?"

"Can't complain, waiting for a delivery of a few things, easy day. Can I get a cappuccino and a couple of those chocolate orange protein bars please?"

"I saw those Chesterfields you got in. I used to have a Chesterfield," Daryl informed him. "Dog ripped it to shit so had to throw it eventually. Family all OK?"

"All fine with us, how are yours?" Seb asked in return.

"Same old, our eldest has come home, didn't like university. I take that to mean it involved actually doing some work and not just getting pissed up with his mates and shagging freshers. Mary is still a grumpy witch, riddled with bronchitis and emphysema, her own fault for smoking so damn much of course, but I love her anyway."

Daryl was still talking when he turned the coffee machine on, and Seb couldn't make out what was being said over the noise.

"You always lived around here?" Seb asked him.

"Got to be about forty-five years now, so yeah, it's nearly always. Why?"

"You ever go up on the cliff-top, past the fort?"

"Sometimes through the summer, not often. Why, what do you want to know?"

"There's a house up there, not far from the fort, little stone-walled garden. I just wondered who lived there?" Seb said, wondering how odd a question it was.

The Broken Doll: Book One

"No idea mate, I vaguely remember a house being there, but I've never seen anyone going in or out. Is it for sale?"

"Huh?" Seb grunted, "Oh, I see, no. Well not that I know of. There was a woman in the garden last week. It looked like she'd been slapped about, but she didn't want to talk to me."

"Ah, so you'd like to be her knight in shining armour, eh? You'd be surprised what goes on behind closed doors. Best to stay out of it. You've got a family, not worth losing over a bit of skirt, trust me, I know."

"It's not like that," Seb tried to explain, not very convincingly. "I was just a bit worried about her. I went back and saw her again, but she didn't say much."

"£4.20," Daryl stated. Seb paid for his snacks and drink and turned back towards the lock-up. "Stay out of it is my advice," Daryl called after him.

"I'll try," Seb shouted back, against the wind, knowing full well that he needed to see the woman again, and soon.

After a couple of hours of pottering around his storage unit, cleaning a few items and listing some new bits on his website, a chubby, balding man in his early fifties turned up in a Luton van. Seb went out to help the man unload the items into the space he had cleared earlier, hoping that these new pieces would sell quickly. He had taken advantage of a sale online of some home items, nautical in theme, and admired the two seaside designed drinks' trolleys. *At least, they're nice enough to keep if they don't sell,* he thought, contemplated having a drinks' stash at the lock-up. However, the Chesterfields were his priority today and although they were in good condition, he gave them a wipe over and called the takeaway owner. No reply on his mobile so he decided to take a wander up there and locked up.

The Broken Doll: Book One

Ten windy minutes later and he was inside the takeaway which had recently been refurbished. A lot of money went into the place, newly decorated with a selection of mismatched, vintage, and trendy furnishings.

"Sid about?" he asked. One of the girls working there came over to him. He couldn't remember if this was Sid's wife or not as there were two, which looked similar. Both brunette, pretty but trashy looking, well aware that their figures were the best thing they had going for them, as long as they didn't talk.

"He's away, visiting family," she told him. "I'm his wife, can I help?"

"Oh hi, yes maybe. Sid asked me to find him a couple of settees for this place, and they are ready, so I need to arrange to bring them up and get payment."

"Sorry hun, don't know nothing about no sofas. How much he meant to be giving you?"

"£1000 for the pair. When's he due back? I can hang on to them for a few days if it helps."

"£1000?! Shit, that's pricey. I wouldn't think he has that much to splash about. Leave me your number and I'll get him to call you when I talk to him, might not be for a few days though."

"OK thanks," Seb replied, disappointed to not be getting it sorted now and concerned about the air of uncertainty around the purchase. He kicked himself for still not getting around to creating some kind of binding order form, having always relied on a verbal agreement. Of course, this carried the risk of the customer changing their mind after he had paid out for the stock, usually with no way of returning the item himself. Seb handed her his business card and headed back to the lock-up, unsure what to do with himself now. He tried to call Sid again but had no luck so called Natasha instead. He updated his wife on what he'd been up to so far and said he may as well head home.

The Broken Doll: Book One

"I'm out for lunch with Dee," she informed him. "Sorry honey, I wasn't expecting you back yet."

Seb told her that it was fine and to have a nice time, he'd go for a swim and maybe make a start on tidying the garden. After gathering his swimming bits, he gazed out at the garden and decided that it was too gloomy outside to start on that project, and even to venture to the pool, opting instead to switch on the television while he waited for it to be time to go on the school run.

Natasha had a pleasant, healthy lunch with Dee, a friend of sorts (another mum from the school whose company was much less irritating than most). She mentioned that Seb had seen a woman hurt at the house on the cliff-top. Her tone and expressions must have been such that Dee asked Natasha if she thought her husband was being unfaithful. Natasha looked shocked.

"Of course not!" she said immediately, but on thinking it over again, went on to say, "but I am worried he has some interest in her. He may just be concerned and feeling obliged to do something, at least I hope so! But he talks about her more often than he seems to notice if that makes sense? And there is a fondness when he mentions her."

"What's her name?" Dee asks. "I might know her, if not I'll find her on Facebook."

"I don't know; I don't think Seb knows. He said he tried to talk to her once, but she ran in the house."

"I wouldn't worry about it Nat, he's probably just got a crush. They all get them because men are only little boys in bigger bodies. It'll pass."

Natasha didn't like the idea of Seb having a crush on someone else and so changed the subject. She received a text from Seb saying that she need not hurry home as he was there to do the school run. Dee did, however, also have to do the school run so when she left at two-thirty, Natasha took the opportunity to have a look around the few shops that were nearby, picked up a pair of shoes and treated herself to a couple of gin and tonics in a pub overlooking the river.

Natasha returned home just before 5pm to find all three children sat around the table doing homework, dinner was on, and Seb was looking gorgeous with scruffy, windswept hair and holding a glass of bourbon.

"All under control," he reported as she entered the kitchen.

"Wonderful! Well done darling," Natasha replied, content at home with her family now.

SIX

Ella's evening was worse than most. The vicious fights had become more regular; this was for certain. However, it was very rare for her to have been hurt when she still carried bruises from a previous encounter. She remained on the floor for hours, unable to move. She was trembling all over, in agony and, without any doubt, wanted to die. *This is no way to live. I don't deserve this, but I cannot change it; I can never escape. I have to lie here in agony, whilst he's probably back in the pub with his mates.* Her mind ran over many ways for her to end her life before that monster returned. She had painkillers but wasn't sure if there were enough to do it properly. There was only beer to wash them down, nothing stronger. Hanging herself seemed too difficult, and she wasn't aware of any rope in the house. *I can't imagine it's very easy to drown yourself,* she pondered. She considered using a knife, a simple cutting of the wrists or femoral artery in the bath and she should bleed out in no time. Then she struck gold! *Why should I leave anything for Lee? Why not burn the house down with me still inside it?* Her mind turned to the garden and not wanting to ruin it, as unimportant as that sounded under the circumstances. The thought of being burnt alive sounded pretty horrific too, so she scrapped that. *What about burning the house down (the garden is no use to me when I'm dead), but I disappear? He'll find me, there will be no body. Hmm, burn the house down and jump off the cliff? Yes, that suits, relatively painless and Lee loses everything.*

It was saddening for Ella. Not her decision to take her life so much, more the fact that she had no one worth leaving a note for, no one who she thought would be bothered, or even attend the funeral. She managed to get herself up from the floor and focused on her mission, her goal clear in her head. She felt a relief as she contemplated her final time, perhaps only twenty to thirty minutes left to live. She searched the products under the kitchen sink for anything which said it was flammable.

Then the unexpected happened. With a loud crash, the front door swung open, the handle banging against the wall. This was followed by another crash. Ella rushed into the living room to see that Lee was home, but not in good condition. He had burst through the door and fallen onto his armchair, sending it backwards, and now lie sprawled across the chair and the floor. *For fuck's sake,* Ella thought. *I don't think I can burn it down with him in it. Maybe he'll choke on his own vomit if I leave him there tonight.* However, the sound of gurgling coming from Lee wasn't vomit, it was blood. A lot of blood. He gurgled something and tried to talk; Ella just about made out the word 'ambulance'. *Oh shit, what's happened?* Ella approached him and saw that his face was bruised. His nose looked wonkier than usual and had been bleeding, and he was holding his abdomen. Ella lifted his shirt and recoiled in horror. There was blood, more than she had ever seen, but not only that. Lee had a wound which ran the width of his belly, deep enough for some of his insides to now be protruding outside. Without a medical degree, it was impossible to say which bits they were; everything was just very red.

"Get me a fucking ambulance!" Lee spluttered, much more quietly than he intended. Ella just stared at him. *What happened? Was it an accident? Was he attacked? Should I call an ambulance?*

"Hurry up you stupid cunt, I'm fucking dying here!"

"Yes. You are." Ella said and turned to walk to the kitchen. She rolled a cigarette and went to sit on her bench, to smoke, and to wait. The wound looked fatal; it shouldn't take long.

The Broken Doll: Book One

Ella was in shock, her mind reeling from the situation. In the space of a few minutes, she had gone from making plans to burn down the house and jump from the cliff-top, as her only option to escape Lee, but now he lay dying on the floor, and a new escape plan was put into action. She had no doubts that she wanted him dead but had always known she couldn't do it herself. She rationalized her actions now by convincing herself that he wouldn't make it anyway, which he probably wouldn't, but why take the chance? She wanted another cigarette, but it was too windy outside to roll, so she moved to the kitchen and made one. Then she lit it. Indoors. *What a rebel I am!* she thought. She walked to the living room, smoking, to see if she was a widow yet.

"Oh fuck!" she exclaimed aloud, gazing at the overturned chair which contained no dying morons. A thick trail of red led towards the front door which was still wide open. Just beyond it, between the house and Lee's car, was Lee. No movement, no sound. He must have decided to get himself to the hospital in desperation but hadn't got more than a couple of metres. The car's headlights were still on and shone on to his body, a pool of blood spreading beneath him. Ella moved around the body and checked for a pulse. Nothing. He was gone. A stench of blood, alcohol, and shit emanated from his corpse. She turned the headlights off and locked the car up with the blood-soaked keys Lee held in his hand.

Now I can call the ambulance, she decided. *Or should I? Don't they say that most murders are committed by a spouse? And it does look like he's trying to get away from me. The police will see he's been beating me and think I reacted out of self-defence, but that's still a manslaughter charge though.*

Ella needed time to plan, not feeling confident that telling the truth would be enough. However, she couldn't plan much with his body outside

The Broken Doll: Book One

for anyone to see. She checked the time; it was almost midnight. She wondered if she could move him back inside; he was much heavier than her, and she was in a lot of pain already, but she had no choice. She managed to roll him onto his back to minimize the blood spilling any more than it already had, and dragged him, inch by inch, into the house. It took Ella almost twenty minutes, but she did it. She looked at the bloody trail outside with a torch. It looked bad, and that was in the dark. *I'm going to have to try to wash it away,* she told herself. She grabbed a bucket of hot water and bleach and tipped it over the area. And again. And again. Eventually, it looked much less noticeable, but she decided to stay up until dawn to check again before anyone came past.

Ella wondered who would notice that Lee wasn't around. How easy would it be for him to disappear? If anyone did notice, she would have to explain why she hadn't reported it. *Simple, he was a wife-beating piece of shit that walked out one night, and I haven't seen him since. I assumed he'd left me and good riddance!* But why is his car there? *He was too drunk to drive when he left, guess whoever he has shacked up with has given him a car, or he's bought another one.*

It was weak; she'd certainly be under suspicion. Especially as the house was covered in gore, and it would be virtually impossible to clean it up. She considered taking the carpets up, but it would be hard to get rid of them. They had an old metal barrel in the garden which she'd used to incinerate garden waste before, the carpet could go in that. She made a step-by-step plan, on paper (perhaps foolishly), and it read as follows;

How to cover up a murder (that I didn't commit!)

1. No murder weapon so don't have to worry about that

2. Get rid of body. Burial seems the only choice

3. Get rid of evidence, in this case blood-stained carpets.

4. In summary; bury the body, including everything in his pockets except wallet and phone. Destroy the phone. Hide wallet (or at least bank cards). Take up whole carpet and cut into small pieces. Incinerate, but in the daytime with garden waste to avoid suspicion. Replace carpet (after checking for staining underneath).

Ella made a large cup of strong coffee and took three codeine-based painkillers. *Once this is done, I can sleep for days; time is of the essence though.* She made her way to the garden, keeping the light off, and began to dig the bed on the far right where the shrubs were planted. It saddened her a little to have to pull them up, but it was necessary; they could be burned with the carpet pieces. She had no idea how easy it would be to pull the carpet up, but that could be tackled after digging a grave.

It was starting to get light by the time Ella had finished digging. She looked like the poster child for some gruesome horror film, covered in mud and sweat, patches of Lee's blood forming stains on her clothing. She liked her comfy clothes and was sad that they too would have to be destroyed. It took all her strength to drag Lee's huge frame towards the garden, panicking a little as the daylight became brighter. She briefly toyed with the idea of chopping him to pieces but considered the mess it would make, and that she didn't really have the stomach for dismemberment, so decided against it. It was a little after 5am; she reckoned she had about an hour before any dog-walkers or joggers appeared. In the end, it took her thirty-five minutes to get her husband's corpse to the hole and fill it in, chucking some rubbish bags and plant pots on top for good measure.

The Broken Doll: Book One

Task one was complete, and she sat herself on the sofa staring at the bloody mess around her. *What was I thinking? This is too much to get away with!* Even so, there was little choice now. Even if she did call the police, she'd still have to explain why she buried him. Daylight streamed into the living room, and she went to check outside the front, where she had tried to wash away the pool of blood. *Thank God,* she thought, unable to notice anything suspicious there. The car, however, was a mess. Blood had run down the driver's door and made a puddle in the foot well and around the pedals. She grabbed a sheet to chuck over the small part that was visible from outside the car, went inside and locked the door, soon falling asleep on the sofa against her will.

Seb awoke feeling refreshed after an early night, almost leaping out of bed at his six-thirty alarm. Natasha was starting to stir too; the rest had been much needed after their night of gin and sex.

"I'm going for a run," he told her. "Thought I would get it out of the way before the kids wake up."

"You're mad," Natasha teased, "it's still so early." Seb got some suitable clothes on and kissed his wife on the forehead.

"I won't be long," he said.

Seb knew exactly where he was going but didn't know what to expect. Would she even be awake? He only hoped for a glimpse of her, maybe in the garden or through the kitchen window again. Just to see if she looked alright. It didn't take long for him to come out of the woods and onto the cliff-top, soon reaching the stone wall of Ella's garden. It looked different, messy. There was a chunk of dirt, which looked freshly dug, maybe yesterday, despite the grey weather. *What is she doing there? It looked good before.* There was no sign of her anywhere and as there were a couple of pensioners walking their Border collies towards him, he couldn't very well peer through any windows. *Hmm, better head back then. Maybe I'll walk the dog later,* he thought, clearly finding an excuse to come by at a more sensible hour.

Seb was home fifteen minutes later and showered, ate some porridge with the children, and made himself a list of tasks for the day. He would come along on the school run this morning, and then had a few deliveries to do. He must chase up Sid about the Chesterfields. They were too bulky to hold on to for long and buying them had made a real dent in his finances. All-in-all, his day passed like many others, back and forth on deliveries, popping to the bank, home for a little lunch with Natasha (who was having a housework day). All the while, his mind was on the woman, her well-being, her legs, and her newly altered garden.

Ella awoke just before midday, not from having slept for long enough, but due to the discomfort caused by sleeping on a sofa whilst covered in bruises. With little thought or emotion, she replayed the events of the previous night. *Right, carpet,* she thought. *The car will have to wait until after dark.* She had a quick shower to remove the mud and blood and put some clean clothes on which covered her injuries as much as possible, then made her way to the car in search of Lee's toolbox. She located it in the boot and brought it into the house. From the toolbox, Ella removed the Stanley knife, hammer, and pliers. She pulled at the edges of the carpet with her hands and found that it came up much easier than she had expected. Once she had the carpet detached from one side of room, she hacked at it with the Stanley. It was exceptionally sharp and went through the carpet without any problems. This became the day's activity; a long, laborious process dissecting the carpet to pieces less than a foot across. She loaded the pieces into garden sacks and piled them in the kitchen as she worked her way along.

Moving the furniture was painful, but she managed eventually, fuelled by coffee and codeine. She was thankful that there was no big display unit or anything heavier than a two-seater sofa. In the worst affected area, blood had penetrated the carpet and stained the underlay. She took this up as well, although this was more firmly attached and took a lot more effort. After six hours, the carpet and underlay were both in small pieces in bags. Burning would have to wait until tomorrow now as it was getting dark outside.

Ella moved across the floor with the hammer looking for carpet tacks. She had trodden on two so far, and it hadn't been a pleasant experience. Once she had deemed the floor relatively safe, she decided to tackle the wall that Lee had somehow managed to bleed on. She took a bucket of hot water and various cleaning products and went to work, scrubbing the wall and the skirting. The skirting was no problem at all, as with the coffee. The blood came off the wall quite easily too, but so did the paint. *Shit!* she thought. *I'm going to have to repaint as well.* The enormity of the job was beginning to get to her. *Painting can wait, if there is no blatant evidence left, and it's not likely that anyone will come by any time soon.*

Jobs left to do – incinerate carpet (tomorrow along with other items), clean car (tonight after dark).

She made more coffee and sat on the sofa, in pain and emotionally distraught, yet somehow relaxed and proud of what she had managed to achieve so far. She smiled to herself as she rolled a cigarette and smoked it on the sofa, not even having to hide the tobacco afterward. Once her next dose of painkillers had kicked in, and it was properly dark outside, Ella grabbed her cleaning products once again and went out to the car. In case anyone happened to be watching a woman cleaning her car at night, she began on the back seats and gave it all a wipe over, ending up on the driver's seat. The fabric on the seats was black, luckily,

The Broken Doll: Book One

and by torchlight there was little noticeable staining. Ella proceeded to mop up the blood from the foot well, cleaned the chrome plates and pedals, and wiped down the door. If you weren't looking for signs of foul play, you wouldn't notice anything wrong in the car. Ella checked over the outside for anything out of the ordinary but found nothing, her mission was almost complete.

After dinner, Seb put on his trainers and fetched the dog's lead. Natasha was clearing up, and he told her that he would take the dog out for a bit while it was still dry. Natasha looked at him lovingly, almost managing to avoid the jealous thought that he may be sneaking off to see someone else.

"Where are you going to walk?" she asked.

"Not sure," he replied, "probably along to the beach and back." With that, he left, heading straight towards the cliff-tops and the mysterious young woman. Seb had been in a rush to get out and forgotten his phone, and therefore, torch, so decided to approach from the other direction, the way he would usually come home. As he came onto the path leading along towards the house, he could see it from the front. There were lights on at the front windows but with closed curtains. *Someone must be in. She might not be alone though,* he considered, becoming nervous as he got closer. There was a flickering white light outside the house, and he could just about make out a silhouette of a car and someone small, most likely her. Seb decided to take a chance and stroll around the front of the house this time; if it wasn't her, he would simply keep walking. If it was her, he wasn't sure what he would do, but he would just see what happened. As he approached, he could tell that it was her, unfortunately not in a dress, but in a baggy tracksuit-type affair. His footsteps crunched on the stones as he got closer, and she spun around, clearly startled. Her torch shone at him and he looked away from the glare.

"Guess that's only fair after I blinded you last time," he said cheerily, thankful for an icebreaker.

"What are you doing here again?" she asked, quietly.

"Just passing," Seb told her, "walking the mutt. How are you?"

"I'm fine, I told you that last time."

"You know, it's easier to clean a car in the daytime, a bit tricky when it's pitch black out."

"Ha ha, yes, well, I forgot to do it earlier so I'm just sprucing it up a bit," Ella said, quickly locking the car. She put down the cleaning bucket and the torch. "So, tell me, why does a handsome stranger keep coming by to check up on me?" she asked.

"Does he?" Seb asked in mock-surprise. "Who is he?"

"You are a funny one, Sebastian," she said.

"You remembered my name.... Interesting," Seb said, feeling a flutter as it was getting a little flirtatious. "What's yours then?"

"Ella. So, what are you after?"

"I'm just a concerned citizen, checking on the welfare of a pretty lady," Seb said, smoothly.

"And how does your wife feel about that?" Ella asked, nodding towards Seb's wedding ring.

"I'm not doing anything wrong am I? Why would she have any concerns?"

"No, you're not. Although the way you look at me makes me wonder if you want to?"

"If I want to what?" Seb asked, wanting her to say more.

"I don't know.... Have me on the bonnet of this car? I'm not offering, by the way, just wondering what you're after from me." Seb felt a bit embarrassed, as though she was mocking him. He decided it best to leave as he felt awkward.

The Broken Doll: Book One

"I'm glad that you're OK. Here's my card if you need any help in the future. Sorry to have bothered you." And with that, he headed back the way he had come, leaving Ella to smoke another cigarette on her sofa, thinking of Seb. *He definitely wants me.*

SEVEN

Natasha woke up at 3am to find herself alone in bed. She jumped up in a panic, unused to Seb not being there, and found him fast asleep on the sofa. There was a glass of bourbon on the coffee table, and the television was on with the sound low. She poked him in the cheek.

"Come on, piss-head," she said, "Time for bed." Seb dragged himself up, and they headed upstairs.

"Sorry, I couldn't sleep so thought I'd watch some television," he told her, not fully awake.

"That's fine darling. I just wondered where you were. I thought maybe you went for a night-time stroll to check on your girlfriend."

"What?!" Seb exclaimed, a bit surprised.

"I'm teasing," Natasha said, "Why are you looking so guilty?"

"I'm not, I just don't like being accused of whatever you're implying." With that, Seb got into bed and fell back to sleep.

When the time came to actually get up, Seb could hardly move. His head pounded from the whiskey; he was tired, and his first thoughts were of his wife accusing him of having an affair, or something along those lines. *Was she joking?* He couldn't remember exactly what she had said. After an hour of hitting the snooze button on his phone's alarm, he managed to drag himself downstairs and asked his wife what she was up to today.

"Food shopping, then seeing some friends. Are you OK to do the school run?"

"Not sure," Seb replied, vaguely. He had no real plans for the day but felt sure he'd visit Ella. It was as if it were something that he had to do, rather than a conscious decision.

"I can get Dee to pick them up if you want? She's been offering to have them round for dinner."

"Yeah, OK do that. I'll let you know when I know what I'm doing." Just after eight-thirty Natasha left with the children in her car, planning to head straight to the supermarket from the school.

"I'll be an hour or so," she told Seb. "Will you still be here when I get back?"

"Er, dunno, probably. I'm going to freshen up and check my emails before I head down to check over the stock."

"See you later then," and Natasha was gone, seemingly quite moody but Seb decided to ignore it and went for a shower. His emails contained no orders or even enquiries, leaving Seb at a loss for what to do with himself. He considered exercise; he hadn't used his gym membership for a while but was still tired and couldn't be bothered. The weather looked better and so he contemplated taking a wander up to Ella's house. She had been slightly more talkative last night, after all. He hadn't liked the way she made him feel though and was unsure if he would be welcome. *Perhaps I should wait and see if she gets in touch with me?* he thought. *She has my card and could make contact if she wanted to. It may seem a little creepy if I head up there so soon.*

Seb resisted the urge to pay Ella a visit and instead tried to get some of his less popular items listed on some auction sites in the hope of making some space in his storage room. He tried to call Sid again but with no luck. As he made a second attempt to contact Sid, Natasha walked back into the house, muttering something about having forgotten her purse.

"Who were you calling?" she asked, not in a very friendly manner.

"Sid, from the takeaway. He's meant to be buying those two Chesterfields this week, but he's gone away, and I can't get hold of him. Bastard owes me a grand. Even his wife can't get hold of him."

The Broken Doll: Book One

"Hmm, someone else's wife you've been talking to is it?" Natasha sounded angry, but Seb couldn't figure out why.

"What's up with you?"

"Nothing dear, you just seem to be going off for a lot of walks and runs, more than usual, since you mentioned that woman."

"Don't be silly. I love you," Seb told her, kissed her forehead and left the house. *Would it make me a total bastard if I head up to Ella's now? Well, Nat will be off to spend the afternoon with the yummy mummy brigade where she can slag me off to her heart's content. I need something to do....*

Seb didn't find it hard to convince himself to wander to the cliff-top; the weather was a little better than yesterday with less wind, and he didn't view his actions as a betrayal to his marriage. This time he approached from the usual direction, finding Ella in the garden, smoke billowing everywhere from a metal barrel. Before he could speak, she shouted over to him.

"Do I have a stalker?" she asked. "Just so I know."

"Sorry. I didn't mean to act weird. I do honestly come this way quite often; I love it up here. You're very lucky to live here."

"I know. It's beautiful isn't it? So, you just happen to be passing again this morning?"

"Nope, I wanted to see you. Sorry if that is creepy or anything. How are you? Honestly."

"I'm really good actually," Ella told him. "Just getting this garden straight."

"It looked pretty straight before. That's quite a bonfire in that barrel. What's burning?"

"Mostly garden rubbish; I got rid of the shrubs along the side, chopped some wood, and I had some carpet remnants to take to the tip so thought I'd chuck them in too." Ella had noticed Seb looking at the garden sacks and there were pieces of carpet visible in

The Broken Doll: Book One

them. Best to mention it in passing rather than look like it's a secret.

"You married?" Seb asked.

"Well you do get straight to the point!" Ella replied, playfully.

"Just wondered, you know that I am after you were checking for a wedding ring."

"Yes I am. And no, not happily before you ask. And yes, he gave me the bruises. He's an arsehole and he walked out yesterday, and I don't know if he's coming back. Furthermore, I've chucked some of his favourite clothes in the fire, just for fun. Does that answer whatever you wanted to know?"

"Shit. I'm sorry he hurt you. You don't want him to come back then?" Seb asked, realizing that Ella was in a bit of a mess.

"He was drunk when he left so I'm hoping he fell off the cliff, if that answers your question? Maybe I'll start to miss him, but at the moment I'm enjoying the peace. Do you want a coffee?" This question surprised Seb, but Ella was even more shocked by what had left her mouth. She had never invited anyone into the house before.

"Yeah actually, that'd be nice, thank you." Seb entered the garden and followed Ella into her little kitchen. He stood awkwardly while she made two coffees, and they went through to sit in the living room. The only seating now was the small sofa. The armchair had been soiled with Lee's guts and so Ella had stashed it in her bedroom out of sight until she could take it apart for the fire, something she had planned for this coming evening. Seb sat down first and Ella joined him; they were close but there was little choice on the small two-seater.

"Are you getting new carpet? Looks like the remnants you're burning could have been useful!"

The Broken Doll: Book One

"New one is being fitted so I had to take up the old one. Do you smoke?" she asked him, changing the subject as quickly as she could.

"Sometimes," he told her. She rolled two cigarettes, and they smoked them in near silence while they drank their coffees.

"Is it safe to leave the fire like that, unattended I mean?" Seb asked her.

"Hmm, good point. I'll make another coffee and meet you in the garden, can you just check it hasn't burnt anything else down please." Seb went out to the garden and poked at the fire with the metal pole Ella had been using. It was dying down, so he went to grab another few bits of carpet from the bag. He was startled by a bang on the window.

"Coffee is ready," Ella called to him. *That was close,* she thought. *Don't be digging around in the evidence bag!* Ella thought it was too risky to keep pulling bits out of the bag in front of Seb, and so chose to let the fire die off rather than sending him away. Once it was out, they moved back inside and sat on the sofa once more.

"I'm going to stink of smoke now," Seb said, wondering what Natasha would say and trying to think of a believable explanation. Ella looked flushed. She had almost offered Seb use of the shower, not that it would get the smell from his clothes, but her fantasy from the evening in the bath came flooding back. She looked him up and down; her heart quickened, and she felt herself dampening a little between her legs.

"What's wrong?" Seb asked.

"Nothing. I was going to say you can use the shower if you're worried about your wife smelling smoke on you, but that won't get it out of your clothes."

"Don't worry, I'll think of something to say. It's not as if I'm doing anything wrong." As Seb made this last comment, he was aware of how feeble it

The Broken Doll: Book One

sounded, an attempt to convince himself, which wasn't entirely working.

"So, she knows you're here?" Ella asked. Seb could tell where this was leading; if he didn't feel that he was doing anything wrong, then why hide the fact he was there.

"No, but she gets jealous. It doesn't mean I'm being disloyal, just keeping the peace. Am I keeping you from anything?" Seb asked, not wanting to overstay his welcome but also not wanting to leave.

"Not at all. It's nice to have some company. So, I guess your marriage isn't too great either?" Ella asked.

"Actually, it's pretty good really," Seb replied. "We get on well. We have three kids; we're just busy all the time."

"What are you doing here then? Don't say it's out of concern for my well-being; I mean it may have started off like that, but I've seen the way you look at me." Seb blushed. He was stuck for words; the flirting was nice. He hadn't been like this with anyone for a long time, and he was sure Ella liked him too. Nevertheless, he didn't plan to act on it; he had too much to lose, and he really did love his wife.

"Yes, I find you attractive, who wouldn't?" he began, "but I'm not after anything. I couldn't do it to my wife and kids. I am enjoying your company though, and I would like us to become friends if that's OK?" *Phew,* he thought, *that was definitely the right thing to say.*

"That's absolutely fine. My husband could come back at any time so it wouldn't be worth the risk anyway. He would actually kill both of us! Plus, I'm no home-wrecker."

"Great!" Seb said, relieved mostly, and slightly disappointed she didn't just jump him, although he was slowly losing faith in his ability to say no so this was probably for the best. "Can I pinch another ciggie?" he asked, "then I'd better get back."

"Yes, help yourself," and Ella passed him the tobacco tin. "I'll be back in a minute, just want to get changed out of these smoky clothes."

Surely, she can do that when I've gone, Seb thought, a nervous panic rising in him. He began rolling two cigarettes when Ella came out from what he presumed was her bedroom. She was in her underwear, black bra and knickers, wearing her hair down now. She looked incredible as she walked past him, gave him a look with her 'come-to-bed' eyes, and picked up a dress from the clothes airer in the kitchen.

"Sorry, I was looking for this one. I thought it was in my bedroom," she said, half-smirking as she noticed the effect her state of undress had had on him, despite the dark, purple bruises which were prominent along her sides and back. Seb chose not to mention the bruises, but it was clear she had really taken some punches. *Holy shit, she still looks incredible though,* Seb told himself. *I need to go before I make a huge mistake.* They smoked and chatted a little and then Seb left. There was an awkward peck on the cheek as he went, mumbling something about coming by again the next day. Ella had told him that she would like that. Seb wanted to believe that he could just be friends with this woman, but he doubted he had much chance of saying no if she tried to seduce him. *I need to stay away from her,* he told himself. *I just don't think that I can.*

EIGHT

Seb's mind was racing; he wanted Ella badly. There was a raw sexuality to her that made him feel powerless. He imagined all the things he wanted to do with her, how exciting an affair with her could be. He tried to justify acting on his feelings, now in no doubt that Ella was also interested. Even so, he couldn't. Natasha was a good wife and an excellent mother. As far as he knew she had never been unfaithful to him and the sex was amazing, even after all these years. There was no sexual act that he could not perform with his wife, so what satisfaction could he gain from sleeping with someone else? Nevertheless, he wanted to, and this bothered him. Ella seemed well, at least well enough not to need checking up on, so his reasoning for visiting her often was now looking unnecessary. *I need to stay away.* Seb became disappointed in himself and his weakness, genuinely scared that he could not resist this woman, and that he was soon to make a life-shattering mistake.

He headed to the takeaway in town to find out if there was any news on Sid but found it closed. This was unusual as it was open from breakfast through to early evening all year round. There was no explanation on the door, and no-one to ask, so he headed home and sat down at his laptop with a coffee. It was approaching three o'clock, but the children were going to Dee's, and he had no immediate responsibilities to adhere to. He logged on to his social media profiles and checked his business page, which showed nothing of any interest or urgency. He found the page for the takeaway which had had no updates for the last few weeks. After another failed attempt to reach Sid by telephone, he searched for Sid's wife online and sent her a message asking for an update as to when she expected her husband to return home, and whether or not she had had any contact with him. Images of Ella walking around in her underwear flooded his mind, and he could feel himself becoming aroused. He thought about going back to her house but knew that was crazy, and it was really just his cock doing the thinking for him. *Maybe I should fix that?* he thought. Unsure of when Natasha would return home, and worried that asking her would make her suspicious, he decided to lock himself in the bathroom and satisfy himself in there. It was a brief act, images of Ella enough to bring him to climax within a few minutes. He cleared up the mess he'd made and called his wife, letting her know that he was home.

Ella spent the rest of the day destroying evidence, beginning with the rest of the blood-stained carpet and moving on to dismantling the chair and burning that. Aside from the decomposing corpse buried in the garden, there was little proof of any foul play having occurred at the house. Once she had achieved as much as she had the strength to do, Ella slumped onto the sofa and began to think over the events of the last few days. She had been on autopilot, carrying out tasks, which seemed to be out of her control, duties which she had no choice but to do. Reality was starting to sink in, and she began to cry. She'd been hurt both physically and emotionally; her husband was dead, and his killer's identity was a mystery. She could face prison if anyone found out that she had hidden the body and destroyed evidence, and, to top it all off, she was now becoming somewhat besotted with a handsome stranger who seemed to have feelings for her. *Maybe he just wants to fuck me,* she thought. *If that was the case, he would have made a move when I was half-naked, surely? He clearly fancies me.... Maybe he is genuinely interested in me?* Ella's mind wandered to thoughts of Seb and the possibility of a relationship; she fantasized about him visiting regularly. She daydreamed about them snuggling up in the evenings with books and films, making love in the shower, him leaving his wife and moving in with her. She even saw herself as a stepmother to Seb's children and imagined family outings. Of course, it would be awkward with his wife. She would be bitter and angry, but people move on. It was with this fantasy that Ella fell asleep where she was sat, smiling to herself about a happy future with a married man she hardly knew.

The kids burst through the door throwing their coats to the floor and running off to their bedrooms.

"Pyjamas!" Natasha shouted after them, scooping up coats and school bags and hanging them on pegs by the front door.

"Hello," Seb said as she came down the stairs into the kitchen. "How was your day?"

"Fine," Natasha replied as she put the kettle on. "Drink?" she asked.

"Tea please," Seb requested. "You OK?" he asked, sensing that something wasn't right with Natasha.

"Fine."

"It doesn't sound like it, what's up?"

"Nothing. What did you do today?" she asked him. Seb felt anxious. It was as though she knew the answer and was testing him.

"Pottered around online for a bit, went to the town to look for Sid, went to check over the stock so that I can clear some space down there. That's about it."

"Oh, right," she said, clearly not saying what she wanted to.

"Why? What do you think I've been doing?"

"Help me get the kids ready for bed. If you actually want to know what's wrong, we can talk about it when they're asleep. Not unless you plan to go for another wander tonight?"

The Broken Doll: Book One

Shit, does she know I went to see Ella? I didn't actually do anything wrong, so I should just be honest, but would I believe her if it was the other way around? Fuck, see what she says later.

This confrontation was unlike Natasha and had Seb feeling on edge. He was eager to get to the bottom of whatever the accusation was going to be, so speedily got the children to bed, convincing them it was too late for stories despite it being half an hour earlier than usual. When they were all in their beds, Seb found Natasha stood in the kitchen with a glass of white wine.

"Tell me again what you did today," she demanded.

"I was here for about an hour after you left, I went down to the lock-up to sort through some stuff, went by the takeaway on the way back, which was closed, and then came home. I tried to call Sid, but he didn't answer and so I messaged his wife but haven't heard back from her either. Then I called you to tell you I was home. Why? What am I supposed to have done?"

"I don't know. Maybe spent the day with that fucking woman?"

"Don't be ridiculous, why would you think that?" Seb asked, trying to sound shocked but really trying to find out if Natasha actually knew, with any certainty, that he'd been there.

"I thought you'd be sorting through your stock, so I went by earlier and you weren't there."

"What time? You must have missed me."

"Just before you called me, maybe half three."

"Right, well, as you know, I called you to say I was home so obviously I'd already left there. Well done with your investigation Miss Marple, but I haven't done anything wrong so give it a rest."

"Hmm, I spoke to that weird guy with the food trailer; Darren is it? He said you hadn't been there all day."

"Daryl. He must have missed me too, maybe he didn't notice me go in or out? You're jumping to conclusions."

"I don't think I am. You'd better not be fucking about mister." Natasha gave him a slightly sad look, like something had gone wrong between the two of them.

"I'm not fucking around. I wouldn't, and you should know that. You should trust me. I trust you. I don't demand you tell me every place you go and who you see all day," Seb replied, slightly hurt and feeling a little guilty. He wanted to walk out, but that would only exacerbate the situation so endured an evening of awkward silence in front of the television instead, followed by, unsurprisingly, a sexless bedtime.

Ella awoke in the early hours still on the sofa. Her train of thought continued from where it had left off as she had drifted to sleep. She pondered her future with Seb. She felt herself falling for him despite hardly knowing him, but still sure that he had shown kindness and saw him as almost a saviour to her. Of course, he didn't know that Lee wasn't coming back, but she could tell him he had been in contact and that they were to be divorced. That may be enough to get him to admit to his feelings. He was unhappy with his wife, probably some fancy looking bitch; he had to be, otherwise why was he so interested in another woman's welfare? Ella could understand his commitment to his children, but they would be resilient enough to cope; after all, most marriages end in divorce, and children deal with it reasonably well. She was certain that Natasha would make things difficult for them though, and she was unsure how to deal with this obstacle. There had to be a way to get her out of the picture but, despite choosing to let her husband die, Ella couldn't imagine herself actually killing someone.

The Broken Doll: Book One

Before she realized it, the sun had appeared, and the day was looking bright. Having convinced herself of the certainty of her relationship with Seb, Ella got herself ready and wrote a list of chores to complete. She was in desperate need of some household essentials, primarily coffee, and required access to money. The small amount of cash she had taken from Lee's wallet would not be enough, and she didn't have access to his bank account. Once Lee had taken his last breath Ella had turned off his mobile phone and hidden it away, afraid of someone calling. It was, however, the only place that she thought Lee may have his PIN stored, if anywhere at all. Nervously she turned the phone back on, jumping at the sound as each text message from the last few days was delivered. Ella was no technical wizard and was therefore thankful that Lee didn't have the sense to lock his phone with a code. There were a few messages, which seemed to be junk mail. Two from sleazy Graham; the first of which read 'Sorry mate' and was dated the night he had fought with Lee. The second, sent yesterday, eloquently stating 'Fine, fuck you then, said I was sorry. We were pissed, you're lucky I didn't press charges the mess you made of my face.'

Ella took this to mean it was unlikely he was the murderer, unless the second text was a clever ruse to make him look innocent although she strongly doubted that he had ever done anything that clever in his life. There were a couple of boring texts from other guys regarding pool matches. The interesting ones were from a number only named as 'C'. There were eleven messages, between the two of them, spanning the last week or so. To begin with, 'C' was trying to arrange to see Lee for more 'fun', then 'C' (a female Ella assumed) was worried that she had put him off seeing her, for some reason. A couple of attempted seduction texts were sent 'I want to feel you inside me xxx', 'Please let me know when we can get naughty again' etc. Lee

The Broken Doll: Book One

hadn't replied to these last few messages. The most recent simply read 'I guess that we're done then? You know that little skank won't please you like I did. I'll be in the pub if you change your mind' followed by a sad face. This last message was dated the night Lee had died.

Ella decided to look through for more information on this 'C' and scrolled through the photos on the phone. There were very few; a couple of pool evenings, drunk looking apes propping up a bar. A few of old tarts that they must have been chatting up on nights out. And one photo of some tits. Not Ella's, and they didn't look like they were from a website, the picture was too amateurish. *Great, so her name starts with a C and I know what her tits look like. However, I do have her phone number.... Maybe there's a way to find out who she is from that?*

Ella remembered what she had been looking for before getting distracted and went through the list of contacts. There was nothing called 'PIN' so maybe he was slightly brighter than she thought. She began clicking on each name to search for a 4-digit number. No luck until reaching the names beginning with 'N'. Nat – 7414. Her first thought was that Nat could be Natasha, Seb's wife. However, that would be crazy and then the penny dropped; he banked with NatWest. Bingo. Detective work complete, Ella turned the phone back off and grabbed her bag, plus Lee's bank card, and headed to town.

After a quick trip to an Express (overpriced) version of a regular supermarket for a few necessities, with the relief that she was able to use the bank card until the funds were no longer sufficient, Ella pondered her next move. *Take the shopping home or go somewhere else? There are so many hours to kill in a day!* Ella thought of Seb and was curious to see where he had his business set up. *Surely, I can pop by and have a look. It's open to the public after all.* Ella couldn't remember exactly where to go so went back into the shop to ask for directions as she only knew the name of the road, and it was unfamiliar to her. Thankfully, it wasn't far and shouldn't take more than ten minutes to walk to, over the bridge and taking the first right after the train station, according to the overweight till assistant with the gammy leg.

Seb had awoken in a bad mood; Natasha was really off with him, and the lack of sex hadn't helped. Once the children were deposited at school, Seb headed down to the lock-up, deciding that sitting there on his own was preferable to sitting at home under the weight of Natasha's angry silence. He didn't dare to go to see Ella for fear of getting caught. He had just had time to buy a coffee from Daryl and play a game of solitaire on his phone when in walked Natasha.

"Checking up on me?" he asked, not in the mood for her moaning at him.

"Kind of, actually," she replied without looking at him. Natasha looked around the lock-up in silence for a few minutes before speaking again. "I do want to trust you. I just feel as if something is off between us, and I can't shake the idea that you're hiding something. Perhaps I'm being paranoid and if so, I'm sorry. Even so, for my own peace of mind, I will be keeping an eye on you. I'm willing to drop it about that woman and to take your word that you have not done anything that you shouldn't have, but if you have nothing to hide, then you won't mind me keeping tabs on you a bit more."

Seb didn't know what to say, after all it sounded kind of reasonable. If he had nothing to hide, then why would he mind his wife knowing his whereabouts? She had played this well. "You are being paranoid honey, but it's fine. I don't have anything to hide," Seb told her, trying to hide his annoyance at her plans to follow him around. The door then opened again, and Seb's heart skipped a beat as he gazed upon Ella, short summer dress, hair down, shy but seductive look on her perfect face. He quickly looked back at Natasha, worried that the panic he felt would be showing on his face. If it did, Natasha seemed not to have noticed. Thanks to the wonders of make-up, she did not notice any bruising on Ella either, or she would surely have realized who this woman was.

"I'll let you get on then, looks like you may have a customer. I'm going for coffee, so if Sid's place is open I'll ask about these old sofas if you want?"

"Yes please," Seb replied. "I'll see you later then." Without another word Natasha left, a slight pang of jealousy coming over her as she clocked the beautiful woman who was approaching her husband. *She's just a customer,* Natasha told herself. *Now you really are being paranoid.*

"Hi," said Seb, head spinning from having both women in the same room.

"Was that your wife?" Ella asked, a little too loudly for Seb's liking.

"Yes, she was checking up on me actually. Apparently, I've been acting suspiciously. What are you doing here?"

"I wanted to see where you worked," Ella told him. "Is that OK? I kind of hoped you'd want to see me."

"It's always good to see you, I just don't want Natasha getting the wrong idea. I have to go and do some things in a minute so can't chat for long, sorry."

Ella looked disappointed. Seb looked terrified, his eyes darting between Ella and the door in case Natasha walked back in.

"You know if she comes back in, you're going to have to buy something, or she'll be even more suspicious!"

The Broken Doll: Book One

"That's fine Seb. I might buy something anyway. I love these sofas; Chesterfields, aren't they?"

"Yes, certainly bigger than the one you have at the moment."

"And they look so comfortable," Ella commented as she sat down on one. "I often fall asleep on the sofa with a book, so it would need to be comfy."

Seb couldn't look away as she slid herself across the Chesterfield and lay face down across its length, her feet at the end where Seb stood. She wriggled herself about, pretending to be getting comfortable, deliberately causing her dress to rise just enough to expose the lower parts of her buttocks and some black, lacy underwear. Seb's blood was pumping, rushing to the area that Natasha alone should have access to. *Shit, I could lock that door and take her right there. Way too risky though, leave before it's too late!* he thought in a bit of a panic.

"The Chesterfields are reserved at the moment, but I'll let you know if they don't sell. I really must go out now, sorry. Good to see you though." Seb tried to be friendly and keep his behaviour towards Ella purely platonic.

"Could you call by my place later for a coffee? I want to talk to you about something. Unless you have time now?" Ella asked sweetly.

Unable to trust himself alone with Ella any longer, Seb said that he would try to see her that evening but really had to go and run some errands now. Ella gave him a raunchy smile, stroked his hand for a split-second, and left.

The Broken Doll: Book One

NINE

Seb was struggling. He wanted to visit Ella, but knew it wasn't wise and had almost resigned himself to the fact that he would eventually end up sleeping with her. He wondered what the outcome really would be if he had an affair. He was terrified of getting caught, of course, and Natasha had been clear that she would be checking up on him. They had always said that if one of them was unfaithful, then the relationship would be over but Seb felt that, in time, they could work things out. Nevertheless, it would be damaged, that was for sure. *If only I had a believable excuse to leave the house,* he thought. Going for a run or walking the dog wasn't going to cut it anymore. He rarely went out for a drink without Natasha, and she knew all his friends so could easily verify his whereabouts, there was no way he would ask anyone to cover for him, mostly because all his friends liked Natasha a lot and he didn't trust any of them to keep his secret. The only other thing he did on his own some evenings was to go to the gym. *Natasha could call the gym to see if I'm there. Although that's pretty extreme. But she might.* Seb decided it was risky, but worst-case scenario he could say that he had changed his mind and been running instead; she probably wouldn't be too convinced, but she couldn't prove otherwise. *I'll need to come home looking like I've had a decent workout, but if Ella gets her way that shouldn't be a problem!*

Seb made this plan with himself, slightly excited about the secretive nature of his actions, partly hating himself for it, and still justifying his actions to himself as he had not physically cheated on Natasha. As the evening went on, Seb got into his gym kit without saying anything.

"I'm going to hit the treadmill for a bit, if that's OK darling?" Natasha looked at him suspiciously.

The Broken Doll: Book One

"Hmm, make sure you go straight there and back then, remember you're under surveillance," she replied. Natasha had a way of making things sound like a joke that really weren't.

"I know. I won't be more than an hour and a half. Love you." And with that, Seb left. He headed toward the gym but then turned to the right, jogging along the river and up to Ella's house. Seb was on autopilot and deep in thought about what may happen when he saw her. For the first time, he thought about Ella's husband and began wondering why he had not yet returned. As he approached the little house, the front door opened and Ella was standing there in a dressing gown, her hair wet, a cigarette in her hand.

"Hi," she said. "I didn't think you'd make it. Wife let you out then?" she teased.

"She thinks I'm at the gym, so I can't stay long," Seb told her as he entered the house. "Have you heard from your husband?" he asked. "I just wondered what was going on with him, it's a bit odd to just go isn't it?".

"He called yesterday, said he's had enough of me, met someone else apparently. It doesn't look like he's coming back," Ella told him deceitfully, looking away, unsure of how to reply.

"Are you OK with that? What happens to the house?"

"I'm glad he's gone; he's a nasty prick. It's sad in a way. I never saw myself as the divorced type, but it's definitely for the best. And it means I get to see you more often."

Seb felt awkward. This last sentence had made him uncomfortable, as if it were confirmation that they were starting a relationship.

"Do you mind?" Seb asked, pointing at Ella's tobacco.

"Help yourself, do you want a drink? I've got some nice bourbon."

"I'll have one small one if that's OK, don't want to smell like booze when I get home." Seb rolled himself a cigarette, and they sat in near silence, sipping at the whiskey. Seb knew he had to go, or he would have been out too long. There was no time to do anything physical with Ella anyway, so he finished his drink and got up to leave. As they approached the front door Ella took his arm, turning him to face her. Their eyes met and she made her move at last, kissing him deeply. For a second or two, he returned the kiss but managed to regain a thread of self-control and pulled away.

"I have to go."

"Are you sure?" she asked him, dropping her robe to the floor, revealing her complete nudity beneath. Like a petrified adolescent, Seb ran out the door and began jogging home, fully aware it was now decision time – either have a steamy, incredible affair with, certainly, a terrible outcome and a future filled with regret, or never see Ella again. Seb was, however, beginning to grasp the fact that the choice may not really be his to make, and that Ella seemed to be the one in control, transforming from a helpless victim to seductive temptress virtually overnight. *I'll end it with her, but in person. I can't just cut her off like that, it's not fair on her.*

Natasha seemed absolutely fine when he returned home, thankfully, and went to bed soon after. Seb sat on the sofa for a while trying to work out how to phrase things with Ella to avoid upsetting her, hoping he had the strength to go through with it and to resist her should she make another move. His mind wandered to the image of her full nakedness, and he couldn't help but sort himself out before climbing into bed with his wife. *God, I'm a dick,* he thought, as he drifted off to sleep.

Ella stared at herself naked in the full-length mirror, pinching the tiny amount of excess skin around her belly. She had always felt quite attractive, despite everything Lee had done to put her down, and so Seb's rejection of her was surprising, and a little hurtful. *He must want me,* she thought. *Men don't generally say no to anyone, and he has been keen to see me. However, he is married with children. He can't possibly find that wife of his more attractive than me. It must be the kids, guess he's worried about losing them. Suppose that confirms that he's a decent person at least. If only his wife truly loved him, then she could see that he would be happier with me and just let us be together.* Ella had no doubt that Seb represented her one real chance at happiness in life and was almost equally convinced that he felt the same way. The only person that stood between them now was Natasha, and Ella had had enough of people coming between her, and the life that she wanted.

The next morning Ella threw on a skimpy summer dress and headed into town to visit the library, grabbing a coffee from the bakery opposite first. Although the sun shone brightly, it was not as warm as she had hoped or, indeed, dressed for. After examining the section entitled 'Staff Choices' and finding them all to be novels about dogs and their adventures, Ella imagined that the 'staff' consist of teenage girls and single women in their fifties. After a half-hour of mooching around the shelves, one of the computers became available and Ella started browsing online. With a limited use of the Internet, she was distracted by some clothing sites for a while and then, when stuck for topics to Google, she put in the name of Seb's business. A few links came up to his social media and website, followed by one detailing the company profile listed with Companies House. She clicked on the link and was presented with Seb's full name, address, trading history, and so on. The listed address was not the same as the address for the lock-up as he had expanded to this after beginning the business from home and had not updated the details online. Ella wasn't familiar with many road names, so she entered the address into Google and found that he lived a minute or two's walk from the town centre, very close to where she now sat.

"Do you have a pen and a piece of paper I could borrow please?" Ella asked the young man behind the desk, looking him right in the eye, trying to decide if he enjoyed canine fiction. He smiled and passed her a scrap of paper, nodding towards a black Biro which was already on the desk. She returned to her station and made a note of anything she felt may be useful; email address, home address, contact numbers. After returning the pen, Ella headed back out into the high street and decided she would enter the raggedy old bric-a-brac place a few doors down.

The place was small, or maybe just seemed that way due to the huge stacks of books, puzzles, and ornaments, in no recognizable order. It smelled funny in there too, a bit like attics and charity shops. Dust lined most of the books, but it was exciting, and there were barely any titles representing mainstream bestsellers in this potential treasure trove of literature. The man who owned and ran the shop was busy sorting through a box of toy cars. He seemed content and did not speak to Ella. Having never seen anyone in the shop before, and the state that it was in, Ella wondered if the man ever made any money, or perhaps he didn't need to, and this was a hobby of sorts. She could have easily spent the whole day there but scanned the more ornate spines looking for something out of the ordinary to treat herself to. There weren't many novels in the shop, it was mostly reference titles on rather obscure subjects, largely bird-watching, but also science-based titles from the 1940s, cookery books, toy and model collectors' guides, and a few on vehicle mechanics from the 1980s. There was a small pile of books, which seemed to be a set, entitled 'The Complete History of Antiques: A Buyer and Seller's Guide'. She found four of these books, fortunately parts I – IV. *Seb would love these!* Ella approached the man who was now lazily watching the passers-by through the window.

"Excuse me," Ella said, almost shyly, not wanting to disturb him.

"Hello," he replied, in a much jollier tone than his expression had led Ella to expect. "What can I help you with?" Ella picked up Part I of the set of books.

"Firstly, I have found four parts to this set, do you know if there are more or is this complete?"

"I have no idea," the man replied, unhelpfully, but honestly. He opened one of the books to look for more information but could not find anything to suggest more titles in the series.

"OK," Ella said, "Four seems like plenty anyway. How much are they?"

"That depends how many you want. I'd say £10 each or if you want all four you can have them for £35."

Ella looked through her bag, pulling out two £10 notes and some change. In total she had £25.16 on her and had not brought Lee's bank card.

"Would you do the set for £25?" she asked, smiling sweetly.

"Sorry love, £35 is a bargain as it is." Ella put her hand on the shop owner's hand and leant forward. Using her other hand, she tugged at her dress causing more of her cleavage to be exposed.

"But I really, really want it," Ella said in her most seductive voice.

"That won't work with me dear; you're not my type," the man stated, a bit taken aback by Ella's forwardness.

"And what type is that? I can be anyone's type you know."

The Broken Doll: Book One

"Well if you had a cock it'd be a good start." Ella hadn't seen that coming and now felt very foolish.

"Sorry," she mumbled and went to leave.

"Don't be silly love, no harm done. Even so, the price is still the same. You want them?"

"Yes please," Ella managed to say quietly, "Just Part I for now, and I might come back for the others if you still have them." Ella paid and quickly left, doubting she'd have the courage to return for a while. The best plans came together over coffee, rather than alcohol, so she resisted the temptation to grab a whiskey from the pub, which was just opening its doors, and popped into a small café for a cheap mug of Americano.

The café was basic, but affordable, and seemed popular, certainly with the over seventies anyway. She sipped at the lukewarm coffee and wondered how to get the book to Seb. *I need him to appreciate how serious I am about him. If he finds out I've discovered his address he'll see how dedicated I am. On the other hand, I may come across too strong.* Ella had difficulty gauging whether her behaviour was being clear about her feelings or appeared more sinister. Nevertheless, she knew she wanted him, and she also knew that he would love the book. *What if his wife sees it? Worst-case scenario she gets angry and leaves him. Which is also best case.* Having convinced herself that it was a win-win plan, Ella paid for her coffee, pocketed a pen from the café counter, and headed up the road towards Seb's house. She paused for a moment to write inside the cover '*Seb, I found this and thought of you, hope you like it. E xx*'

As Ella approached the house, she became nervous, unsure whether or not to knock on the door (it could be unpleasant if Natasha answered) or to put the book through the letterbox. When she arrived, it became apparent that the latter wasn't going to work; you would have been lucky to fit a Friday-Ad through that tiny opening. Ella was too worried about Natasha answering to knock, and so left the book leaning against the front door, hoping desperately that Seb would find it first.

Ella's stomach was full of knots as she made her way home, nervous about someone other than Seb finding the gift she had left. A part of her wanted Natasha to find it, to cause an argument in the hope that Seb would come running to her. She worried that Seb would be angry with her though and debated going back and removing it from his doorstep. If it had already been picked up, then it may be unwise to go near the house so soon after, she decided, choosing instead to continue her slow wander home. Ella had other things on her mind, pressing concerns, which kept creeping into her thoughts. She wondered how long she could use Lee's bank card for before it ran dry, unsure of any incomes that he may have besides his wages. She thought about turning on his phone again, certain there must be messages from people he knew trying to find him by now. The thought terrified her, as if turning it on would make it traceable like in a film. Of course, it may well be traceable, but Ella had no reason to think the police would be doing that if they hadn't first been to the house to check on him. Ella thought about getting some bourbon on her way home and couldn't decide whether it was a waste of money or a well-earned treat. The range at the only shop on the way was somewhat limited, so she decided to look and if nothing took her fancy, leave it. She gazed at the spirit shelves with disappointment, not one bourbon on offer, just generic blended Scotches and Jack Daniels. She opted for a half bottle of Jack, as she couldn't stomach the sweetness enough for a whole bottle, grabbed a bag of ice, and decided that she would sit in the garden and wait patiently to hear from Seb.

The Broken Doll: Book One

Seb was sat in the kitchen, staring at the laptop when Natasha walked into the house. "Hi handsome," she said, sweetly. "What are you up to?"

"Trying to sell some things, it's been ages. I've not been having much luck in the auctions so thought I'd try some selling pages, Friday-Ad, found some selling apps on the phone. What have you been doing?"

"Not much, have we got any wine?" Natasha asked.

"There is a little white in the fridge, just about a glass each, maybe."

"Great," she replied, grabbing the wine from the fridge and drinking it straight from the bottle. Seb looked at her with an uneasy glare, confused as to why she hadn't poured two glasses.

"So, I got you a present today. Do you want it?" Natasha stated in a tone which wasn't as friendly as when she had first entered the house. Seb became nervous; something was clearly wrong but there was no way that she could know about him being kissed by Ella.

"Sounds exciting, what is it?"

"It's a book, about antiques." Natasha held the book up for Seb to see. He looked genuinely pleased with it.

"That's really nice of you darling, thank you." Seb managed, with genuine appreciation.

"I even wrote a message in the front cover, just for you."

Seb opened the book and read the handwritten message inside. He could feel his pulse quicken in preparation for the impending argument. He couldn't think of anything to say at all; Natasha wasn't stupid.

"I can't help it if she bought me a book," Seb muttered feebly. "There isn't anything going on."

The Broken Doll: Book One

"She knows where we live?! It was a lovely thought, and you should thank her for it," Natasha said in a sarcastic, angry tone. "Thank her, in person. As in go to her, now, and get the fuck out of this house." Her voice only rose a little as she said this to her husband, managing to maintain her composure as much as one can when chugging wine from the bottle.

Seb looked terrified, unsure of how to respond. He immediately felt guilty for his first thought, which was to say 'Fine. I'll go and thank her. Really hard.' So, instead, he told Natasha that she was being unreasonable, and he would go to the lock-up for a bit to give her time to calm down, telling her to call him when she wants him back and if necessary, he'd sleep there tonight. However, as soon as he closed the front door he knew where he was heading.

It was still light out as Ella sat on her garden bench, sipping Jack Daniels on ice, staring at her phone in the hope that Seb would text. Nothing. *Maybe he hasn't found the book, perhaps he can't contact me because of HER.* Ella longed for Seb to call her, to thank her, to come and see her. As she looked out to sea from her garden, twilight creeping in, she was startled by a familiar voice.

"We need to talk."

Ella's heart skipped, overjoyed to see Seb, but this immediately faded as she realized that he was not happy.

"Hey," she said.

"I don't want to seem ungrateful. The book is lovely, but Natasha found it and threw me out. She's really pissed off, thinks we're having an affair."

"Sorry, I didn't think," Ella lied, "I saw it and thought you'd like it. Did you explain that we're just friends?" she asked.

"I told her that there is nothing going on, which there isn't." Seb stated, not entirely convincingly.

"Well I didn't mean to cause any trouble. But as you're here, whiskey? What time do you have to be in?" Ella asked with a bit of a piss-taking tone.

"Tomorrow by the sounds of it, I told her I'd stay at the lock-up tonight." Ella's stomach felt funny, excited perhaps, as an opportunity had arisen for him to stay the night. She grabbed a glass from the kitchen and poured Seb a generous shot.

Seb slumped down on to Ella's sofa, whilst she went to grab her tobacco from the window sill in the kitchen. She sat down next to him, slightly closer than was necessary.

"How long is she likely to be pissed off with you for?" Ella asked him. Seb looked troubled, unhappy.

"I have no idea, probably only for a day or two. I just need to get her to believe that I haven't done anything wrong."

"So, I guess staying here tonight wouldn't help matters?" Ella asked, looking him in the eye, making her offer quite clear.

"No, it definitely wouldn't help. And I really can't stay over, even if nothing happened, she wouldn't believe me. She may well come to the lock-up and check on me anyway." Ella looked away, trying to conceal her feelings not only of disappointment but also embarrassment. She had been sure that Seb would seize this opportunity to spend the night with her, but he was too worried about getting caught. *He should get caught,* Ella thought. *At least then she'd bugger off.*

"Hypothetically," Ella began, "If you weren't with anyone, would you be interested in me?"

"Of course," Seb replied, with certainty. "I'm sure you can tell that I'm attracted to you, and I'm flattered that you like me too. But, I'm married, and I don't want to lose that. It's been hard for me not to start something with you but, unfortunately, it isn't going to happen."

The Broken Doll: Book One

Ella began to well up as she rolled a cigarette, trying to hide the tears that were forming. *He wants me, but we can't be together because of her.* Ella thought about telling Natasha that they had been having an affair, hoping that she would leave Seb. He'd be angry though, it could backfire if he just denies it. Natasha would have doubts, but without proof then she would, or at least should, stand by her husband. *I'd need evidence of an affair, but if he doesn't stay over what can I do?* Ella decided that her only option was to try her best to seduce Seb tonight. She refilled their glasses and went to get changed. When she came back to the living room, Ella was wearing just a nightie, not too short or sexy, but enough to get Seb's attention. He immediately noticed the lack of a bra, her small, pert breasts outlined perfectly with visible nipples. Ella sat back down with him, this time a little further away, as if she had taken the hint that nothing was going to happen, but fully aware that his eyes were all over her. They chatted for hours, finished the whiskey, smoked too many cigarettes. The conversation came naturally, with no particularly deep subjects, just a general 'get to know each other' discussion. Seb was enjoying himself; the whiskey had relaxed him, and he was conscious that there was a level of flirting taking place. He would sneak the odd glance at Ella's chest whenever she leant forward to pick up her drink and was aware of a nagging voice inside his head telling him to leave soon. Even so, the hours passed; he was still there, and Ella made a move. She wasn't particularly subtle, and was also a bit drunk by this point, but Seb was still taken by surprise as Ella stood up and quite deliberately dropped the lighter. She faced away from him and bent over to pick it up, her nightie rising enough to reveal no underwear and give a brief, but a very clear, view of everything. As she turned around Seb looked away.

"Did you like that?" Ella asked.

"I should go," Seb replied, without actually moving.

"Yes, you probably should." Seb stared at her, trying to find the strength to get up and head to the lock-up. It was still early enough to say he had been in the pub if Natasha had been to check up on him.

"Can you do me a favour before you go?" Ella asked him as she knelt on the floor in front of the sofa.

"Maybe," Seb said with uncertainty.

"Will you come in my mouth?"

TEN

Natasha was rather drunk. The small amount of wine that had been in the house earlier had long gone and the children were in bed, so it seemed like a good idea to call Dee and ask her for some company and plenty of alcohol. Natasha explained the situation and Dee just nodded, muttering a few statements about how all men are shits. Understandably, Dee took Natasha's side in things, but she was also the type of person to enjoy the drama. This meant that she didn't have anything particularly helpful to say, and from previous experience, genuinely thought that all men were either violent, unfaithful, or, in the case of her first long-time partner, both.

"So, assuming he's banging that skinny bimbo, what's the plan now? If you let him get away with it, he'll just do it again, and what's to say she's the first!" Dee stated.

"I've never had any reason to suspect him before, and the way he's behaving now he doesn't seem able to keep secrets very well. If he is cheating, then it'll be over, we've always agreed on that, and he knows that's the deal. I just don't know if he really is. Not for sure anyway."

"Where's he gone now? Are you sure he hasn't gone to see her?"

"Fuck knows. I really hope not. I've had way too much wine to drive about spying. I want to trust him, but it's difficult when he's acting so oddly. However, maybe it is just her; she could simply be a creepy stalker trying to cause problems," Natasha wondered, the thought formulating in her head.

"So, confront her. Tell her to back off. If she insists that they've been having an affair, then tell her to prove it." The wine had a part to play in Natasha agreeing to a confrontation. Rowing with Seb about it was entirely different to getting into an argument with a virtual stranger.

"I'll go by her house tomorrow and talk to her," Natasha decided.

"I wouldn't wait. I can stay with the kids, go up there now. At least you'll know for sure if he's with her, and he won't expect you to be out of the house because of the kids. If he's not there, then you can tell her to back off, if he is there, then at least you know," Dee insisted. Natasha felt that she had to go along with the idea, Dee was quite a dominating person. She also wanted to go, fantasizing about smashing that bitch's teeth in. Adrenalin had already begun pumping, nervous about a confrontation, more frightened that she may catch her husband doing something that she dreaded.

"I need a cigarette," Natasha mumbled as she stood up, wobbling a little as the wine took a firmer grip on her senses. As she returned from the garden, Dee was ending a phone call.

"Taxi will be here in ten minutes," she said.

"Really? I'm not sure this is sensible. I don't even really know where she lives."

"It'll be fine. It's got to be done, trust me. It was Barbara at the taxi place; she's going to drive you up there and wait outside to bring you home again. She'll know where to go, there aren't many houses up there."

"You didn't tell her anything did you?"

"No, just that you had to pick something up from a friend's house, and I told her roughly where it was."

Seb felt helpless, lust taking over. He remained sat on Ella's sofa with her knelt before him. She gazed up at him and began undoing his trousers, causing very noticeable movement inside them. His head tipped back, and his eyes closed. He let out a little moan as he felt her slightly cold hand take hold of his cock. Then the warmth of her mouth enveloped his whole shaft. However, his mind immediately wandered on to thoughts of his children and Natasha. He jumped up, his sizable erection almost hitting Ella in the face.

"I can't. I have to go." Without any further conversation, he put his bits away and, once again, almost ran from the house.

For fuck's sake, he thought. *Now I've done it. Pretty sure that's cheating. Can't take any risks like that again.* Seb headed through the wooded area down to the road and walked briskly towards home, determined to fix things with his wife.

The roads were quiet as the taxi sped along, the driver trying to work out the best approach to the house on the cliff-top as it was dark and largely gravel paths. As they passed the bottom of the wooded area, a figure emerged whom Natasha could have sworn was her husband, but there was wine involved, and it was dark.

After a bit of driving about up a couple of dead-end lanes, the taxi stopped as near as possible to the house without approaching closely enough to be obvious. Natasha decided she would rather surprise Ella and hoped sincerely that she was alone. The curtains were closed, but a light was on inside. Natasha's heart was racing as she knocked on the thin, wooden door. As it opened, just enough for the occupant to see who was calling, Natasha could see that Ella had been crying. *That's a good sign,* she thought. *Maybe that was Seb, coming to tell her to leave him alone.*

"You know who I am?" Natasha asked.

"I can guess. What do you want?"

"I don't know what's going on with you and my husband, he says there is nothing, and I hope to God that's true, but you need to back off. He's with me. He has children. There are plenty of desperate men around here that would be happy to give you some cock, but Seb isn't one of them. Take this as your only warning." Natasha could feel the anger in her voice, the volume rising. She had planned to be calm, to explain that Seb was off limits and leave. Ella just cried, constantly, irritatingly.

"What the fuck are you crying for? And don't say it's me because you were crying when I got here. Has he been by? Has he told you to back your skanky ass off him?"

"Fuck you," Ella said through tears. "He doesn't want you anymore. He's going to be with me so just leave us alone." Ella went to shut the door, but Natasha had seen red at this point and pushed it open, slapping Ella hard enough around the face to knock her to the floor.

"You're a lying whore. I think he's been here to tell you to stay away." Ella slowly stood up, facing Natasha. Her face was red on one side, eyes puffy from crying.

"I'm crying because I feel bad for you and your children, but we can't help who we fall in love with. Seb is too good for you. Yes, he was here. We had some drinks, and he has left to go and end things with you. And before he left, I gulped down his come; it was the best head he'd had, he said. Apparently, you hardly bother anymore."

Natasha didn't lash out. She could feel tears welling up and didn't want to break down here. She bolted from the door and returned to the taxi, dialling Dee's number.

"Hi," Dee said. "Seb's just turned up looking for you, I told him you went to get wine."

"He's a fucking prick and that little bitch can fucking have him. He had already left and apparently, he's there to tell me we're finished. I'll only be a few minutes. Don't say anything to him until I'm back."

The Broken Doll: Book One

"OK, see you soon," Dee replied, trying to sound jolly and not alert Seb to his wife's mood.

Ella's stomach churned, adrenaline still pumping from her confrontation with Natasha. She had set things in motion which couldn't be undone, hoping that she had made it easier for Seb to leave his wife. Ella was sure that this is what he really wanted, certain that they could be happy together. She clung on to her phone tightly, awaiting something from Seb. She was sure that he would be on his way back to her soon, probably quite emotional, but it would be the first night of their new life together. Ella couldn't sit still; things needed to be perfect. She pottered about the small house, tidied the kitchen, and then went to the bedroom. No one had been in there since Lee had 'disappeared', and so it was still full of his things, something she hadn't paid much attention to as she often fell asleep on the sofa. She began by changing the bed, and then grabbed some black bags from under the kitchen sink. She wondered about hiding a certain amount of her husband's belongings, to add some support to the story that he had simply left. However, it didn't seem necessary; no one knew how many clothes he owned, and there was no way of validating this either way. He owned very little, with most of his money going on beer and cigarettes, so it only required a few bags to get all his clothes, and a few toiletries, out of sight.

Ella took the opportunity to make sure the room was appealing, threw the bags out into the garden with the intention of asking Seb to dump them tomorrow, or perhaps incinerate them, reapplied her makeup, and gave the bathroom a quick once over. An hour had passed and there was no news. Feeling a need to keep busy, Ella started going through the drawers of the television cabinet in the living room, picking out any of Lee's DVDs and CDs that she had no use for. The only trace of her husband that now remained inside the

The Broken Doll: Book One

house was a photograph of the two of them, taken when they were first dating. Ella gazed at it, remembering how happy they had been at that time and wondering why, and how, it had all gone so horribly wrong. She was undecided about getting rid of the picture and placed it in a drawer, feeling that it was inappropriate to have it gazing down at her and her new lover. As Ella rolled a cigarette on the sofa, she thought about her husband. More accurately, she thought about his corpse under her garden. Gradually, since his very discreet burial, she had begun moving some bits around outside, meaning that now that particular area was under some large stones and plant pots. There was no noticeable aroma wafting up from the grave and no sign of any animals trying to get to it. Ella didn't dare to go digging about, especially as she had no idea how long a body takes to fully decompose. Once she had Seb's help, she planned on having the area paved, or at least something more secure to prevent any future discovery. Two hours and still nothing. Ella presumed that Seb had a lot of things to pack up, maybe conversations about contact with his children and so on. *Surely, he will be here soon; he's worth the wait.*

Seb sat on the sofa that he had chosen with his wife less than a year ago. Dee sat opposite him, on one of the matching armchairs, sipping her wine in an awkward silence. She had clearly had a few glasses as her speech had begun to slur a little. She looked nervous, as if they had been talking about Seb, and he had now interrupted this. Fortunately, the silence was broken by the sound of a car pulling up outside, followed by the loud sound of a car door being shut. The front door opened and in walked Natasha, face puffy from crying, anger glistening in her eyes. She didn't look too steady on her feet, which Seb put down to the wine. She was one of those people that could drink steadily for some time with no noticeable effects, and then suddenly be completely wasted. She seemed to be about to hit that point. Seb also noticed that his wife did not have any wine with her, suggesting that Dee had lied about her whereabouts. The car was a surprise as well, presumably a taxi as her own was still parked on the next road over. Then something clicked, suddenly her whereabouts became apparent. No wonder Dee did not know what to say to him. Immediately he was on edge, irritated, and expecting a fight.

"You forgot the wine," he stated, making it clear he knew he'd been lied to.

"I should probably go," Dee said as she started to rise from the chair.

"Probably," replied Seb, imagining that Dee had got his wife all riled up.

"I'd like you to stay please," Natasha told her. "Please. There won't be a fight, I just would like my soon-to-be ex-husband to get a bag of his things and leave the house." The calmness in her voice bothered Seb; he wanted her to shout at him, get it all out, and then he could have his say. However, she didn't. Seb was torn, undecided whether to accept it for now and try to talk to her tomorrow when she would be calmer and sober, or whether to state his case right away to avoid things escalating. A trait of his personality, one which irritated himself as much as his wife, was his inability to just quietly go away, and this had an overbearing effect on any important conversations, this one being no different.

"Why?" he asked, "What am I supposed to have done this time?"

"Are you fucking serious? You know what you've done, and I'm not having an argument here and now in case the kids hear us."

"No, I don't know, so why don't you tell me, or is it just your paranoia again?" he retorted, trying to keep the anger from his voice. Natasha stepped closer to him and, as calmly as she could manage whilst holding back the tears, told him where she had been.

"I went to see your whore. I couldn't decide whether you were being honest with me or not, but I hoped you were, and that you were just being harassed by that woman. I thought if I went there, and you were there, then I'd know for sure."

"But I wasn't there, so what's the problem?" Seb asked, confused by her argument.

"I spoke to her; she was crying when I arrived. I told her to back off you, I fucking defended you. Stupidly I thought she was crying because you'd told her to leave you alone. But she was crying because, in her words, she felt sorry for me as the two of you were going to be together."

"Don't be so fucking stupid, if she did say that, then it didn't come from me. I don't want anyone else but you," Seb replied, trying to process this in his head, trying to work out what Ella may have actually said and what Natasha's drunken misinterpretation of that could have been.

"Maybe she just has the wrong impression; she does seem to like me, but I thought we were only being friendly. If she thinks I want more then she is mistaken," Seb told Natasha.

"Yeah maybe, although I guess fucking a girl in the face may make her feel like you want more than just her friendship!" Natasha stated curtly.

Shit, thought Seb. He knew he wasn't a very good liar and didn't feel ready to deny it yet. He was angry that Ella had told her, but he was guilty, so he couldn't very well put all the blame on others. *Better get out now and deal with this tomorrow,* he thought, storming upstairs to grab a bag of essentials and walking out of the house. He decided to take the car, despite being well over the limit, and headed down to the lock-up, not wanting to see anyone at that moment, so he could evaluate the situation and try to salvage something of his marriage.

"What a fucking arsehole!" Dee said, a little shocked at how the conversation had gone. She expected Natasha to make an accusation, Seb to deny it, and they end up going to bed grumpy. Even so, she didn't expect Natasha to say all that.

"Is that really what she said to you? He didn't even try to deny it."

"Yep, she said he was leaving me, had gone home to tell me, and that he came in her mouth before he left. Apparently, he said I never bothered sucking him off any more." At this point, Natasha began to cry, knowing that although the sex she had with Seb was incredibly good, it had been much less often than it used to be. *But that's normal isn't it?* she wondered to herself.

"Well I hope you smacked her in her spunky, whore mouth," Dee stated. "So, what happens now? You always said that if he cheated, then you'd be done with him. Do you think you'll end it completely? Or just let him suffer for a while?"

"I have no idea!" Natasha blurted through floods of tears. "I can't stand to look at him, but I don't want to push him away and into her bed. I suppose he's heading there now. I hate to think about it, I'll call him tomorrow. I just want to sleep now." With that, Natasha stood up and made her way to bed. Thankfully, the wine had made it a little easier for her to sleep, and she was quickly out, exhausted from sobbing. Dee sat in the living room alone and decided that she should stay the night in case her friend needed her. She called home to let them know and curled up, wondering what would happen tomorrow, and how much she should be involved. Ultimately her only role was to support Natasha, and she wondered if pushing her into confronting Ella may have been a mistake.

ELEVEN

Ella looked at the clock through bleary eyes. She must have nodded off for a while. 3.10am and no Seb. It didn't make sense; surely, he wasn't still with *her. Why had he not come running back here? He had to have gone to his storage place, maybe he was worried Natasha would follow him and make a scene. He could just be trying not to hurt her more than necessary, or even trying to protect me.* Ella decided to get dressed and headed out into the darkness, she had to know why he wasn't with her, and she told herself that if he doesn't want to come straight to hers, then she needs to accept that; they can make all the arrangements properly at a more sensible time. Something nagged in Ella's mind, a worry that he may still be with Natasha, a fear that she tried to dismiss but found difficult to shift. It was virtually silent out at that time of the night; the few local pubs had emptied hours beforehand, and the only sound was the lapping of the river against the jetties and the distant rumbling of a fishing boat's engine; even the seagulls were quiet, taking a break from their usual horrendous din. As Ella made her way over the bridge which led to the station, she startled as something ran across her path. She hadn't been in the more built-up parts of town this late at night for a while and was surprised to see a group of foxes scurrying about. She felt jittery. The silence and darkness were eerie, and she began to feel vulnerable, as though anything could happen to her and no one would know. She began to take quicker steps, despite understanding that her imagination was getting the better of her, and that she had quite effectively scared herself for no logical reason.

It wasn't long before she reached Seb's lock-up and was relieved to see a car parked outside the entrance. There was no sign of life, but with the shutters down it wasn't possible to tell if a light was on, or to detect any movement within. Cautiously, Ella knocked on the metal door which formed part of the corrugated shutters. Although she hadn't knocked hard, the combination of the silence outdoors and the material itself meant that the knock reverberated loudly, taking her by surprise. She looked around in a panic, worried that she may have woken someone nearby, but nothing stirred. Ella thought about knocking again but soon heard movement coming from inside. A bolt slid across with a squeak and the door opened a fraction revealing the unhappy, and exhausted looking, face of the man she now believed belonged to her.

"Jesus. What do you want?" he asked, in a tone which wasn't very friendly. Ella tried to hide the sadness she immediately felt with this greeting. She reminded herself that he had chosen not to come to her tonight, and she needed to respect this; after all she had only really wanted to make sure that he wasn't with Natasha.

"Sorry, I didn't like the way we left things. I was kind of expecting you to come back tonight."

"Are you serious? Natasha told me what you said to her, about us being together! I really am sorry if you feel that I've led you on at all but there is no 'us', I'm staying here tonight, and tomorrow I intend to go home and try to fix the damage you've done to my marriage."

Ella's face changed somehow with this statement. The disappointment of Seb not being pleased to see her became a look of anger.

"So, you can just stick your dick in my mouth and then make out I'm the one ruining your marriage. Typical fucking man. I told Natasha everything, there is no way she'll want you back, and you know you don't really want her. All you're going to do is hurt more people for longer; she knows it's over so now there is nothing stopping us being with each other. We can make an arrangement for your kids once she's calmed down a bit and start our life together. It's going to be perfect; I'll be so good to you."

"Look, I'm sorry that you're alone and I'm sorry that your husband left. I understand that you want company, and I think I'm some kind of rebound reaction for you, but I have told you before we can never be together. Yes, I have come close to being seduced. You're beautiful, and I'm sure it would be fantastic. I'm flattered that you've been so persistent, and I guess I'm at fault for letting you keep on trying with me; I just enjoyed the attention. Even so, it's a definite 'no'. I don't feel like we can even be friends really, I almost went too far with you earlier, and I can't risk it. This is it now Ella, go home." With that, Seb closed the door before Ella could speak, worried that she would attempt to seduce him yet again. Ella turned away from the building, tears streaming down both cheeks, feelings of anger, sadness, and embarrassment overwhelming her.

Ella looked at Seb's car. Next to the drain in the road, she spotted a piece of brick, about the size of a fist. She bent down to pick it up, glancing across to see if Seb had reopened the door. Everything was silent and still. She thought about putting the brick through one of the windows, but it would be easily fixed and would only make him angrier with her. She had to make sure that he had to come to her. The anger and frustration that she was feeling rose to the surface and, with the brick in both hands, she slammed it into her own face. The pain jolted through her entire body as her nose cracked, blood pouring like a burst pipe, drenching her clothes. She couldn't breathe through her nose and so had to open her mouth, but as she did it was filled with the warm, rich taste of blood. Once she had regained her composure a little, she sat herself down on the pavement, her back against the side of Seb's car. She rested her head against the passenger-side wing, making sure there was some blood left behind. She waited a few minutes, formulating a plan, and stood herself up. She threw the brick into the shrubbery at the side of the pavement and slowly made her way up through the town and to the police station.

Dee was snoring away on Natasha's sofa when there was a bang on the door. She grabbed her phone to check the time, not quite 6am. *It must be Seb,* she thought, *guess he didn't take his keys.* Dee felt a moment of panic when she answered the door to two police officers, wondering if they were here to see her or Natasha.

"Natasha Briggs?" the female police officer asked. She was much shorter than Dee, barely five feet tall and had the frame of a small boy. Dee doubted she could be very effective in a confrontational situation, although perhaps she suffered with Short Person Syndrome and was frighteningly aggressive.

"No, she's still in bed, I think. What's happened?"

"Can we come in?"

"Yes, of course. I'll go and get her." Dee headed upstairs and found Natasha fast asleep, still mostly dressed. She started to wake her friend, but Natasha startled, quickly sitting upright.

"What's going on? Did you stay over?" she asked.

"Yes, I thought you might need the company. You need to get up. The police are here."

"What the fuck? Why?"

"I don't know. They want to talk to you." Natasha grabbed a robe and headed down into the lounge to find two police officers sat on her sofa. Her mind raced as she wondered who had been hurt, this being the only explanation for their presence that she could imagine.

"Mrs. Briggs?" the small female officer asked her.

"Yes. What's happened?"

"Is your husband Sebastian Briggs?"

"Oh God, what's happened to him?" Natasha asked as she took a seat. All she could think was perhaps a car accident, he had driven off smelling of whiskey after all.

"Nothing has happened to him," replied the male officer, a tall, red-headed man with unusually large arms. "We have him at the station at the moment; he was arrested last night for assaulting a young woman. Do you know where he was?" Natasha looked, and felt, shocked. She assumed that the young woman was Ella but couldn't imagine her husband actually hitting a woman. He'd been a bit aggressive in the past but only verbally; he'd never laid a finger on her.

"Er, we had a fight, and he left here quite late, maybe around eleven but I'm not sure. He has a storage unit near the train station, so he said he was going to stay there, and I haven't heard anything from him since. What's actually happened then? Seb wouldn't hurt a woman. I don't believe that."

"I bet it's that skank causing trouble," Dee butted in.

"Who's that?" the small officer asked.

"Some slapper has been trying to get Seb into bed, seems to think he's going to leave Natasha, and they'll live happily ever after. She told Natasha that Seb was leaving her, but Seb denied it. That's why he wasn't here last night. Neither of us know whether he's been having an affair, but this woman seems a bit nuts," Dee continued.

"Do you have a name for her?"

"Ella something. Apparently, her husband left her recently so Seb has been comforting her, whatever that means." The ginger officer was taking notes and then looked at the ladies.

"Mrs. Jenkins is the one who was assaulted. Do you think that your husband tried to end an affair with her, and things turned violent? Would you say that would be likely?"

"No way!" Natasha said. "Seb may, or may not, have been a cheating prick, but he wouldn't attack anyone."

"What if it was because he thought this woman was going to expose a secret or try to break up his marriage?" the officer asked. Dee and Natasha sat in silence thinking this over.

"Thank you for your time," said the female officer as they stood up to leave. "We'll be in touch shortly when we have more information." The police left, and Natasha and Dee stared at each other in disbelief. There was no way either of them could now go back to bed, so Natasha went to the kitchen and put a pot of coffee on.

"Well that was unexpected," Dee said, unsure what to say on the subject.

"What the fuck has happened?" Natasha asked, half to herself. "There's no way that Seb would hit a woman, although I thought there was no chance that he'd cheat either. Maybe he tried to get her to back off, and she got aggressive with him. Perhaps he just pushed her off him in self-defence?" she suggested, hoping that this was what had happened.

"If that was the case, then I don't think he would have been arrested, unless she's made it out to be something different," Dee said, a little unhelpfully. "You have to go and see him, get his version."

"Do you think they'll let me?" Natasha asked. "They said they'd be in touch. Seb could have called me, do you think he had the one phone call? Like on television, or is it not really like that? It's not as though we have a solicitor whom we use for things like this!" she exclaimed. "Jesus, I guess I'll have to wait for a bit and see if the police call back. If not, I'll go down there later and see what's happening." The women spent the next hour or so drinking multiple cups of coffee and

The Broken Doll: Book One

gazing in almost complete silence at the kitchen walls, each of them concocting theories in their heads as to what could have actually taken place. The one thing that they agreed on was that something didn't add up, the situation felt wrong and worryingly serious.

Seb sat in a cell, not for the first time in his life but certainly not for at least twenty years. He'd been in a similar position on three occasions between the ages of seventeen and twenty-four, although each of those times it was related to drunk and disorderly conduct, usually culminating in some kind of brawl. It had never been serious enough to require legal representation or for charges to actually be made, more a case of sleeping it off in a cell and getting a caution, if that. This felt significant. The aggressiveness of the police officers battering on the lock-up was terrifying. It couldn't have been more than twenty or thirty minutes since Ella had left before he was taken away in cuffs. His head was spinning, completely bewildered by the situation. He'd been shown photographs of Ella, soaked in blood. Her nose looked broken, and her cheek was grazed. Someone had clearly hit her hard, but it wasn't him. So why was he here? The police had told him that Ella had accused him, but her story seemed vague. Her statement said that she was grabbed by the hair from behind as soon as she had walked away from Seb's place and then hit in the face with something, causing her to slump to the floor. She didn't get a good look at the attacker but no one else was around, and they had just had an argument. She told the police that she 'thought' it was him, enough of a suggestion to have him arrested but vague enough to mean he probably wouldn't be prosecuted.

Seb had been playing over every scenario he could come up with and ran it down to two. Either someone had randomly attacked her as soon as she had left him (which seemed extremely unlikely in this area) or someone had attacked her with a motive. The only person Seb could think of was Natasha, and it was a scary thought. It wasn't beyond the realms of possibility though, Natasha could be extremely defensive of her family and, very occasionally, had demonstrated a shocking loss of temper. The thought of another woman tearing her family apart could have been enough for her to become violent. Seb decided that this was much more likely than a random attack but there was something with the timing which bothered him. It had been a good four hours since he left the house; how likely was it that his wife had been waiting around, watching out to see if Ella came by? He needed to speak to Natasha but couldn't do much from inside the cell. After what felt like a long time, an officer came by with some government-funded breakfast; cold toast and some kind of egg-based slop. He washed it down with some weak tea and waited for news. A few hours must have gone by when a different officer, a pretty female one with a chubby face, came to tell him he was being released; he just had to sign some papers.

"Don't be going out of town any time soon," he was told by the sergeant. "We still may have some more questions for you."

"I won't be going anywhere," Seb replied. "And feel free to ask whatever you want. I didn't do this."

"That's what we're here to find out," the sergeant said, in a tone which suggested he believed Seb to be guilty. Seb gathered his belongings after he had filled in the bits of paperwork and decided he needed to head home and talk to Natasha, to try to get to the bottom of this as well as attempting to fix what was left of his marriage.

The Broken Doll: Book One

TWELVE

As Seb left the police station, exhausted from the night's events, he wandered home via the newsagents near the top of the high street and picked up an energy drink and a pack of Marlboro menthols. Next door to the newsagents the takeaway remained closed with no indication as to why or when it would re-open. Seb gazed through the window as he lit a cigarette. Everything seemed to be in its usual place but with no sign of life. Other than the display counters, which now sat empty of the usual cake slices and snacks, there was no visible change inside; it was as though they had closed one evening as usual but just not reopened since. All Seb knew was that the owner had gone away for a few days, hence he still had the Chesterfields, but it was becoming a concern, particularly due to the amount of money he was now owed for the settees.

"There's something funny going on here," a voice said, startling Seb. It was one of the local oddballs, a guy whom Seb had seen around quite often. He gave off an impression of someone who was homeless, but he was too clean. His clothes were very mismatched, his hair grey and wild, his voice extremely well-spoken. On the other hand, Seb had seen him rooting through bins on more than one occasion. *An eccentric, I suppose,* Seb had thought previously. *Probably a multimillionaire that has got a few screws coming loose.*

"Yeah," Seb agreed. "I know he went away for a few days but thought he'd be back open by now."

"Yes, it is rather mysterious," the stranger said. "Perhaps he had enough of that wife of his and has moved on to greener pastures. Knickers like a yo-yo, so I'm told."

Seb looked, and felt, genuinely surprised by this. He didn't know them well enough to be able to judge the accusation fairly, but his surprise stemmed more from whose mouth the words came from. After all, this guy didn't seem to be entirely sane. Even so, he was always about in the town, who knows what he may have overheard somewhere.

"I don't really know them," Seb informed the stranger. "I'm hoping to hear something from Sid soon as I've got some sofas for this place. Hopefully, it'll be business as usual before too long." With this, Seb walked the last few minutes' home, his mind refocusing on the impending conversation he was about to have with his wife, wondering if she knew about his night in a cell and, if so, sincerely hoping that she had no doubts about his innocence.

Ella woke suddenly from a painkiller-induced sleep to the sound of her mobile screeching at her. The codeine had been enough to send her to sleep a few hours earlier but was wearing off now, and her whole head throbbed. The call was from a private number, and she debated whether or not to answer it, thinking that being asleep would be a good enough excuse to ignore the caller. Before she could make up her mind, it rang off. She waited for a moment and there was no notification of any voicemail. It was hard to get comfortable with such a bruised and swollen face, memories of fights with Lee now coming to the forefront of her mind. She wondered if this had been a stupid thing to do, questioning why she had done it, knowing full well that her actions hadn't been thought through or premeditated. The anger she had felt towards Seb for his rejection of her had triggered something inside her which scared her a little, and now she had done something which she could not take back easily. Ella made her way to the kitchen for some more codeine and some water, rolled herself a cigarette and sat outside with a duvet wrapped around her. A part of her felt pleased with what she had done, now having control over whether Seb gets charged with a violent crime.

Although there is nothing honourable in having to blackmail someone to commit to a relationship, Ella felt that it was in everyone's best interest in the long run, that she was giving Seb the push he needed to leave his wife. The other part was one of complete stupidity. She had made a serious allegation which would undoubtedly mean more contact with the police, even if she does not press charges. Police attention is not something anyone would want when they have their spouse's corpse buried in the garden. Ella decided that today she would try to relax and wait patiently to hear from Seb, whenever he is released, aware that it would seem strange if she was to call the station, or Seb's mobile, to see how he was.

Natasha was still stood in the kitchen, having hardly moved since this morning. The kids had sensed something was wrong and thankfully went about getting themselves ready promptly and leaving the house with Dee. Natasha was struggling to grasp the events unfolding around her, her husband's apparent affair, the somewhat ludicrous suggestion that he had attacked a woman, the fact that he wasn't here when she just wanted him to hold her and make everything OK In all the years they had been together, Natasha had never had any reason to doubt Seb's honesty and faithfulness. Her mind was now torn between either keeping firm in her belief that he was, essentially, a decent man, or accepting that perhaps he was a totally different person to what she had thought, capable of being both unfaithful and violent. If he could act in this way now, then it was highly likely that there could have been incidents in the past as well, maybe previous affairs. Nevertheless, the more rational thoughts were still outweighing the terrifying ones. Seb's version of events suggested that he was pretty much stalked and (almost) seduced by this woman, all the while doing his utmost to remain faithful. She had yet to have an opportunity to discuss the assault allegations with him, but she couldn't imagine it was something he had done, or ever would do. As with most things in life, the truth was most likely to land somewhere in between these two versions. Natasha had begun to accept that her husband's relationship with Ella was probably not as innocent as he had made out. If he had slept with her, then it was something that Natasha would be willing to discuss, as the reality of them separating would be too complicated and traumatic for everyone. Natasha doubted that it would have been an affair though, she knew her husband and although she could, just about, imagine him giving in to temptation if the seductress was insistent enough, she is sure he would have felt terrible afterward and made sure it didn't happen again. It was as she was having these thoughts, ones which motivated her to get Seb's honest version and to stand by her husband, that the doorbell rang.

"Hi," was all Seb could manage as his wife opened the door to their home. Natasha hugged him tightly, fighting back the tears. Seb began to well up as well, this affection taking him completely by surprise. The hopeless, frightened feeling he had had on his way home from the police station melted away, and he began to feel a little better, supported and wanted. They made their way down to the kitchen, Natasha clicking the kettle on. Seb stood in silence, unsure of how to begin a conversation.

"I've been at the police station," he said, wanting to get that news out of the way first, perhaps for a little sympathy before discussing any infidelity.

"I know. The police came around at six this morning. They said you'd been arrested for assaulting a woman."

"I didn't do it. You know I wouldn't do anything like that."

"Of course, I know you didn't do it," Natasha replied, pouring two mugs of tea. "But someone did."

"I thought maybe it was you," Seb admitted, a little reluctantly.

"As much as I would love to smash her face in, I'm afraid I was in bed. You actually think I would have done that?" she asked, a little bemused.

"I don't know, but I did wonder. It turned me on a bit actually, thinking you'd be that protective of your man," Seb told her, playfully.

"If I had done that, it would have been more for my own pride. But I didn't, and neither did you. So, who did? And did she actually think it was you or is she just a spiteful cunt?"

"That's down to the police to sort out, although they seemed quite sure it was me. Ella making a statement saying I did it is pretty strong evidence, even if it's bullshit. I don't understand why I was released though, apparently the police will be around later, and I'm not meant to go anywhere today." Natasha looked thoughtful, playing out different scenarios in her head. She read a lot of crime novels and, despite it being a horrific situation for them to be in, she was weighing up possibilities as though she was the lead detective.

"Grab a pen and paper," she told Seb, who obediently found them and sat at the kitchen table.

"Draw two columns, one headed 'whodunit' and the other 'who Ella thinks did it'."

Again, Seb did as he was instructed.

"Down the first column, we need any possible suspects, even the ones we know are innocent. So, you, obviously, me (as I have a motive), a stranger not known to her. Is that it? I can't think of anyone else."

"Dee?" Seb suggested. "She can be a bit aggressive. Remember when she threatened to rape that guy in the pub with a cider bottle after he squeezed her tit?" Natasha laughed a little, the story sounding funnier now than it had been at the time.

"You can put her down, I guess she had motive, and she was the one who told me to confront Ella at her house. But, of course, she has an alibi; she stayed here all night."

"But she could have slipped out when you were sleeping, couldn't she?"

"Jesus Seb, Dee didn't actually do it."

"I know. I'm just playing Devil's advocate. So that's three of us, all with opportunity and motive. All of whom are innocent. Just leaving the 'mysterious stranger' theory. What's his motive?"

"It could be anything," Natasha said. "It could be someone else that she's been fucking about with. It could have been some nutter who just hit her. Maybe a piss-head chatted her up, and he didn't get his way so lashed out? Although I'm sure she doesn't turn anyone down." Seb felt that the last comment was unnecessarily bitchy, but it seemed completely inappropriate to try to stick up for Ella in the circumstances, and he kept quiet.

"Right, so what goes in the next column then Miss Marple?"

"Next to your name, i.e. you did it; Ella obviously knew it was you, and this fits with her reporting it to the police. Next to my name, imagining it was me, either she knew it was me, or she didn't. If I had done it, then it's more likely she would have reported it to you in an attempt to get you on her side. Unless she thought that I was you but that's unlikely. The same situation applies if it was Dee, I don't know if she would know she's my friend but either way I don't see why she would blame you. Plus, we know it wasn't any of us, which just leaves a stranger; the motive, therefore, could be anything. Unless she plans to use this as some kind of revenge for you ending things with her, which you better have done, or some kind of control over you, then I don't see her motivation. It's really fucking bizarre."

The Broken Doll: Book One

"If it had been a stranger, and happened outside my shop, I would have thought she would have come back to me for sympathy, or help, rather than heading up to the police station. And if she intends to use it to hurt me, or us, then it seems like quite a coincidence for her to be attacked and afterward come up with that plan. Plus, attacks like that are pretty rare around here. It's only really the odd fight at pub kick-out time." Natasha's mouth opened a little, as though she was about to speak, her eyes' widening.

"Of course, there is one other suspect," she pointed out.

"Two, actually," Seb replied.

"Her husband!" Natasha exclaimed. "You said he was violent; that's how you met her. Maybe he saw her talking to you and got angry. She would have been too scared to tell the police it was him, and so she blamed you!"

"Possibly, but it doesn't explain why she was at the police station on her own. Also, I don't think she ever reported the violence before so if he had hit her, then why didn't they just go home."

"Hmm," Natasha murmured, slightly annoyed at Seb for picking holes in what she had thought was a perfect explanation. "Hang on, two? Who's the other person?"

"This might sound a bit nuts, but what if she got someone to do it deliberately to frame me? Or," Seb hesitated, "what if she did it to herself?!"

THIRTEEN

Ella was becoming frustrated. She was generally a patient person but had experienced a huge change in her life; she had gone from wanting to be alone, so that Lee would not hurt her, to desperately craving attention from Seb. She had blocked herself into a corner with the accusation of violence, and now she could not contact him without it looking suspicious. He was unlikely to contact her either, so the intention to blackmail him into seeing her was appearing rather poorly thought out. She had started to worry extensively that the police would begin to look at her past and discover she had a missing husband, something that most people would have reported at least. Up to this point, she hadn't been very concerned about getting caught; worst-case scenario she could explain the history of domestic violence, and that she had panicked on the night he died. However, if Seb managed to convince the police that he was innocent of this crime, if the truth was discovered that she had hurt herself, it would cast a doubt over any allegations she made about Lee's attacks on her. After a lot of considerations and weighing up of her options, she decided the only choice was to drop the charges, hoping that the police would not follow up the matter themselves. The day was disappearing quickly, and she decided to walk back to the police station rather than telephoning them, as she didn't want an officer sent to her house. The walk was only about twenty minutes, but there was a strong wind blowing, and it made the journey uncomfortable. When she arrived at the station, she was greeted by a different desk sergeant, a middle-aged lady this time that looked concerned as she studied Ella's bruised face.

"Hi, I came in last night to report an assault. How do I go about dropping the charges?" Ella enquired, slightly nervously, worried about being accused of wasting police time. The desk sergeant

The Broken Doll: Book One

looked at her sadly as she took Ella's name, date of birth, and address, along with the crime reference number.

"Take a seat please and someone will be out to see you soon." Ella sat down in the empty waiting area, gazing around at the posters for local support groups. She was surprised that there were so many, unable to imagine herself ever attending anything like that. There were the usual topics, Alcoholics Anonymous, Narcotics Anonymous, Domestic Violence Support, plus a whole range of others such as Suicide Help Group (badly worded in Ella's opinion), Sexual Abuse Survivors, and a workshop which seemed to help elderly people avoid being conned out of their life's savings by dodgy builders. As she sat wondering whether attending the domestic violence group would have helped her deal with Lee more effectively, a tall, stern looking officer approached her. He looked as though he was in his late fifties, fairly handsome for his age, almost rugged.

"Mrs. Jenkins?" he asked. Ella nodded silently. "Please follow me." Ella followed the officer through a door with a pass-code, to an interview room where she sat in the furthest of three chairs, next to the window. The room was tiny, aside from the chairs there was only an indoor plant of some kind, quite tall with big, dark-green leaves, and a small desk on which sat a machine to record conversations and a jug of water with three upside-down glasses next to it. The officer clicked on the recorder and took a seat. After stating the names of those present, and the date and time, the officer looked up and addressed Ella.

"I understand you have decided that you no longer wish to press charges against the man whom you allege assaulted you in the early hours of this morning? Can you please confirm this for the benefit of the tape, please?"

"That's correct," Ella stated, clearly.

The Broken Doll: Book One

"Could you please explain what led you to this decision, as the records show that you were, understandably, upset when you came in and keen for us to prosecute the alleged offender." The officer seemed irritated, as though this was a waste of his time. Ella assumed he was thinking she was being silly, someone who had argued with a lover and forgiven being hurt in this way, wasting the police's time trying to get someone in trouble and then changing her mind. It probably happened quite often, Ella thought as she looked at the man's uninterested expression.

"It wasn't entirely his fault. Seb, I mean. We had an argument, and I was being very unkind to him. He's still married you see, but he's leaving her, and I told him that if he didn't do it soon, then I would tell his wife. He got angry, but I shouldn't have threatened him. It was just an argument that got out of hand; he has never done anything like this before, and I don't want to get him in trouble. It's been a difficult time for him, and he's under a lot of pressure," Ella explained.

"I see. Well if you do not want to press charges, then there isn't very much that we can do about it, as long as he hasn't frightened you into withdrawing your statement?"

"No, not at all," Ella assured him.

"One question before you go. I see you are *Mrs.* Jenkins. Presumably your husband is aware that you are seeing Mr. Briggs?" *Shit,* thought Ella, *I didn't see that coming.*

"I don't see how that is any of your business really. Sorry, but it's not relevant to this," Ella replied, trying not to sound confrontational as she did not want to appear to be hiding anything.

"Of course," the officer stated, whilst looking at her in a way that suggested he was thinking something over. "You're free to go whenever you're ready." With this, he turned off the recording device and stood up, holding the door open for Ella to leave.

The wind was still high as Ella left the police station, the drop in temperature noticeable. The trees were having a difficult time keeping hold of their leaves, and the seagulls appeared as though they were flying sideways. As Ella headed for home, wanting to hide under a duvet somewhere warm, she pondered her options. She wondered what the police now thought of her, the response to her dropping the allegation had raised some kind of suspicion with the rugged-looking officer. Maybe he thought that she had been coerced into dropping the charges. Perhaps he thought she was just a vindictive bitch trying to get her lover in trouble, which wasn't all that far from the truth. So long as there was no further investigation, Ella decided it didn't really matter what he thought. The walk home felt as though it was taking much longer than usual, especially once she had cleared the protection of the houses and trees and was suddenly exposed to the elements on the clifftop. The last few minutes of the journey left her with windswept hair and a salty taste to her skin as the gusts blew in from the sea. As she closed the door behind her, Ella dropped her coat to the floor and cranked up the thermostat. Summer had been lingering well, but this year seemed to have forgotten about autumn completely and skipped straight to winter. Ella had absolutely no intention of leaving the house again at any time soon and so ran herself a hot bath, filled the largest mug she could find with black coffee, and grabbed her softest, thickest nightwear from the bedroom. She undressed herself carefully, grateful that she had worn a button-up blouse and therefore did not have to lift anything over her bruised face. It was still cold inside the house, the bath slowly filling up, as she stared at herself, fully naked, in the mirror, clutching on to the warm mug. Her breasts gave a good indication of the temperature, and she saw that her ribs were now noticeable. She appeared malnourished, rather than thin. A diet of nicotine and caffeine wasn't enough to support her, and she was in need of more than just the odd slice of toast. Ella was not a vain person but had always been happy with her appearance; she knew that she was pretty. As nasty as Lee had been, he had rarely called her ugly or fat, or made any other comments to lower her opinion of herself physically. Even so, she did not see someone pretty in the mirror; her face was a mess, and she now worried about it healing well enough. Her body looked uncared-for, and she knew, if she was to keep Seb, she would need to make more effort. She slipped into the hot bath and began to plan a fresh, healthier routine to ensure that she was ready for her new life with her new man, determined not to give him any reason to turn her down.

"You've got to be a total fucking nutcase to smack yourself in the face and blame someone else," Natasha stated.

"Yeah, well we don't know for sure, although it's certainly possible, I think. Maybe I underestimated her, she's clearly got some issues. Even if she did, we can't prove it, so it'll be her word against mine, and I don't have an alibi."

"Shall I go to the police station? I can find out what's happening and suggest our ideas. At least it would give them something to think about, maybe raise a few doubts in her story?" Natasha offered. Seb looked as though he was welling up. He stared at his wife.

"Thank you for believing me," he said. "I love you so much."

"Just because I don't believe that you would batter a woman with a rock doesn't mean everything is fine between us. I merely think she may be a bit crazy, and perhaps you haven't played up in quite the way she makes out. You have been seeing her, cheating emotionally if not physically, lying to me about your whereabouts, and up to God knows what else. I don't think you've fucked her; I sincerely hope you haven't anyway, because if you've done that, or if you lie to me again, we are finished. I know when you first met her you were just trying to help, but it's become more than that, and it must stop. No more chances."

"That's fair. And, no, I haven't fucked her. And I swear that's the truth, and I never would," Seb told her, fighting back tears. "I guess the police would be the next step as I haven't heard anything from them. Should we go together?"

"I would like that," Natasha told him. "At least then I know where you are, and that you're not hiding anything from me. We need to get across to the police that she is basically an unwell stalker, and hopefully they will need more evidence than just her word to prosecute you."

At the police station, Natasha took the lead and approached the desk, explained that they were there with some new information relating to her husband's case from the previous night, before taking a seat in the waiting area. Natasha looked determined, knowing what she had to get across to the police, fearful that her husband may actually be the victim of unwanted attention from someone unstable. There was a nagging in the back of her mind that told her she didn't know all the facts, perhaps he had slept with her, maybe even hit her. She strongly doubted the latter, but it seemed unlikely that anyone would pursue someone if they had been told no enough times. Seb categorically denied having sex with Ella, and she saw it as her duty, as his wife, to accept this as the truth. She looked at her husband; he looked exhausted, upset, slightly puzzled by everything. It wasn't the look of someone who had been caught misbehaving; it was someone who felt ashamed for allowing something unpleasant to happen to themselves and their loved ones.

The Broken Doll: Book One

"Mrs. Briggs, Mr. Briggs?" said a man in his late fifties. He was a large man, tall, and muscular for his age. "I understand you have some information for me?"

"That's right," said Natasha.

"Come through please." Natasha and Seb followed the policeman through to a small room with an indoor plant, a desk, and some chairs. It was not very spacious, but still a little bigger than the cell that Seb had been released from only a few hours earlier.

"I will be recording this, in case the investigation goes any further." With that, the officer pressed record on the machine on the table, stating the names of those present. "What can I help you with?" he asked.

"Right," Natasha began. "We have been trying to work out what actually happened last night and as my husband has already stated his innocence, which I have no doubts about, we have arrived at the two most likely scenarios. We thought that we would let you know what we had come up with and see what you thought about it, as other lines of inquiry?"

"I see," said the officer, not looking too impressed at being told how to do his job. There was a long pause as Natasha realized that was all he was saying, and it was now her turn to explain what theories they had put together.

"Either it was Ella's husband, who has a history of being violent with her, perhaps he had discovered she was chasing after Seb and got angry..." Natasha began. The officers face registered something which Natasha couldn't place. Perhaps he was unaware of the domestic violence that Ella had experienced, which made sense as Seb had thought it had never been reported.

"Or," she continued, "she did it to herself." Natasha let this hang in the air, accepting that it sounded pretty crazy.

The Broken Doll: Book One

"OK," the policeman said, scratching his cheek, whilst he thought of what to say in the correct way. "Regarding previous domestic violence, we have no record of any complaints from Mrs. Jenkins. Now, of course, this doesn't mean it hasn't happened, a large proportion of abuse victims don't report the incidents for obvious reasons. It is certainly an avenue that we can look into. As for self-inflicted injury, it is also possible as you say, and it isn't as uncommon as you would think, or like it to be. Mrs. Briggs, would you mind stepping outside so that I can speak with your husband in private please?" Natasha shot Seb a glare, concerned about what couldn't be said in front of her.

"She can stay," Seb replied, "I don't have anything to hide from her."

"Very well. Mrs. Jenkins came to the station today, not long before you both arrived actually," the officer began. "She came to drop the charges against you. It is unclear at this moment what her motivation was for doing this, but her reasoning was that, although she still maintains you attacked her, she said it was following an argument that you had had. She explained that the two of you were having an affair, one which had become serious enough for you to be leaving Mrs. Briggs soon. I enquired as to the reaction from Mr. Jenkins to this news, and she did not want to discuss that. So, as things stand, you are free to go and there is currently no case against you. However, I would suggest that both of you keep as far away from Mrs. Jenkins as possible, and I will be advising her to stay away from you. I do not know what the truth to this is, and it has the makings of something potentially damaging to everyone involved, but as far as the police are concerned, there is no longer a criminal case to pursue. If you have any need to discuss anything in relation to this in the future, then feel free to come by but, for now, our involvement has finished. I hope this all makes sense?"

The Broken Doll: Book One

"Not really," said Natasha. "So, assuming Ella is making all this shit up about him leaving me," at which point Seb received another quite frightening glare from his wife, "Seb is now in the clear and just has to stay away from her? And if she begins pestering him? Presumably we can come to you?"

"Yes of course, any further incidents, please do let us know, and we can deal with it at the time." Seb and Natasha thanked the officer and made their way out of the station.

"Wine?" Seb suggested.

"Gin. Dee said she's happy to keep the children overnight. Let's just get drunk and start trying to fix this fucking mess you've made." Seb liked that idea a lot, hoping that this meant Natasha was open to some make-up sex soon. There was clearly too much going on with Ella for him to have any more association with her, and he decided that now, finally, it was time to cut off all contact.

FOURTEEN

Ella decided that she would wait for Seb. Not for long, although that was, perhaps, not her choice, but at least for a few days spent lying low and giving him a chance to make contact with her. Well, that had been the plan, anyway. By late afternoon, the following the day, Ella found herself going a little stir-crazy. She had heard nothing and had occupied her time ensuring that the house was spotless. It was, of course, not a huge house, and with her being the only occupant it did not take long for it to be presentable. The weather was in no way inviting enough for her to potter round the garden, and she was reluctant to touch much out there anyway for fear of disturbing the corpse buried within. It wouldn't take much for the rotting body to give off an odour to attract some local wildlife, and she didn't fancy trying to apprehend a fox wandering off with a body part. She had been contemplating for some time about searching online for information on body decomposition rates, but her only Internet access was at the library, therefore linked to her library card, or could be noticed by a nosy local looking over her shoulder. She wondered if it was the sort of search that flags up with the police, but assumed she was probably being a little paranoid. Not that she ever intended to dig Lee up, but she decided to let nature take its course out there, and she would approach the situation when the spring arrived, possibly enlisting Seb to help pave the area, enough time having passed by then not to raise any suspicions. Her mind was now back on to Seb, dreamily imagining him shirtless, labouring hard in the garden while she sipped a crisp gin and tonic with a slice of lime, reading a book perhaps. She stood in the kitchen, gazing out across the garden. The rain was beating down, and the wind was still persistent. As she stood there alone, she couldn't imagine herself further from that fantasy. Another glance at her phone confirmed her solitude, and she decided to be strong and not to contact him. The only distraction she could hope for was sleep and so, after a couple of sleeping tablets, she curled up in bed trying not to worry about the future, certain that, eventually, Seb would be where he belonged.

Seb looked up at his wife from his position on the floor, kneeling before her as she sat on the sofa. His face was wet from her; his ears slightly reddened as she had pressed her thighs tightly against his head as she reached orgasm. He began to unbuckle his belt.

"What are you doing?" Natasha asked him.

"It needs to come out before it goes in," Seb replied, rather poetically.

"Er, no one said it was going in. To be honest you're lucky you got to eat me, but you are ever so good at it and I was feeling a little frisky. Nevertheless, I'm sorted now, so thank you, and that's it for tonight. Think of it as you making amends for your behaviour." Seb looked disappointed to say the least; he thoroughly enjoyed going down on Natasha but felt a little used now. However, he knew better than to complain, and she did have a point about him owing her something to make amends.

"Fair enough," he told her, "Maybe tomorrow then?"

"We'll see. I might just want to be eaten each day for a while before I think you deserve any pleasure. If I want more, you'll know about it." The remainder of the evening was spent in the way that most evenings had been spent before Ella had been around, snuggled on the sofa, a few gin and tonics, until one of them was tired enough to sleep. Seb was hoping Ella was out of their lives now but there was a nagging feeling which bothered him greatly, a fear she would somehow make contact with him, that she would change her mind about pressing charges, that she still thought they could be together. If she had hurt herself deliberately to frame him, who knew what else she was capable of?

The following morning it was as though nothing had happened, as if Ella had never existed. Natasha was up before Seb for a change and brought him a coffee in bed. She was already dressed, looking as though she had made an extra effort. Seb wondered if she was trying to look nice to keep him interested in her.

"I'm going to pick the kids up from Dee's soon, is there anything you want to do before I go?" Natasha asked.

"Hop on my face if you want? Breakfast in bed?!" Seb suggested, hoping it might lead to more.

"Aww, that's really romantic!" Natasha told him, in a mocking tone. "Tempting darling but I'm already dressed, and you'll get all excited again. Don't want you wanking all around the house while I'm out." Seb huffed a little as he picked up the coffee.

"Fine," he muttered. *Wanking sounds like an idea,* he thought, now looking forward to her going.

"So, what are you planning to do today? You haven't seemed to have sold much recently with the distraction of Little Miss Psycho. Maybe you should get some work done, bring a bit of money in?" Seb hated it when Natasha got bossy with him but was well aware that he had to go with the flow if he wanted things to improve between them.

"I was kind of banking on selling those Chesterfields, would have been enough to see us through a few weeks. The takeaway is still closed, and I'm not getting any response from Sid or his wife; there is something really odd about it all. I looked through the window, and some homeless-looking guy said Sid's wife had yo-yo knickers! He didn't look like a reliable source of information, but who knows? Think I'll have to try to sell them elsewhere, but it's a pain, and I probably won't get as much for them."

The Broken Doll: Book One

"Have you asked anyone else who was working there what's going on? I'm sure there were another two or three girls who waitressed there. One of them is usually at the school, I don't know her name though."

"I'll see what I can find out," Seb told her. "If there's no joy, then I'll put them up online." Natasha walked around to Seb's side of the bed, kissed his forehead and, simultaneously, gave his cock a little rub through his pyjama bottoms, just for a second.

"I'm going to head off then. I'll grab a few bits from the town and pick the kids up. Dee will probably want to know the gossip, so I might be a couple of hours but stay in touch please. And stay away from you-know-who!" As soon as Seb heard Natasha's car start he grabbed his phone and found some porn. He opted for one of the videos in the 'Glory-hole Secrets' series and enjoyed it so much that he didn't even last the full four minutes running time. He was sufficiently impressed by the chubby redhead's apparent lack of any gag reflex and her desire for a very sticky chest. Once Seb had mopped up the mess with yesterday's boxers, which he found on the floor next to the bed, he headed downstairs to prepare for the day. There was nothing to be done about Ella, other than having no contact which shouldn't be too difficult. It was time to focus on the business and start bringing some money in, beginning with the mystery of Disappearing Sid.

Once Seb had made another coffee he sat down at his laptop and began searching online for anyone else associated with the takeaway, or any other way to contact Sid. He dialled the number which he had for him but, as before, it went straight to voicemail. This time Seb left a message, trying not to sound as though he was chasing for money, wording it more in a way that showed concern for his acquaintance who had gone AWOL. Sid would have seen the missed calls previously, and had not called back, so Seb didn't pin much hope on getting a response. It was unlikely that Sid's wife was as uninformed as she had made out, but it could well be a private matter that Seb had no right to expect to be informed of. Seb decided to call the takeaway's number on the off-chance that someone was on site. There did not appear to be a voicemail system attached to this number, and it just rang and rang. It was another dead end. As Seb was gazing at the laptop screen, perplexed at what was going on, his phone, which was on silent, vibrated loudly across the oak dining table. It startled Seb enough for his mug of now lukewarm coffee to almost slip from his hand. He was disappointed to see that it was only Natasha, and not someone returning one of his calls.

"Hi," he said, still pondering the Sid situation.

"Right, I've asked Dee and she said the woman from the school who worked at the takeaway is called something like Chantelle, or Crystal, or something very Jeremy Kyle sounding. It begins with a C anyway. If that's at all helpful?"

"Yeah maybe, thanks. I tried calling Sid on his mobile and land line but no answer from either. I'll see if I can find this woman online then. So, all OK there?"

"Yes fine, just having a coffee. Probably stay here another hour or so, but I have my house keys in case you need to go out anywhere."

"Right, well I'll let you know what I'm doing when I know. Love you."

"You'd better. Love you too." Seb logged on to his social media account and searched for Chantelle. No one came up who looked familiar or knew anyone in common. He tried Crystal, finding two who live locally enough to work there. One looks as though she is about fourteen, and that's with all the makeup and terrifying eyebrow 'enhancement', so Seb ruled her out for now, making a mental note to come back to her if everything

The Broken Doll: Book One

else led nowhere. The image he had of all the female staff at the takeaway was skinny, brunette dolls; as far as he could remember they had all looked the same. The other Crystal appeared to be on the bigger side than he had imagined and had dyed black hair. Her face was also covered in piercings. Seb doubted that this would be the sort of person Sid would have employed as he was a bit of a sleaze, taking on people he found attractive, and he had a particular taste, i.e. Barbie.

With his online attempt at detective work proving futile, Seb decided to head to town and see what he could discover in person. He intended to spend his day on the matter, and if no further information could be gathered, he would call it quits, mind his own business (quite literally), and start trying to sell the sofas elsewhere. As a last-minute thought, Seb printed a photograph of the sofas on a sheet of A4 paper alongside an ad for them, planning to put this up in the newsagents. Not only did this make him feel as though he had been proactive in trying to shift them, it also gave him an excuse to talk to the staff in the shop which was located next door to Sid's place. It was probably another long shot, but perhaps someone there knew something.

FIFTEEN

The sun had begun to appear through the clouds and, despite the fall in temperature, it was much more pleasant now that the wind had dropped a little. Seb crossed the road at the top end of the town and passed the closed takeaway, entering the newsagents next door. He grabbed a Double Decker and decided to pick up a small pouch of tobacco, suddenly craving nicotine, his Marlboro's having long since run out.

"How much to put a for-sale poster in the window?" he asked the young male behind the counter, who was rather distracted by two teenage mums perusing the magazines, incredibly underdressed for the temperature outside.

"Fifty pence for a week if you use one of the little cards, A4 is a quid a week."

"Yeah, it's A4. OK, I'll put it up for two weeks and be back if I need it renewing."

"That's seven forty-seven altogether then," the assistant told him, eyes flicking between Seb and the young mums. Seb handed the poster over.

"It's for some Chesterfield sofas I'm selling," Seb told him. The guy tried his best to appear interested but only managed a little smile and a mumbled 'OK'.

"Customer let me down," Seb went on. "They were actually meant to be going to the place next door, but it's been closed for a while. I don't suppose you know if they're opening any time soon?"

"No, sorry mate. I haven't seen anyone going in or out for the last few days at least."

"You talking about next door?" chirped a voice behind Seb, who turned to see the scantily-clad mums had begun to queue behind him.

"Yeah," Seb replied, hopefully.

"Well, we don't know anything for a proper fact or nothing, but I heard, down the King's Head, that the guy that owns it found out his wife was a bit of a

The Broken Doll: Book One

slag, used to flash her tits for drinks. Not that they were very nice, far too plastic looking. Anyway, that's what I heard so maybe he left her. Old cow was probably desperate for some attention. I'm surprised it took so long for him to find out; I thought everyone knew what she was like."

"OK, thanks" Seb managed as he rushed out of the shop, the woman's voice grating on him as soon as she had begun to talk. *It seems like the old tramp might have heard the same rumours,* thought Seb. *I guess the King's Head could be a fountain of knowledge, if by knowledge you mean local gossip about which women are the easiest.*

Seb made his way down the virtually empty high street, withdrew ten pounds from the cash machine, and approached the King's Head. It had not long been open but there were already a couple of patrons outside with cigarettes, looking as though they were in until closing. Inside was quite empty, with two old guys at a table by the window, settled in with ale and newspapers. A guy whom Seb recognized as the bar manager was wiping down the tables, and a barmaid, Seb assumed, sat at the end of the bar staring at her phone whilst eating some pork scratchings. She looked familiar, although it was a small town so quite a few people looked familiar. Seb had intended to get a coffee but felt a bit conspicuous if he didn't order alcohol and decided on a pint of one of the local ales. The barmaid hadn't moved from her spot and so the bar manager had had to interrupt his cleaning to come and serve Seb. Once the drink had been paid for Seb, took a seat and rolled himself a cigarette. His first attempt had gone awry as he placed the cigarette paper on a table which was still damp with surface cleaner. He tried again, this time more successfully, and made his way out the front. The two people who had been there as he came into the pub were no longer there, having gone back in but to the other side of the bar, through the saloon door. Seb

The Broken Doll: Book One

virtually downed the pint, aware that he needed to buy another in order to strike up conversation with the bar staff. Seb ordered another pint and began to cautiously strike up a conversation with the man behind the bar.

"Do you know the guys that own the takeaway at the top of town? Sid and his missus. I heard they drink in here? I haven't seen them about for a while," Seb asked.

"He doesn't come in here often, never did really. His missus, Maggie, used to be in here a lot but not that recently. Why do you ask?"

"Oh, I have some stuff for Sid, furniture. I was supposed to deliver it, but they've been closed for a while, and he's not answering the phone. I needed to see if he still wanted it before I sell it to someone else."

"Well I don't know why they've been closed, I'm afraid. One of the regulars in here was asking after Maggie last night actually, said he'd seen her somewhere looking really upset. They had a funny relationship from what I could tell," the man said, leaning in closer as though to prevent anyone overhearing despite the bar being almost empty. "It was no secret she was carrying on with a taxi driver; he always came and picked her up at closing time. Think they were having a bit before she got dropped home. Maybe her husband found out, and he's buggered off."

Seb thought this over. He was beginning to get an impression of Maggie which wasn't very pleasant, and not really any of his business, but he couldn't help wanting to know more.

"Someone else said she had a bit of a reputation, so maybe he has left her. Although, from what I heard, it wasn't one particular guy, could have been anyone."

"She's a wild one that girl, acting like she's eighteen without a care in the world. I can see why people would say that, she was all over whoever showed an interest, but only usually left with the same guy when the cab arrived."

"Usually?" Seb repeated. "Did anyone else leave with her?"

"I can't remember specifically when but maybe last time she was here, or the time before, she was snogging one of the girls she works with, you know, as a bet from some of the guys. They'd buy them drinks in exchange for putting on a bit of a show. That night I didn't notice a cab, she walked off with her workmate and one of the builders, reckon he was trying his luck with them on the way home."

Seb sipped at his pint, thinking this all over. The fact that Maggie was still in town, and Sid was not, coupled with her apparently quite well-known reputation, pointed almost certainly to a breakdown in their relationship. Sid wasn't answering the phone, and it didn't seem as though he was coming back. Seb would just have to move the sofas to another buyer.

Ella woke up later than usual, feeling groggy from the sleeping pills. Once she had dragged herself out from under the duvet and made a coffee, she spent her morning pacing the house, unable to find anything more to clean or rearrange, so she tried to read. Her mind wasn't in the right place, the lack of contact from Seb occupying her every thought. She was agitated, desperate to know if he was alright, and not too angry with her. After managing to pass the first hour of the afternoon staring blankly at the television, she tried to force herself to eat. The cupboards were virtually bare, but she found an old tin of soup in one of them which she heated up and drank from a mug. Once she had washed up the saucepan and mug, she decided that she could wait no longer. Not knowing what was happening was unbearable, and so she decided to try to call Seb. Ella fully expected there to be no answer the first time, or for that bitch wife of his to answer it if she

The Broken Doll: Book One

had somehow begged him to stay at their house. Nevertheless, she decided that she had nothing to lose and, once she was comfortable on the sofa, called his number. It rang a few times then went to voicemail. *Shit,* she thought. Ella tried again, and this time her call was received.

"Hello?" Seb answered, gruffly. Ella was speechless, gasping a little at finally hearing Seb's voice, then composing herself.

"Hi. It's me."

"Yes, I know who it is. Why are you calling me?" Seb responded, curtly.

"I wanted to check that you were OK, and to apologize really. I'm sorry about the whole police thing; I was just upset. I dropped the charges though; did they tell you that?"

"Yes, they told me. Are you expecting me to be grateful or something? I wouldn't have been there if it wasn't for your bullshit. Did you do that to your own face or get someone to do it for you?" Ella was starting to feel worried. She knew Seb would be a bit angry about the police, but no real harm had been done.

"That doesn't matter now. Your wife knows about us, and we can be together. I've been cleaning up the house so it's ready for whenever you want to start bringing your things around. It's going to be great."

"What the actual fuck are you talking about? I told you I was not giving up my family. I nearly lost them because of you. I thought I was helping you, but you're not fucking right in the head. Don't call me or come near me again. Ever." The line went dead, and Ella stared at the phone. *What had just happened? Why is he still with Natasha?* It was all too much for Ella to cope with, and she walked to the kitchen, picked up the mug she had used for her soup, and hurled it across the living room. Pieces of red china scattered across the floor. She walked across the shards in her bare feet, feeling sharp pricks to her soles. Her whole body

The Broken Doll: Book One

trembled uncontrollably as she grabbed the television from behind and threw it off its stand, the screen cracking. Ella took a seat on the sofa and surveyed the mess, noticing a trail of blood, which must have emanated from her feet. She examined the injuries, her left foot appearing to be intact but her right foot showed two fairly deep cuts. Ella decided that they weren't worthy of stitches and tried to ignore the throbbing pain. She felt overwhelmingly angry, with herself, with Seb, with Natasha for taking him back. She felt an urge that she had not felt for some time, a dark cloud appearing over her, a suggestion of suicide. She did not want to die but, at that moment, it was a temptation purely as revenge for the way that Seb had treated her. Instead, she took a kitchen knife, one of the sharper ones, with a smallish blade and a black handle. She sat on the sofa and, being fully aware that physical pain can help relinquish emotional distress, even if only temporarily, she began to make small cuts to her forearm. There was a sting as the blade pierced the skin, drawing just enough blood for the dark-red droplets to make their way along her arm. She chose her forearm as it was harder to hide and hopefully, at some point, Seb would see what he had done. Each cut made Ella feel a little better, until eventually, eight cuts in, she decided to stop. Her head felt clearer now, and she dressed her wounds, swept up the fragments of china and stood the television back in its original place. *Right,* she thought. *Weak crap out of the way. Time to make a plan. Natasha doesn't get to keep my man, and she needs to accept that.*

Leaving the last few mouthfuls of now warm ale in the glass, Seb made his way out into the daylight and wandered home, deep in thought. Everything seemed to point to a breakdown in Sid's marriage, and he felt it would be inappropriate to hassle him for payment of the sofas, despite the inconvenience of having to try to sell them elsewhere. Seb fumbled in his pocket for his house keys and found Natasha in the kitchen, peeling potatoes. It had been a while since they had all sat down to a meal together, Seb realized.

"Ooh, what's for dinner?" he asked, leaning in and giving her a kiss on the cheek.

"Sausage and mash, later. I picked up some of those sweet chilli sausages we had before. So," Natasha continued, "do you want to tell me why you smell of booze this early in the day?"

"That, my dear, is because I have been to the pub," Seb informed her. He then went on to explain all the gossip he had found out about the takeaway owners and informed her that he would, most likely, need to source an alternative buyer for the items.

"It's a pain," Seb told her, "but I'm probably wasting my time keep trying to contact him."

"Seems like no one in this town believes in monogamy," Natasha stated, a little under her breath.

"Don't be like that, I thought we were alright now?"

"Sorry, I didn't mean to be bitchy. It's a bummer about Sid, but you did say they'd sell easily enough so maybe you should get on with that sooner rather than later."

Seb took a seat at the dining table and opened his laptop. He was debating whether or not to tell Natasha about the phone call from Ella but decided against it. No point making her more paranoid and there was no reason to think that Natasha would find out.

"So, this gossip..." Natasha said, the juicy nature of it holding her attention, "it came from some tarts in the newsagents, a homeless guy, and the barman?" The phrasing and tone suggested that the information was unreliable, which Seb thought over; however, these seemed to be the sort of people that Maggie had, and probably still did, socialize with.

"It was from different people, all of whom were aware of her reputation. No reason to think they're conspiring to bad mouth her without good cause. Why? Do you think it's all bollocks?"

"No, I guess I'm just a bit surprised, and they don't sound like particularly trustworthy sources. Did you not find that waitress girl?"

"Not with either of those names. I don't think it's worth any extra time really. If you want to know any more, I'm sure you'll see that woman on the school run."

After a few minutes spent putting photos of the sofas up on some second-hand sites, Seb stood up, walked over to Natasha and forcefully kissed her. She was taken by surprise and pulled away slightly, trying to hide a smile.

"What's up with you? How much did you drink?" she asked.

"Let's go out," Seb suggested firmly, "We can take the dog and the kids for a walk, maybe stop at the park." Natasha looked at her husband, thankful that the man she used to know was beginning to reappear.

"That sounds lovely," she told him. The weather outside was still rather cold but the sky was clear and the children, wrapped in thick coats, didn't seem to notice the temperature. To any passers-by, it was the perfect picture of a happy family. Seb smiled to himself, feeling content with the life he had, only by a thread, managed to keep hold of. He felt ashamed that he had been willing to risk all of this for another woman's company, starting to take on board just how fragile everything was.

As the family made their way past the lifeboat station, Penguin excitedly pulling Natasha in all directions, Seb heard the sound of a text message being received. Both his and Natasha's phones made the same sound, but she seemed not to have heard anything. Seb

The Broken Doll: Book One

pulled his phone from his pocket and felt a little rush of panic as he noticed who the text was from.

'I'm really sorry about the way things went with us; I know we can't be together, but I don't want to leave things this way. Can we please meet up, just for a few minutes later? I promise I won't try anything on. E x'

Shit, Seb thought, deleting the message and switching his phone to silent mode. Natasha was focused on the dog and didn't seem to have noticed anything. *Ignore her and she'll go away,* Seb told himself, rather optimistically.

It didn't take long before the children all began to complain that they were suddenly starving and, after a ten-minute climb about in the play park, the group made their way home. The sky had stayed clear but as the afternoon went on the drop in temperature became much more noticeable.

"We should have grabbed some wine on the way home. The house is dry!" Natasha said in mock panic.

"It's bloody freezing, so I don't think I want anything cold," Seb told her, putting his coat back on. "But I don't mind popping out to get something."

"Red?" Natasha offered.

"Nah, it makes you sleepy, and I may have plans for you later. My tongue could use a workout!" Natasha let out a little giggle. "Well, if that is the case, it'll have to be spirits. Either gin or whiskey, but if you don't want anything cold, then I'm sure I can manage some straight bourbon."

"Sounds delicious, I'll see what I can find," Seb told her as he picked up his wallet and walked back out into the crisp air. *Bread,* thought Natasha, having forgotten to ask Seb to pick some up whilst he was out. She pulled her phone from her back and called Seb's number. She immediately heard a buzzing coming from

The Broken Doll: Book One

the kitchen, and as she approached, saw that he left his phone on the work surface along with his keys.

For fuck's sake, she thought. *Guess I'll have to send him back out when he gets in.* The screen on her husband's phone showed three notifications, one being the missed call from herself, one being an email icon and one a text message. Natasha, unable to resist, opened the message. At the top, it showed 'Ella' and time stamped only six minutes ago. 'Please let me see you one more time; I just want to clear the air. I'll keep asking until you give in. At least reply instead of ignoring my messages, it was so nice hearing your voice earlier, E xx'

Natasha could feel herself shaking, the adrenalin starting to flow. She took Ella's number from Seb's phone and stored it in her own. She paused for a moment, planning what to say. It was far from an eloquent message, but Natasha at least made sure the intent was clear enough. 'This is Seb's wife. Leave him alone you crazy skank. He's not interested and if you contact him again, we will be going to the police. Find some other poor bastard to wiggle your anorexic arse at.'

Natasha was busy staring at the phone, wondering if she would get a reply, when Seb walked through the front door, a bottle of Jim Beam in hand. "This was all they had that wasn't too expensive I'm afraid," he shouted down to the kitchen. "When the sofas sell, I'll get us something a bit more upmarket." As Seb came down the stairs to the kitchen, he saw the look on Natasha's face; she seemed angry about something.

"What?" he asked, apprehensively.

"We need bread," she told him. Seb audibly sighed in relief that it wasn't anything serious. "Also, your girlfriend texted you."

Fuck! Seb thought, desperately hoping it didn't mention the earlier contact.

The Broken Doll: Book One

"What did it say?" he asked.

"She wants to meet up, one last time, something about you ignoring previous messages. She liked hearing your voice earlier and it made her all wet. OK, I made that up, but apparently you spoke to her earlier. Now it seems odd you would forget to mention that to your wife, and I very, very much hope that, if at all, it was by phone and involved you telling her to fuck off."

"She called me earlier, wanted to see me. I told her not to call me ever again, I thought she understood. I didn't want you worrying. Guess I'll just have to ignore the text and hope she gets bored soon."

"I replied. From my phone, told her to stay away, or we'd go to the police. If you hear anything from her, I'm trusting you to tell me immediately, no fucking about. If I think you're hiding anything from me again, you'll be out. Now pour me a whiskey and tell me what you plan on doing with that magical tongue of yours."

"Fine," Seb replied, a little grumpily, worried that Ella wasn't going to let up and hoping Natasha hadn't made anything worse. He looked at his wife who looked a little puzzled.

"Fine?" she repeated. "Is going down on me that much of a chore?"

"Sorry, I didn't mean that. Of course, I'd love to."

Natasha was evidently in the mood for some affection and, after an enjoyable family meal, the pair quickly moved the three children through the process of baths, stories, and bed. Once they were satisfied that they would not be disturbed, Natasha took her husband by the hand and led him to the living room, where she proceeded to close the curtains. She gazed into his eyes as she removed her jeans and the black lace knickers that she knew he liked. As she sat on the sofa, legs open, she gave him his command, loudly and sternly: "Eat me!"

The Broken Doll: Book One

Seb dropped onto his knees in front of her and began to run his tongue all over his wife, slowly making his way up the inside of her thighs, teasing the most sensitive parts. When Natasha was worked up enough, she demanded that he enter her, and they made love, roughly. Despite obviously enjoying the events, Seb had been a little distracted by the sound of a few vibrations coming from the kitchen, sounds which most likely were coming from his phone on the kitchen table. He worried it was Ella, a sense of dread coming over him as he feared that she may not be giving up on him as easily as he had hoped.

Once they were dressed, Natasha went into the bathroom, and Seb took the opportunity to check his phone alone. Two messages by text; both from Ella.

'I know things have gone a bit shitty between us; I just had the wrong impression. Can we meet up?' This was followed by 'If you really don't want to see me again, then I need to hear it from you, in person, otherwise I can't give up on what we had, please meet me.' *Shit,* Seb thought. *Natasha wouldn't be happy with this.*

"OK?" Natasha asked as she entered the kitchen, startling Seb slightly. He tried to hide the guilty expression that he knew had appeared across his face.

"Yeah. She texted me." Seb immediately felt better for having decided not to hide it.

"For fuck's sake," his wife replied, "I may have to actually kill her soon. What does she want, or shouldn't I ask?"

"She said she can't give up on me, unless she hears it from me, in person, that I want her to leave me alone. What should I do?" Natasha thought for a moment, fantasizing about throwing Ella into the river, slightly disappointed that it wasn't a reasonable plan.

"Meet her, be clear with her. But I'm coming too."

"I don't think she'd accept what I'm saying with you there, she'll think I'm just saying it for your benefit. I'll do it; you'll have to trust me. I'll tell her to make it somewhere public." Seb took his phone and replied to the messages, saying that he would meet her in an open place, in half an hour and asked where she would suggest. He then grabbed his trainers and his car keys and prepared himself for, what he hoped, would be his last encounter with Ella.

SIXTEEN

After almost twenty minutes, Ella received a reply, relief sweeping across her as she saw that the message was from Seb and not Natasha. *He wants to meet! God, I hope he comes on his own.* Ella thought about locations; he wanted somewhere public and she would rather be alone with him, so she suggested meeting by the beach. There could be a few dog walkers about, and it was outdoors, at least, but not too busy that they couldn't talk properly. Ella saw this as her last shot, and she needed to take drastic action to win her man, certain that it was in everyone's best interest in the long run. It was far too cold outside for a dress, so Ella grabbed a long coat and a hat, putting them on over a tight, white jumper, and black leggings. Seb had told her that he would be driving, and she should come and find his car. Ella picked up her handbag and headed out of the door, turning on her pocket torch to avoid stepping into any rabbit holes on her way towards the more manageable path. Nervously, she headed for the rendezvous point, wondering if Seb would actually come alone. Ella felt unsure if he was, again, stating his intention for them not to see each other anymore, or if he had accepted that they were destined to be together. Ella felt as though she was on autopilot, each step she took seeming out of her control, with no real time spent thinking through her options. She was aware that she was being persistent with Seb, understanding that it may be viewed as a little excessive. She could, however, feel herself falling for him and pushed aside any doubts, or considerations, that she could have fallen for just about anyone in her current state. Ultimately, she was alone and did not like it. Ella was certain a future with Seb would be perfect, and that she deserved it. She was determined to make it happen whatever it took to achieve, as she had decided it was what she was entitled to; a happy relationship, a future that held

The Broken Doll: Book One

some excitement, the chance to be loved rather than simply owned.

As she passed the pub near the beach, she felt her stomach turn a little, her nervousness making itself known. From the barriers which signalled the entrance to the parking area, she could see Seb's car, facing towards the sea. It was very dark at this point, not helped by the lack of street lights or other cars. The only other vehicles were two motor homes parked up on the grass verge, both bearing French number plates, the occupants of which appeared to be out, possibly at the nearby pub. Seb must have noticed her approaching and appeared from the driver's side, standing next to the car which was now lit up as the door had opened. He was looking towards Ella, but not saying a word. *Maybe he's not sure if it's me yet,* Ella thought, a little disappointed there was no excited hug or any sign of affection.

"Hey," Ella called as she became close enough for them to see each other more clearly.

"Hi," Seb replied, curtly. "Get what you want to say out of the way, and then I'll say my bit, and we can both go home." Ella tried to hide the hurt from her face, telling herself this had always been a possibility, and that she just had to get across her intentions in a way that Seb would respond favourably to.

"OK, thanks for meeting me. I wasn't sure if you'd be able to get out or not," Ella began, trying to establish whether or not Natasha was lurking anywhere nearby.

"I told her I was meeting you, that it would be the last time."

"I see. Well, I didn't like the thought of leaving things the way we did and I just, well, I wanted to say I'm really sorry for the thing with the police. I know that changed how you thought of me, and I feel as if I've ruined what we had. I know it must be hard for you to decide what you want, and difficult to leave your family. I shouldn't have put so much pressure on you."

"I had, and very much still have, no intention of leaving my family. We were friends, and yes, I liked the fact you wanted more from me, and yes, I was tempted. What man wouldn't be? Even so, it was never going to be a relationship, or even an affair. If I was the type to cheat, I would have done it when you first offered. I do feel a little bad that I may have led you on, well I know that I did, but this is it now. We can't see each other anymore."

Ella could feel her eyes welling up. He seemed genuine, and she was now able to see that she had really messed it all up by involving the police. She felt that she should have been more patient and eventually, hopefully, she would have been capable of seducing him. Surely that would have helped? The idea of accepting Seb's decision barely entered her head though. She took her tobacco from her coat pocket and began to make a cigarette, something which proved difficult with the cold wind blowing in from the English Channel.

"Do you mind if I sit in the car while I roll?" Ella asked, her voice trembling. Seb felt guilty. He could see that he had hurt this woman, she looked close to tears. However, he was also wary of her seductiveness, cautious that she may be planning to try something on. *I've resisted plenty of times before, and that was before I knew she was a bit nuts,* he thought, nodding at her and resuming his position in the driver's seat.

The two of them sat in silence, the interior light off, as Ella rolled two cigarettes. From her bag, she took a quarter bottle of whiskey which she had grabbed from home before she left, in case it was required. Seb looked at the bottle; maybe it was the coldness of the evening, or perhaps the desire to escape the current situation, but he wanted some. Only a little of course, he was in the driving seat, but a bit wouldn't hurt. Ella saw him looking at it and passed it to him along with one of the cigarettes. Once Seb had turned the key to allow the windows down a little, they sat and smoked, Seb taking a few large gulps from the bottle. As they passed it back and forth in the dark, Seb did not notice that Ella had merely held the bottle for a few minutes and handed it back to him. He, therefore, had no reason to be suspicious of Ella's intentions until the dizziness started. Before he knew it, all had gone black and a fog of sleep had enveloped him.

"This isn't what I had wanted," Ella muttered to him as she reached across to the key and closed the windows.

Natasha was on edge, the knowledge that her husband was with that psycho was, understandably, making her feel uneasy. Although Seb had been clear that he was making sure things were finished, she didn't trust Ella not to try something on. Even if Seb could turn down some pussy (which shouldn't be too hard as he'd not long had some), who knew what Ella was capable of. She had gone to the police claiming assault after all. He'd only been gone half an hour, so she decided to wait until it had been an hour, and then she'd call him. *Surely an hour would be plenty of time to get across to her that she needs to just fuck off.* So many different scenarios kept running through Natasha's head though, making it impossible to for her to stay still or get anything else done. *Was he fucking her? What if she has gone nuts and attacked him? Maybe he has attacked her? What if they were having a blazing row and someone had called the police? That wouldn't be good with the previous accusations.* There was nothing that could be done except to wait, and so Natasha decided to clean the bathroom as a kind of distraction. At least while her mind was running wild, she would get something useful done at the same time. With some thick bleach and a wire brush, she went to work on the patches of black mould, which seemed to be dominating the lines between the tiles around the bath, scrubbing at them ferociously as she fought back images of her husband with another woman. Eventually, impatience got the better of her, and she sent Seb a text, telling him he was taking a bit too long and to give her an update as she was beginning to worry. This only made the feeling worse as no reply came through, time seeming to slow down unbearably.

Ella got out of the car and looked around, still no sign of the holidaying French campers, no sign of anyone nearby. She was unsure how long the sleeping pills would last for, hoping to be able to wake him when the time was right. Ella's mobile phone wasn't particularly modern and, therefore, the camera on it wasn't very good without some decent light. This added to the risk, but Ella felt that the coast was clear enough to take the chance. She also wasn't sure how unconscious Seb was, and how much he could manage in his current state. She called his name a few times but there was no response, so she began to undo his jeans and, with a bit of a struggle, managed to pull out his flaccid penis. *If they wake up with boners, then this ought to work,* she thought to herself as she took him into her mouth. It took a little bit of time, but she began to feel it grow in her mouth until it was almost fully erect. Ella doubted he would be able to climax whilst asleep, although wet dreams exist so maybe, and took a few photographs of herself, mouth open, the end of his cock against her lips. That was all she had thought of doing, giving herself enough to blackmail Seb with. She saw her actions as being for the greater good, a way to achieve their happily-ever-after. She had underestimated how much she was going to enjoy the experience, however, and after another quick look around found herself removing her leggings. The seriousness of her actions hadn't fully been taken on board, perhaps because she was female, and things weren't the other way around. All thoughts of wrong and right disappeared as she climbed on to Seb's cock, feeling it slide inside of her. He was completely out for the count, but it was so hard that, with a few moments of riding him, she shuddered from an intense orgasm. She snapped a few more pictures of their genitals, trying to show that he was inside of her without giving away the fact that he was not consenting. Ella got herself dressed and pondered the next move, thinking that Seb needed to wake up soon so that he wasn't found asleep. Ella wondered if an orgasm would do and continued to play with his cock, but despite it becoming sticky on the end, there was to be no full finish.

Ella placed what was left of the whiskey into her bag, put Seb's bits back in his jeans and stepped out of the car. Feeling pleased with herself, she resisted the urge to send any pictures to Natasha yet but headed home to make a coffee and prepare for dealing with Seb, certain he would call when he came around. *I bet he wakes up horny,* Ella thought to herself. *Well, he can have as much as he wants once Natasha kicks him out.*

Seb was awoken by a loud bang against the car window. An older guy, maybe about sixty years old, with little hair and a high-visibility jacket was looking at him, and not in a friendly way. Seb felt disorientated; it was now light, and he was still at the beach. He fumbled for the keys but couldn't find them in the ignition so opened the door.

"You can't sleep here," he was told gruffly, and the man then made his way further along the beach, towards the camper vans. Seb looked out across the sea, the sun not long having risen, the expanse of the English Channel appearing calm. It looked as though it would be a pleasant day, despite the chill he had felt when opening the door. The last thing Seb remembered was talking to Ella. *Had he fallen asleep*

The Broken Doll: Book One

while she was still there? Was it a combination of the whiskey and his general exhaustion that had finally caught up with him? Seb tried to piece together the conversation with Ella, attempting to establish how things had been left between them. He remembered explaining it was finished, that she seemed upset, but they had sat in silence and had a drink. Then he must have dozed off. A wave of panic hit him as he began to see that Natasha was going to be thinking the worst; it certainly wouldn't look good for him to have met Ella and stayed out all night. The car keys weren't in the ignition, and his pockets were empty. *Shit,* he thought, wondering if Ella had taken them to piss him off. After a few minutes of rummaging around in the foot wells, he came across the keys and his phone. The phone was off, presumably due to a dead battery as he usually charged it overnight. Seb had a horrible feeling, like that of a teenager who has stayed out past their curfew, fully knowing that they will be in trouble when they get home. He started the engine, the clock on the dashboard illuminating, informing him that it was not quite 6am. He took the drive home slowly, his head still groggy from being suddenly woken up. He was dreading a confrontation with Natasha and felt unable to explain why he had been out for so long.

As Seb walked through the front door, he was surprised to find Natasha and Dee drinking coffee in the kitchen. Natasha's face looked pale, her eyes puffy, as though she had been crying. She looked startled to see him, her face quickly turning to rage.

"Don't even fucking speak, get out right now before I do something I regret. I don't want you here; the kids will be up soon, and I won't be able to stay calm."

"Fucking hell Nat," Seb said, calmly, "I know how it looks but give me a minute. I fell asleep in the car. I talked to Ella, made it clear that she is to leave us alone, then I woke up this morning. I guess I must have been exhausted." As Seb said these words, he appreciated how unbelievable they sounded, choosing not to mention the whiskey or allowing Ella into the car with him.

"You're a liar. You must think I'm a fucking moron. Get out, I'll let you know later when you can get your stuff."

"That's the truth!" Seb stated, a little bewildered by Natasha's refusal to accept his explanation, and a little hurt that she had suddenly decided not to trust him.

"Seb...," Dee began.

"You can stay out of it. What the fuck are you even doing here anyway? All you do is tell Nat how shit I am."

Dee didn't say another word, instead just stood next to Nat, looking at the floor. Seb could see that they were overemotional and had worked themselves up all night, convincing themselves that he had been up to no good. In this situation, it was pointless to try and reason with Nat, and so he turned and left, got back into his car and headed a little out of town. After about ten minutes of driving, the roads still quiet due to the hour, Seb parked up in a small area which formed part of the nature reserve that stretched across the area between home and the neighbouring town. There he sat, gazing out at nothing in particular, no tobacco to smoke, his phone too dead to use, and wondered what had happened to lead him to this place, at this very moment. It seemed beyond ridiculous for Natasha to end their marriage just because he had fallen asleep, although Seb knew he was oversimplifying matters. *If she is serious, what do I do? How long do I beg for?* Seb was aware of a temptation to go to Ella, if his marriage was truly over, but this all appeared to be working out in her best interests and suspiciously so. He decided to walk off the groggy feeling which still clouded his head, having always enjoyed this area with its tranquillity only interrupted by the occasional jogger.

The Broken Doll: Book One

He headed east, away from home, and strolled along the path, feeling both lost and free at the same time, as though all his problems were in the distance, and could wait for a while before, inevitably, being faced.

Seb felt lost without his phone but didn't think it was a good time to go home so he spent the morning wandering about, grabbing a coffee at the first place he came to. After slowly drinking the hot, black liquid, he had a browse around the shops and came across an electrical place he hadn't known existed. He bought a cable that would enable him to charge his phone via the USB socket in the car and decided he would feel a little better if he ate. It was getting on for eleven and, after some indecision, he voted against a full English breakfast in a cafe and went for a mixed grill in a pub, alongside a pint of local ale and a Makers Mark on ice. *Well, I've got nothing better to do,* he told himself, relishing in the extravagance of drinking so early in the day, dwelling a little in self-pity. The food wasn't great, the medium-rare rump being closer to well-done and the sausages tasting far too cheap in relation to the price he had paid for it, but it was still a good start to the day. He had convinced himself that he deserved a few treats after the way he had been spoken to by Natasha and, by not contacting her, perhaps she would realize that he was not at fault this time.

After three pints and three whiskeys, Seb left the pub, making his way back through the town which was far busier now. He felt a little drunk as he emerged into the sunlight, certainly for the time of day, and knew that he could no longer drive. After picking up some cigarettes, he almost walked past a trendy little bar, full of pensioners having lunch and yummy mummies enjoying a Pinot Grigio in between school runs. With no other plans for the day, and a feeling of recklessness taking over, he decided to go in, get himself a large gin, and relax in the beer garden with a smoke. The first double went down far too easily, and he soon lost count of how many he had had. People came and went; the afternoon became colder as evening approached. Seb's mood changed, realizing that he couldn't go home, at least not in this state. He was stuck with three choices, as far as he could see; spend the night in the car, go to the lock-up, or go to Ella. If he had been sober, then he would most likely have just gone and fallen asleep in his car. However, he was drunk, angry with Natasha for not letting him explain, and in need of some company. Unsure of what would happen, but still willing to take the risk, he walked around the corner to the taxi rank outside of the train station.

Ella spent the day reading, feeling surprisingly calm. There had been no word from Seb, and she had not contacted him, although she did hope that he was OK. She worried he may be angry with her but felt sure it would pass in time. She had also been concerned that Natasha would turn up again, like she had done before, but it appeared that she was beginning to accept the situation at last. Ella had spent hours in bed on the previous night, debating whether or not to send any of the photographs to Natasha. A little after 1am, her phone signalled a text message, and not a very polite one at that. 'Where is my husband? I warned you to stay away from him.'

Ella resisted the urge to reply and left it unanswered until another message came through half an hour later, essentially saying the same thing. Ella wanted to say that he was at her house but if Natasha came there, she would discover the lie and so went for a different story. Ella sent 'He's with me; don't worry, we've just been driving about and talking. He'll let you know when he wants to talk to you.'

Natasha tried to call Ella several times, sending more messages, each sounding more and more desperate. *Seb must still be asleep,* she thought, wondering whether Seb could convince his wife of the truth when he finally wakes up. *Not that it matters, I can prove what a naughty boy he's been.*

After a further hour of ignoring her phone, Ella decided it was all or nothing. *One last message,* she decided; 'Sorry for the delay replying, we were busy.' Ella then put her plan into action, sending this message with two photographs attached. The photos were grainy and dark but there was no mistaking the explicit nature of the content, or who was featured in them. With this, Ella turned off her phone and fell asleep, content that she was on the way to a happy future with Seb, confident that these feelings of upset and guilt would pass with time.

When she had awoken, Ella had not turned her phone back on, a little apprehensive about receiving abuse from Natasha and not wanting it to spoil her mood. She relaxed in the bath with a book, drank tea, read some more. This passed the day wonderfully until she was disturbed by the sound of a car pulling up outside. The lights indoors were off, just a small lamp provided enough light to read by. If it was Natasha, she could pretend not to be in. A more frightening thought was that it may be the police, perhaps Seb knew she had given him the pills. Even so, who would believe him? He had already been accused of assaulting her, there was a suspicion about them having an affair. It would look more like he was trying to cover his actions. She peered through the window, relieved to see it was a taxi. As Seb stepped out of it she noticed him fumbling about in his pockets. The taxi drove away, signifying to Ella that Seb wasn't planning on making any quick escape. *He's hammered,* she thought, watching him wobble a little as he approached the door. As she opened it, she saw sadness in his eyes, as though he was trying to fight back tears.

"I didn't have anywhere to go," he told her. "I'm also a bit drunk."

"It's fine. I'll make some coffee." Seb found his way to the sofa and slumped down, kicking off his shoes. Drinking for so many hours had taken its toll, and he wanted to sleep. He managed to keep his eyes open long enough to take the mug of coffee from Ella.

"You look like shit," she told him. "Do you want to use the shower? Promise I won't peek." This seemed like a good idea, possibly the only way that Seb was going to stay awake for much longer. He nodded, made his way to the bathroom, and locked the door. Ella listened to the sound of the water running, unsure of what to say to him, not knowing what had happened between him and Natasha or what he had been told. Ella sat patiently, resisting going into the bathroom, taking things slowly until she knew why he was here. This soon became clear, however, as the water shut off and from the bathroom came Seb with a towel around his waist, still wet.

"This is what you wanted isn't it?" he asked, dropping the towel to the floor. "I'm here now."

SEVENTEEN

"I don't think your wife would approve," Ella said, smiling, as she tried to assess the situation.

"I don't care anymore," Seb told her. "She's convinced I spent last night with you, and she won't give me a chance to explain. She doesn't want me, and I'm sick of trying to work things out with her when I haven't actually done anything that wrong."

"You know I'm not going to say no," Ella said. "But you are quite pissed, and I don't want to be messed about. I'm serious this time. You can't just turn up here because your bitch wife doesn't want you at the moment, then go buggering off back to her when she's finished her strop."

"I know. And don't call her names please; this isn't her fault."

"Well it is really. She can't have been a very good wife, or you wouldn't be stood there naked. I don't know what you saw in her anyway, miserable looking cow. Chunky too."

"That's enough," Seb warned Ella, suddenly feeling defensive of Nat and not finding Ella as attractive when she was being this way.

"Or what?" Ella asked as she walked towards Seb, a smirk appearing on her face. She could see her comments were getting to him but, as he had said, he had nowhere else to go. She was in command of the situation.

"I can call her whatever I want. She's nothing to me, just the ugly bitch that tried to come between us. She doesn't get to keep you though, I will do anything to be with you, I'll do anything *with* you."

Seb saw a flash of something terrifying in Ella as she spoke these words, something which made him feel as though he had no choice in events, that she could destroy him and his family. He saw red, her words playing on his mind, coupled with his guilt for being there at that moment, and he lashed out. He had never actually hit a woman before. He'd pushed Natasha once, when they'd had a horrible fight, years ago, but it didn't become a big issue. This was different; this was a loss of temper. With some force, more than intended, Seb slapped Ella across the face. She didn't fall or even stagger backwards. Her face quickly turned red and Seb immediately felt awful. *She's been through enough of that treatment with her husband. Jesus, I'm just as bad,* he thought. Ella stared straight into Seb's eyes as she unzipped the grey hoodie she was wearing. She lifted her T-shirt off to expose her bra.

"Do it harder!" she demanded.

The sight of Ella's cleavage has caused a sensation in Seb's body. The slap now felt erotic and, mixed with the alcohol, he paid no attention to concerns he may have otherwise had. He didn't consider it could be some kind of trick, he did not think about his recent police encounter, his brain full of animal instinct, overwhelmed by lust. He slapped her again, this time splitting her lip, so that a trickle of crimson ran down her chin. She smiled as she removed her bra, dropping to her knees. The aggression felt out of control as she took him into her mouth, Seb felt unable to stop his actions. He grabbed her hair and rammed himself deeply into her mouth, causing her to gag. He kept doing it until he felt a sharp pain and noticed that she had bitten down, not hard enough to draw blood but hard enough to make him recoil.

"Oops," she said playfully. "Have I been naughty?" As she said this, Ella went on to remove her trousers so that she ended up on all fours on the floor, with just some black knickers on. Seb slapped Ella across the bottom and ripped her underwear off, literally tearing them. His hand slid between her legs, and he could feel that she was more than ready for him, her inner thighs glistening as her dampness spilled out. He lifted her onto the sofa, positioning her in a sitting pose.

She stared at his cock longingly, insanely hard and juicy at the tip. However, it wasn't going in yet, she soon realized. Seb was on his knees in front of her as he lifted her legs into the air and used his tongue on her. It went deep inside her, lapping up her juices. Her legs were high enough for his tongue to reach both orifices, and she had at no time experienced this sensation. She had also never felt so wet, as though it was just pouring out of her.

"Do you have a condom?" Seb asked when he came up for air. "I don't have any."

"No, don't worry though, just get it in me." Seb didn't argue the point; it was something to think about after the deed. He could always pull out and hope for the best anyway. Besides, she could be on the pill. As he went in, Ella moaned, feeling the full length of him. They threw each other about the room, at it hard and rough, in various positions. Finally, with Ella bent over the arm of the sofa and Seb standing behind her, he reached his body-shuddering climax, not managing to withdraw and thus filling her deeply. She turned around and took his hand, leading him to the bedroom where they collapsed on the bed, sweaty, sticky, and covered in red marks, scratches, bruises, and a little blood.

"You OK?" Seb checked, looking at Ella's naked body, noticing the marks he'd left.

"I certainly am now," she smiled contentedly, pulling up the duvet and cuddling up to him. Seb's eyes quickly felt heavy, and he started to drift off, Ella's head resting on his chest as she lay awake, wishing that this could last forever. Once Seb was fully asleep, Ella crept to the kitchen to get her phone from her handbag. She turned it back on, surprised to see just one message from Natasha, simply calling her a skank in reply to the photographs she had sent. She made her way to the bathroom where she proceeded to photograph herself; the red marks on her face and buttocks, the split lip with its crack of dried blood, and the finger marks around her wrists where Seb had pinned her against a door earlier. Seb had turned onto his side, and she cautiously managed to pull back the duvet enough to get a clear picture of the scratches on his back, the sign of a great sex session, or possibly defensive wounds from trying to fight him off. That would ultimately be his decision, based on how he behaved in the morning. Ella had, after all, warned him that he couldn't have her and then just leave.

It didn't take long for Ella to fall asleep once she had turned her phone back off, closed all the curtains, and pretty much hidden them away from the rest of the world. Ella was, of course, unfamiliar with sharing a bed with anyone now, and she woke several times through the night. Seb was very much asleep though, and her cuddling into him did not seem to disturb him in the slightest. She woke again as daylight began creeping through the curtains, guessing it must be around 7am. She was aroused, in the way that couples generally are at the start of a new relationship, when they can't get enough of each other's bodies. Seb was stirring a little, so she began to touch him, feeling him instantly become hard in her hand. He rolled onto his back, eyes still closed, and murmured a little. She could feel her own dampness and climbed onto him, hearing him whimper as she took his cock inside her. She writhed around on him, building up a sweat, her hands on his chest until she reached her climax. He stayed where he was, eyes closed, but a little smile appeared on his face as he waited to see if there was more on offer. She lifted herself off him and took his hard, wet dick in her hand and worked it until he sprayed all over himself.

"Coffee?" she asked, as he slowly opened his eyes.

The Broken Doll: Book One

"Yeah, and some paracetamol if you have it." He looked down at the mess on his skin. "A cloth or something might be handy too."

"No problem," Ella replied, walking out to the kitchen, still fully nude. *Fuck,* Seb thought. *I haven't been woken up like that in a while. It's going to be a day of some big decisions.*

"Still no word from your husband?" Seb asked as Ella handed him a coffee, placing a glass of water next to the bed with some painkillers.

"No, thank God. I think he was having an affair with some local tart, so he's probably shacked up with her somewhere."

"But he's not been by for anything? It's odd he hasn't been in touch at all, isn't it?" Ella looked away. "Not really, he took what he wanted, and it's not like we have any kids for him to bother with." Ella seemed uncomfortable on this topic. Seb felt that she was not being entirely truthful with him, but it could simply have been that she did not want to talk about her husband whilst in bed with another man.

"Did you not want any children? Or didn't he?" Seb asked, still curious to know more.

"I do want children," Ella replied. "I mean I did. Just not with him being the way he was, it didn't seem right to bring up a child in that environment." Seb had noticed the way she had responded. "You do or you did?" he asked, a little apprehensively as he recalled the unprotected session they had had last night.

"Don't look so worried, I don't know really, certainly not right now. Any idea what you want to do today?" Ella asked, changing the subject. "Do you have anything you have to do, or should we stay in bed all day?"

"I don't know. I'm going to have to talk to Natasha, work out what we're going to do. This has been great, but I don't feel like I can go from one relationship to another just like that."

"She isn't going to take you back now," Ella stated, abruptly. "I told you last night, you can't just use me and go running back to her!"

"I know, and that's not what I'm saying, but I have to think of the children, about where I'm going to go, there are things to sort out." The thought of all the practicalities, and the guilt, were all too much at this hour with the raging hangover banging away at his head.

"You don't need to go anywhere; you can live here. I thought that was the idea?"

"It's too soon for that, but just give me some time to think things through. I do want to keep seeing you, so please don't think I've used you. Do you have a plug with a USB socket? My phone has been dead for ages. I should turn it on really."

"No hurry, let's just rest for a bit longer before we have to face anyone."

After they had finished their second mugs of coffee, and Seb had started to feel a little more awake, Ella climbed out of the bed and headed to the shower. The hot water stung the parts of her body that had taken the most punishment last night, but she was enjoying the reminder, savouring the memory of what Seb had done to her.

"Seb?" she called, over the sound of the water.

"Yeah?" he replied, his head peering round the door into the bathroom.

"Want to join me?" *She's insatiable,* he thought, *but no reason not to.* As he stepped in, the hot water hit the scratches on his back, scratches he did not appreciate the extent of in the heat of the moment. Ella began rubbing him down with some shower gel, her body already covered in a soapy lather. He stood still, enjoying the feeling of her hands working their way over every part of him, paying special attention to his buttocks and cock. He explored her soapy breasts with one hand, placing the other on the side of her face and kissing her deeply. He was hard again, and she began rubbing herself against him. They quickly rinsed all the bubbles off and touched each other, kissing naked in the shower. Seb turned her around and entered her, slowly sliding in and out as he pulled her hair gently. However, this time he was sober, and the contraception issue was still on his mind, so he stopped.

"We should get some condoms if this is going to be a regular occurrence," he said.

"Yes, we'll get some today, I promise. It would probably be for the best. Even so, I can't leave you like that," Ella told him, dropping to her knees and finishing him off with her mouth. She swallowed the whole load before hopping out and brushing her teeth. *At least she didn't spit,* Seb thought, quite satisfied with his two orgasms already this morning.

Natasha was a mess. She didn't know where her husband was, although she could hazard a good guess. She didn't know if he had come home as she had taken the children to stay at her parents, and Seb's phone seemed to still be off. She didn't know if he was safe, or if he was coming back to her. She felt guilty for throwing him out like that, but the evidence was clear; he was a cheat. Ever since they had met, they had always been straight with each other, if either one of them is unfaithful, it's over. Nevertheless, now that it had actually happened, she didn't want it to be over. She wanted him to beg and grovel and cry, to sleep on the sofa, to be there for her to ignore for weeks, to make him do chores, and for him to buy her gifts as an apology. However, she wanted him *with* her. Of course, her parents were livid at what he had done, and understandably so. She knew that they would strongly

The Broken Doll: Book One

oppose her taking him back and would never treat him the same way again. Natasha felt that it may have been a mistake telling them all the lurid details. She wished now that she had told them it was just a silly fight, something forgivable. Their faces when she told them he was photographed with his dick in some tart's mouth, well, shocked would be an understatement. So, they had responded in the way that people of their generation did in situations like this; by making pot of tea after pot of tea, virtually force feeding the children biscuits and hot chocolate, banishing any mention of Seb from their house, and acting as though Natasha and the children were going to move in.

"What are you going to do about the house?" her father asked her. "Are you planning on staying in that area, or do you think it would be wise to move a bit nearer to us? Perhaps sell up? There are some lovely places nearby available at the moment."

Natasha hadn't even considered moving. Their house was the family home; it was the children's home. Both the children and herself had friends there, and aside from the issues between Seb and Natasha, he was the children's father, and he was a good one. An awful spouse does not necessarily equate to a bad parent. She had no doubt he would want to see them regularly and they him.

"I don't know; I haven't thought that far ahead yet. The house is in both of our names anyway, so he'd either have to buy me out, or we'd have to sell and split it, but it wouldn't leave me with enough to buy another house on my own so I would probably have to look at renting. Even so, I really can't deal with that at the moment until I know what's going on."

"OK dear, but don't leave it too long, the children need stability and this sort of trauma that their so-called father has caused can send children off the rails."

The Broken Doll: Book One

Natasha hated the way her parents viewed young people in general, the way that they were convinced that anyone under thirty was a tattoo-faced, unemployed drug addict. They seemed terrified that any emotional upset, no matter how trivial, would be enough to send their beloved grandchildren spiralling out of control and before anyone knew it, they would be mugging pensioners and smoking crack.

"Can we stay for a few days? A week at the most. I'll call the school and let them know. Just while I get a plan together."

"Of course, stay as long as you need. You can even make it permanent if you want to. Just think about it." The thought of moving back in with her parents was more frightening than being on her own by far, but Natasha just smiled and nodded.

"We'll see. But thank you," she told him.

In a nondescript bar, drinking a pint of weak lager, a few hours' drive away from home, Sid sat with a newspaper and scanned through the jobs' section. *Fuck all as usual,* he thought to himself, becoming increasingly frustrated with his situation. He was staying with family, but they didn't get on very well. He had mounting debts owing from the business he had abandoned when he had decided to leave everything, and everyone, behind. He stared at his pint, thinking about Maggie. He knew she was a wild one; that's what he had liked about her, and neither of them had been angels. He'd coped with her flirtatiousness, put it down to just being part of her personality. He even learned to ignore the rumours about her, blaming them on other people's jealousy and assumptions others made about her. Regardless, that night had been unbearable. She'd been seen kissing other people at the pub when she'd had a few too many before, and they'd talked about it. He'd given her a hard time, but he had done the same in the past, so they moved on without too much fuss. He'd been fuming a few months previously when a photo had appeared online of Maggie flashing her tits in exchange for shots, and there had been a bit of push and shove that night, but they had made up, just as they always did. This was different though. It was unforgivable. Sid felt ashamed and embarrassed by his wife. And this time it was too much. Word would get about; everyone would be laughing at him and laughing at her. Sid decided he couldn't stay and off he went, just like that. He wouldn't be able to face the other people involved again without losing his temper, so he disappeared, binned his phone, started afresh. Although this wasn't as easy as he had hoped; the money didn't last long, and he had some legal issues to face after walking out on the business. However, for now, he had a roof over his head and a pint in his hand, so things weren't as bad as they could have been. He felt calmer too, less preoccupied with fantasies of revenge, of hurting the other man, of hurting Lotte. *What's done is done,* he told himself. *She made her choice, and I've made mine. Good riddance.* With that thought, he finished the last of his pint and walked out into the rain, heading back to the house he was temporarily calling home, with people he reluctantly referred to as family.

EIGHTEEN

"I need to pick up my car," Seb told Ella, looking out at the sunny day, planning to walk there for a bit of time alone to think.

"OK, shall I come with you?" she asked.

"No, it's alright. I won't be too long." Ella looked put out.

"Don't worry, I'm coming back. I'll get some of my things while I'm out and be here in a couple of hours." This seemed to cheer her up a bit.

"Fine, I'll be waiting," she told him, playfully. "Shall I wait in bed?"

"Sounds good," Seb told her, somewhat dismissively, and grabbed his keys, phone, and new charger cable as he walked out of the door. The air was fresh, but the sky was clear, at least, good weather for a stroll. Seb estimated that would take about half an hour to walk back to where he had left the car, but he felt in no real hurry; apprehensive about seeing Natasha, nervous about returning to Ella. He felt as though he shouldn't have gone there last night but couldn't deny that he had thoroughly enjoyed it. It hadn't really sunk in that his marriage could actually be over, and he needed to clear the air with his wife before making any further mistakes.

The walk to the car was uneventful as he wandered, deep in thought, barely noticing the dog walkers and joggers. Although the car parking area was free to use, and he had not noticed a time restriction, he was still relieved to find the car without a parking fine attached to it. As soon as he was inside, he turned on the heaters and connected his phone to the USB socket, waited for a few moments for there to be enough charge, and turned it on. He then started the engine and made his way home, or at least to where he had called home until recently, with determination to find some clarity regarding the state of his marriage.

"Nat?" he called, letting himself into the house. "Are you in?" There was no reply. Not even the chocolate brown lab came to see who had arrived. Seb searched the house, beginning at the top, in the master bedroom. It looked a little different; the bed was made, as always, but somehow it looked as though it had not been slept in. There were a few bits from his wife's bedside cabinet missing, but he couldn't place exactly what they were, it just looked a little emptier than usual. As he opened the large, mirrored wardrobe that they shared, he noticed a few gaps on her side; there were definitely clothes missing, but they could be anything as the wardrobe had always been so full. The scene in the children's rooms was the same, with a few clothes gone, favourite teddies, etc. The bathroom looked sparse, with just Seb's toothbrush and toiletries present.

Seb headed down to the kitchen and put the kettle on. He ran back up to the master bedroom to retrieve his phone charger and plugged it in at the wall in the kitchen. His phone had vibrated several times during the drive back but was still very low on battery, so he made a drink and prepared himself to read the messages that he knew would be waiting for him. Ignoring all the email notifications, and things which now seemed trivial, he went into the text messages to find four from Natasha, one junk message offering a loan, and one from the landlord of his lock-up asking him to call. Seb deleted the loan offer message, deciding to call his landlord before reading the messages from Natasha, in case it was urgent. After a brief conversation, Seb discovered that his tenancy agreement was ending in a month, and he needed to decide if he wished to renew. Seb promised to call back later, as this may actually be something which he needed to consider in the current situation, aware, however, that he would need to store the stock somewhere, and God knows where he could take those bloody sofas.

Seb felt on edge as he opened the messages from his wife, all dated the night before last. The first three were all before midnight, all asking where he was, why he wasn't home, if he was safe, but with increasingly concerned undertones. The last message was not of concern; it was blunt and full of hurt. 'Wow, I really did misjudge you, you fucking lying prick. Don't come back, you made your choice. I fucking hate you!' *Great!* Seb thought. *She just assumed I was cheating. Nice. And now I have.*

Seb decided that he couldn't just leave things like that and called Natasha, hoping to find her a little calmer. He half expected her not to answer, or for her to shout at him, but she took the call.

"Hi," she said, sounding sad. "I thought you weren't going to call."

"Hi," Seb said in return. "Sorry, my phone has been dead for the last two days; I just came home to plug it in. And to see you, of course," he pointed out, worried she would think that he only wanted his charger.

"I thought that I had made myself clear, I don't want to see you," she told him.

"Where are you? Have you gone to your parents'?"

"Please don't come here, my dad will probably try to kill you; you're not their favourite person at the moment."

"I understand how it looked by me not coming back, but you haven't given me a chance to explain. After I saw Ella, I fell asleep in the car, she had gone home before that. I swear to you. I didn't do anything wrong."

"So, you're saying you haven't fucked her? I just want to hear that exact sentence from your mouth

The Broken Doll: Book One

before we carry on." Seb hesitated, long enough for Natasha to notice.

"Shit. OK, this is the truth. You won't like it, but I don't see how it could make things any worse. Yes, we had sex. But that was last night, after you'd kicked me out, and I spent the day drinking yesterday." Seb could hear his wife trying to hold in the tears, and he felt himself welling up, knowing that he couldn't go back from this now.

"Jesus, Seb, you offer the truth, and yet you still can't manage it. All you've said is that you fucked her yesterday, but it's pretty much my fault for kicking you out and, because you were drunk, it couldn't be helped. It's pathetic. I know you were at it the night before as well, why do you think I was so angry?"

"I'm telling you the truth, nothing happened that night. I know how it looks, and I can't deny that but if you don't believe me, then that's your choice."

"If," Natasha began, with an impatient sigh. "If you had come home with your story about falling asleep, I would have strongly doubted it. It sounds like nonsense. Nevertheless, as your wife, I would have accepted that, as I have so many of your other stories, unless I had evidence to the contrary."

"What the hell does that mean? So, you're saying that you do believe me? There can't be anything proving otherwise because I know what I was doing."

"I'm not going to keep going over it," Natasha told him, sounding tired of the conversation. "Take what you need from the house, we'll be away for a few days while I make plans. Stay at the house if you want, but don't you dare bring that whore there, and don't be there when we get back." With that, she ended the call and Seb stared at his phone in confusion.

As Seb pulled a cigarette from the packet in his jeans' pocket, his phone vibrated again. He stared in disbelief at the messages from Natasha, beginning with 'This is why I don't believe you' and followed by two photos. One of two sets of genitals, as close to each other as they could possibly be. Familiar looking, certainly, but not necessarily his own. The other was less disputable; Ella's face was unmistakable, even in the dark, and that cock with the tip in her mouth, was most likely his. In the background, Seb's car keys could easily be seen as well as his right hand with the distinctive, titanium ring he wore.

What the fuck? Seb muttered, unable to take in the images before him. *Well, that explains why Natasha didn't believe me! But I don't remember doing that.*

Seb felt a sickening sensation creep across him, trying to recall the events of that night. *We were sat in the car, drinking whiskey, then I woke up. Had she tried it on with me, whilst I was asleep? It would explain how she got the photos. It still doesn't make sense, though. If I had just drifted off, I'm pretty sure her climbing about and grabbing my dick would have woken me up! Unless...*

Seb began to take in what had happened, his mind frantically trying to find another explanation but unable to come up with one. He'd been drugged, but they had both had the whiskey, hadn't they? He racked his brain, trying to recall actually seeing Ella drink any, but couldn't picture it. *What am I doing?* he asked himself. *For fuck's sake, she tried to have me locked up for assaulting her. She's now drugged and pretty much raped me to sabotage my marriage, and there I am, choosing to wake up next to her and actually considering moving in with her!*

He called Natasha back, needing to explain, but she was not interested in any more lies. Seb pleaded his case, explained to her his theory, but his wife sounded as though she would rather not hear any more.

"Either way, you spent last night with her, so we're done. You can't blame that on anyone else, even if she's a nutcase that deliberately set this in

The Broken Doll: Book One

motion, you admitted to voluntarily sticking your dick in her. If you are serious about the drugs and, as ridiculous as it sounds, that she may have raped you, then go to the police and see what they say. However, it's not my concern." With that, the call was over. Seb slumped to the floor feeling an anger rising inside him, anger towards Ella for what she did, anger towards Natasha for not trusting him, but mostly, anger towards himself for being weak and using such lame excuses to justify being unfaithful.

Ella was still lying in bed, wearing just a short nightdress, when her phone rang. She saw that it was Seb calling and expected him to say that he was on his way back to her. He had been gone longer than she had anticipated, and Ella was wondering if there had been any problems with his wife.

"Hello sexy," she answered. "Are you on your way yet?"

"Not yet. What happened the other night, when we were at the beach? I don't remember much."

I guess Natasha showed him the photos then. Ella had thought this through before sending them, and knew that her explanation was weak, but it had had to be done anyway.

"The whiskey hit you pretty hard, you said you wanted some from me, but you were finding it difficult to manage, if you know what I mean. I tried to get you worked up with my mouth, which helped a bit, but not enough to get anywhere. Do you not remember?"

"Nope," Seb told her, firmly. "I don't remember any of that at all. Which is odd. It's also odd that you would feel the need to photograph us and send the picture to my wife." Seb sounded angry, but Ella had expected that.

"I'm sorry; I shouldn't have done that. I was just worried that you would use me and go back to her,

The Broken Doll: Book One

denying everything. You told me at the beach that you wanted me, not her, so I didn't think it would matter which one of us told her."

"Seriously? The last thing I remember is telling you that I wasn't interested, us sitting in the car, then I woke up in the morning. Something isn't right here. Something isn't right with you. I don't think this is a good idea any more. You need some professional help, whatever your issues are they need to be dealt with. If I'm honest, your behaviour scares the shit out of me. I do care about you, despite everything, but I need some space from you; time to get my head straight. You should go to a doctor or something, get some advice, because the things you do are more than a little odd." Seb thought he phrased things compassionately enough; it certainly sounded better than 'Fuck off, you're a crazy bitch!' Ella didn't like it though, her voice rising as she took in what Seb was telling her.

"How dare you? You use me two nights in a row then think you can just bail out? Only a couple of hours ago you were coming in my mouth, and now you want a break from me? That is not an option, I'm afraid. You gave me your word that you wouldn't just fuck me and leave. And I gave you my word that I wouldn't let that happen. Come back, we'll talk, and get things clear. Like you said, you have nowhere else to go anyway so why not be with me and see what comes of it?"

"I don't think it's a good idea at the moment, sorry. I'm going to go now."

"Wait, don't hang up. I'll see a doctor if it helps, but I'm scared to go on my own. Come here and we'll go together. Please?" Ella sounded desperate, frighteningly so.

"No," Seb told her. "You see a doctor, get your head straight, and perhaps we'll talk in the future."

"Then maybe I won't go to the doctor, maybe the police will be more interested."

The Broken Doll: Book One

"Don't start that again, I'm sure the police will get fed up with you keep making things up about me. And threatening me won't make me want to see you," Seb told her, calmly.

"I can change my mind over the assault charge any time I want, and that, coupled with the fact that you raped me last night, could be enough for them to take me seriously. I have bruises on my wrist, my face is marked, my lip split."

"Don't be fucking ridiculous," Seb told her, not feeling as confident as he sounded. "There was hardly a mark on you this morning, and you know full well it was consensual."

"The bruises and hand prints were pretty clear last night when I took photos of them. I gave you the choice, if you want to have me, then it's for good. You can't just slap me about one night and fuck off back to your wife. I won't allow that."

Seb didn't trust himself to say anything else to Ella, so he ended the call, only just managing to resist throwing his phone across the room. *Had she planned the whole thing? The roughness of the sex had been her idea, and I didn't think at any point that she wasn't really into it. Surely the police wouldn't believe her?* Seb wondered. Nevertheless, he was not convinced. Although the evidence was circumstantial, it undoubtedly portrayed him in a bad light. And then there were Ella's photos; whether he could prove that he had not consented on the first night didn't matter, she certainly looked willing in them. A decent barrister would make the obvious point that her being willing one night doesn't mean that she was necessarily consenting the next, but it must at least throw some doubt on her story, especially after accusing him of assault then sucking his dick in a car.

Feeling as though he needed to vent, he called Natasha back, hoping that she would talk to him.

The Broken Doll: Book One

She answered, but sounded impatient, as though she just wanted him to leave her alone.

"I need to talk to you. I'm sorry, but it's serious. I spoke to Ella, about the photos."

"So?" Natasha said. "She sent them, so I'm sure she isn't bothered."

"I don't remember doing anything that night, but it's beside the point now anyway. She's threatened me with a rape charge." There was an uncomfortable silence as Seb awaited a response from his wife.

"Well she looked pretty up for it in the photos. You've got yourself a proper nut job there, not my problem though is it."

"She's talking about last night. Things got pretty rough, but it was all consensual, now she's taken photos of some marks I left on her and said I have to go to hers, or she's going to the police."

"Why the fuck would you think I would want to know that? That you had some steamy, rampant fuck session with another woman? Jesus Christ."

"Sorry, I just don't know what to do, I think she's dangerous. I'll get some legal advice, just in case. You and the kids should stay there for a while longer, until I know what's happening."

"I'm sure we'd be fine; I'm not a threat to her anymore because I don't want you. Even so, we will be staying here for another week or so I expect."

"Good, I'll let you know what happens."

"Don't bother, I'm trying to get away from all this shit. I'd rather you don't call me anymore unless it's actually an emergency. And please don't give me any more of your sordid details, I really don't want to know how you fucked her." With that, the call ended.

The Broken Doll: Book One

Seb turned off his phone, avoiding any further contact from Ella. He wondered if she would turn up at the house, but he had deliberately not mentioned that he was alone and hoped this would be enough of a deterrent to stop her from just dropping by. He plugged in his laptop and started to search online for legal advice, noting down the details of some local firms that may be able to advise him, should it become necessary. It appeared that the onus fell on him to demonstrate his innocence, rather than the police proving his guilt, if there was a credible witness, and so there was nothing stopping him being prosecuted for the assault, and the rape, based solely on Ella's statements. Unless he could discredit her somehow? He learned that the law was very one-sided when it came to rape cases, with females being unable to be charged with the crime. They can, however, be charged with serious sexual assault, and can be charged with rape if they assist another male in carrying out the act. Seb doubted that there would be any way to prove he had not consented to the events in the car, and he would only bring that up if there was any police involvement at all. With no reason to doubt Ella's statements, if she chose to make them, it would create a strong case against him, and Seb began to feel sick with worry. He was fearful that simply telling the truth would not be enough in the eyes of the law. Somehow, he had to prove that Ella was unstable, possibly dangerous. He looked through his phone for messages from Ella, there were only a few as he had deleted most of the earlier ones to avoid Natasha seeing them, and the ones that remained weren't very significant. Yes, she was asking to see him, but it didn't prove anything either way. There was only one thing he could think of doing, one thing which may be enough to protect himself from Ella's threats, and this involved seeing her again.

The Broken Doll: Book One

Ella was crying, angry tears streaming down her cheeks. She didn't want to have to keep threatening Seb, she didn't want the police involved; she just needed him to be there. Even so, she was unwilling to let him just keep coming back and forth, messing her about; she deserved better than that. If he didn't come back by the morning, then she would have no choice, and she didn't expect him to. The knock at the door startled her, and so did the deep kiss he gave her before even saying hello.

"I didn't know if you'd come back," she began. "I'm sorry I look a mess, got myself a bit upset."

"It's OK baby," Seb told her, wondering if this would actually work. "I'm here now. I just had to know what was really going on. I'm not happy that you sent the pictures to Natasha, but I do understand why you did it. Let's just forget about it now."

"Sounds good, I'm really glad that you're here. If you had told me that you were on the way, then I would have found us something to eat."

"I'll get us a takeaway if you want? Chinese or pizza?"

"I'm fine with anything. I never get takeaways, so I'll let you choose. What shall we do while we wait?"

"I don't mind really; I'll order a pizza then." Seb went online and ordered a large meaty pizza before disappearing to the bathroom. He didn't intend to stay any longer than necessary. After he had emptied his bladder and flushed, he turned on the voice recorder on his phone and tucked it into his pocket, with the microphone end poking out.

"Ella," he began, wanting to ensure he got her name into the recording. "What would you like to do while we wait for the food?"

"Have a guess!" Ella told him, excitedly. "I don't want you to spoil your appetite for pizza but feel free to eat me for a bit!" Ella hitched up her nightie enough to reveal that she was not wearing underwear, and Seb approached her, kneeling on the floor.

"Tell me what to do," he said, making it into a game, hoping to get some clear vocalisation rather than a recording of squelchy sex noises.

"Put your fucking tongue right inside me. Now!" Ella demanded, getting into the mood, and as a result, giving Seb what he hoped for.

NINETEEN

"Do you want me?" Seb asked, as Ella slouched back on the sofa, legs spread. He ran a hand up her thigh, feeling her wetness. She moaned a little as two of Seb's fingers entered her.

"Tell me what you want," he whispered to her, hoping it was still loud enough to be picked up on the recording.

"Eat me, and fuck me, stop teasing!" Ella told him. And with that, he stood up and walked away. As he opened the front door, Ella began to see that something was wrong, but before she could pull herself together, he was already getting into his car. She ran out the door after him, but it was too late. He was on his way, the car soon disappearing round a bend.

What the fuck? she thought, completely confused as to what had just happened. Ella made her way to the bedroom to grab her phone, and as she was finding Seb's number, there was a knock on the door. *Is he playing some kind of game?* Ella wondered. She was unable to hide her disappointment when she opened the door to find a middle-aged woman in a blue uniform holding two pizza boxes.

"Shit, sorry. My boyfriend ordered those, but he had to go somewhere, and he has the money on him."

"Well, they need paying for," the delivery person told her.

"Hang on," Ella said, shutting the door in the woman's face. *Pick up, pick up,* Ella thought, as Seb's phone rang and rang. *For God's sake!* Ella opened the door once more and explained that she had no way to pay for the pizza and didn't know how long he would be, causing the woman to grumpily put the pizzas back into her car and drive off without saying another word. Ella then proceeded to try to call Seb again, and again, until she could feel herself becoming angrier each time

The Broken Doll: Book One

the voicemail kicked in. *It must be a game,* she thought. *Maybe he just wanted to tease me, get me worked up, and then he'll be back for some more. What else could it be?* However, the minutes turned to hours and there was no sudden return, no answering of the phone, no explanatory text. Nothing. Ella couldn't figure out what had made him go from touching her like that to walking out, without a word. It made no sense, and it frightened her not knowing why he had done it. Was he unsure about a relationship with her and, therefore, suddenly felt cautious about more sex? Had she done something to put him off? Had he just remembered he needed to be somewhere? Nothing added up and Ella felt out of control, pacing about the house, constantly re-dialling his number. The evening was closing in and outside was virtually pitch black, the nearest light being from the houses nearer the town centre. Ella had an overwhelming feeling that Seb wasn't coming back, and she was struggling to make sense of his apparent change of mind. She had avoided sending him any text messages, or leaving any voicemail recordings, as she did not want any evidence which would cause doubt over her allegations, should she feel the need to make them. Nevertheless, with him refusing to answer the phone, she had no way to resort to threats and did not know of any other way to deal with the situation. *Should I follow through and report him to the police? If I do, what if he comes back, and he does want to be here?*

Ella wanted to wait until morning but was terrified of a sleepless night, her mind getting carried away with Seb's possible motivation for leaving her so abruptly. After another hour of indecision, she got herself dressed and headed into town, determined to get answers.

Seb congratulated himself on his self-control. There she'd been, attractive, ready, and he had just walked out. Overall, he was pretty pleased with himself. He now had evidence to show that she was a very consenting adult in whatever their relationship could be called. He had, he assumed, managed to very much piss her off, and now he had taken control of the scenario and was heading home, with the rather optimistic intention of never seeing Ella again. When he was back indoors, Seb wanted to call Natasha but decided against it. She had asked him not to, and he didn't really know what to say. He felt it was unlikely that she would be that impressed if he explained he had managed to resist fucking Ella, something he should have refused before, of course. And Natasha was not going to want to know that he had even been there, let alone with some wet fingers.

Seb took a seat at the kitchen table, grabbed some notepaper, and began to construct a time line of events. He began, most sensibly, with when he had first met Ella, detailing as much as he could recall about when, where, and why he had had any contact with her. To add to the authenticity, Seb included some aspects of how he had felt about Ella, temptations that he endured, forwardness on her part. This made him feel better, more organized, and it also made his case seem much more solid and believable. There was no intention to take things any further at this point but having everything a bit clearer in his mind gave Seb less to worry about if Ella did anything crazy.

Once Seb had neatly put together everything that he felt was relevant, including the photos Natasha had sent him, and a copy of the voice recording which he had emailed to himself, he decided it was time for him to start taking more care of himself, to try to work toward a resolution to his predicament rather than wallowing in booze and junk food. He grabbed a bottle of water from the fridge, wolfed down a couple of bananas as he had still not eaten, and decided to go for a swim. This certainly seemed more appealing than the gym, as he wouldn't get distracted by his phone, and the pool was usually almost empty at this time of the evening. On his way there all he could think of was Ella, most likely sat on her sofa, crying all over the two pizzas he had ordered. Part of him felt bad, but part of him was pleased with himself; after all, it had been her own doing.

Seb had been quite right about the pool being quiet; it was actually empty. As he stepped into the water at the shallow end, trying to ignore the temperature, he knew that this had been a very good idea. It was quiet, relaxing. The only sound was the hushed chatter between the male lifeguard and a female staff member, someone whom Seb recognized from working on the reception desk sometimes. She was pretty, with dark hair and dark eyes, almost Mediterranean looking. As much as the uniforms at the leisure centre were probably designed for practical purposes, there was no denying it was a plus that this girl's legs were on show. Seb swam a couple of lengths and stopped again as he returned to the shallow end, thankful that he was in no danger of drowning, as the lifeguard seemed preoccupied with the dark-haired girl. It was hard to tell if they were actually a couple, or if they were just flirting, but it was undeniable that there was something between them. As Seb continued to swim slow lengths, he began to make up stories in his head about them. Was one, or both, of them in a relationship and this was an affair? Were they just friends or colleagues and it was completely innocent? Did they have access to the leisure centre after hours and, if so, would they meet up for skinny dipping and sex once the customers had all left? Seb managed to pass over an hour, casually swimming up and down the pool, daydreaming (in quite some detail) about what these two strangers got up to after work.

Once he was showered and dressed, Seb decided to leave his phone turned off. The swim had made him hungry, but despite it being late, he felt

The Broken Doll: Book One

invigorated and chose to walk to the supermarket and put together something to eat at home. It was tempting to go to one of the fast-food outlets, but this would have been foolish after exercise, opting instead to pick up some chicken fillets and vegetables. If Seb had turned his phone back on and seen the messages sent to him by his neighbour, then he would have had a little warning before turning the corner onto his road and finding two police cars parked outside his house, the blues and reds flashing. It would also have been less of a shock when he saw that the glass pane of his front door, and the living room window, were smashed. Seb saw four of his neighbours talking to uniformed police officers, the older gentleman who lived opposite, a couple who lived next door to him, whom Seb spoke to quite regularly and liked, and a young girl who he thought lived in a flat a few doors down from him. As they spotted him, everyone turned in his direction, someone calling him over. Before the police officers could say anything, the older man, William, came towards him.

"I had to call the old bill; some crazy woman was battering on your door for ages. When I came out to see what she was doing she was hysterical, shouting about you being a rapist! I told her I would call the police and when I went inside to use the phone, she must have found a rock or something and put your windows in." Seb didn't say anything, just nodded. One of the police officers verified who Seb was and ushered him into the house. Once inside, Seb pointed to the sofa for the police officers to sit down.

"I know who did this," Seb told them, positioning himself in the armchair. Shards of glass lay scattered across the floor by the bay window.

"So do we, Mr. Briggs. We have Mrs. Jenkins at the station. She came to us. She has admitted to causing the damage to your property."

"Right," said Seb. "So, what now?"

The Broken Doll: Book One

"It depends if you wish to press charges. Mrs. Jenkins has also made a very serious allegation against you."

"Yeah, I bet she has," Seb muttered.

"Mr. Briggs, do you have anyone who can keep an eye on your home, now that it is rather open to the elements?"

"Er, I don't know really. Why? Do I need to come to the station right now?"

"I'm afraid so. Sebastian Briggs, I am placing you under arrest for the assault and rape of Mrs. Ella Jenkins. You do not have to say anything but anything you do say may be used against you in a court of law. Please place your wrists in front of you." Silently, Seb put his hands out as requested, allowing the officer to place him in handcuffs and lead him into the back of one of the police cars, under the whispers and gaze of his neighbours.

"The time is twenty-two forty-seven, November third. Present are P.C. Oliver Smith, D.C. Lorraine Matthews, and Mr. Sebastian Briggs," D.C. Matthews stated clearly, after hitting the record button on the tape recorder, the same one in the same room as the last time Seb had found himself here.

"Mr. Briggs, can you please confirm your whereabouts yesterday evening, and for all of last night," D.C. Matthews went on to say. Seb looked down at the table, feeling overwhelmed, wishing he had had the foresight to bring the notes he had made. D.C. Matthews was not an attractive woman, scrawny, with greying blonde hair, and thin glasses. Seb noticed no wedding ring, which he didn't find surprising, and assumed, by the excessive aging of her hands, that she was a heavy smoker. This also didn't surprise Seb; it was probably a highly stressful job, with a lot of pressure to make the right decisions.

"I was with Ella, at her house. All night."

The Broken Doll: Book One

"And can you confirm what you were doing at Mrs. Jenkins home on that night?"

"We were mostly having sex." Seb looked up as he said this, trying to gauge any reaction from the police but nothing registered.

"Apart from having sex, did you do anything else or did that occupy all the time you were there?" he was asked.

"I arrived early evening. I had a shower, and we started having sex. This went on for a few hours, then we went to sleep. We had some more sex in the morning, then again, in the shower, then I left soon after that."

"That doesn't sound very romantic," D.C. Matthews commented.

"It wasn't supposed to be; it was just sex between consenting adults."

"Ah," D.C. Matthews began. "That brings me to the next point. Consent. How would you describe the sex? Had you been drinking before you arrived at Mrs. Jenkins home?"

Seb was aware of how things could appear, but he was also aware that he had committed no crime so went on to explain the events of that night in detail, excessive detail as far as the police were concerned. He described everything from when he dropped his towel, admitted to slapping Ella, detailed the sex in each position, even telling them when he came. He particularly highlighted Ella's reaction to the sex, her demands for roughness, her insistence on more in the morning. He went on to describe the threats made against him, that she had told him she had photographed the sex 'injuries'. He explained about the pictures Ella had sent to Natasha, that he had no recollection of that evening, and that he had been the victim of a sexual assault. There was still no change in expression on the faces of the officers, and Seb found it

The Broken Doll: Book One

frustrating that he could not tell if they believed him or not.

"Thank you for that Mr. Briggs. I wanted to hear your version before I went over the allegations against you, it provides better clarity that way, and hopefully will help us to get to the truth more easily. Mrs. Jenkins came to the station this evening, visibly upset, and told the desk sergeant that she had smashed two windows at your property. She was remorseful for this behaviour and said it was in response to the way that you had treated her. She says, which is in line with her previous statement in which she alleges you assaulted her, that the two of you were having an affair. She says that your wife has now left you because of it, but she feels that this is not what you wanted, hoping to be able to keep her 'on the side', as she put it. Mrs. Jenkins has told us that she was unwilling to accept you staying with your wife after so many promises to leave her and so, after the two of you met at the beach for sex in your car, she took a course of action which resulted in her sending photographs to your wife, thus forcing the situation along. She goes on to state that you did not handle your wife leaving very well, and went on a drinking binge, turning up out of the blue last night. She says that you were aggressive and drunk, and that she asked you to leave. You proceeded to slap her across the face and rape her. Soon after, you fell asleep and this morning, seeming remorseful, you left Mrs. Jenkins home and have not been in contact with her since."

Seb was looking straight at the officers whilst he heard all of this, very little expression showing on his face. He had already put his version across and, when it came down to it, there was hardly any evidence to support either person's story.

"So, am I being charged?" Seb asked.

"Not at the moment. We will need to see the photographs you allege Mrs. Jenkins sent to your wife, as soon as you can bring them by. Once we have those, and carry out further investigations, we will let you know what, if any, action we intend to take. Do you intend to take action against Mrs. Jenkins for the alleged sexual assault at the beach, or for criminal damage to your property?"

"I don't think that the incident at the beach is going to be possible to prove and, as I stupidly had sex with her the next day, it's not going to be taken seriously is it? With regards to the photographs that she sent to Natasha, I have them on my phone and can email them to you right now if you wish?"

"That would be helpful; the desk sergeant will give you the email address to use. When it comes to the alleged assault that you claim to have been the victim of, it's your decision. But if you can't prove that you were drugged, then no, I don't see it coming to anything if I'm honest."

"But the damage to the windows, yes. I would like to press charges." Seb told her.

"OK, I will sort out the paperwork. I suggest you go and take care of the damaged windows, and if you can get the photographs emailed across to me as soon as you can manage, then that would be great. And don't go too far, we will want to talk to you again I expect, so make sure that you stay contactable. It would be in your best interest to stay away from Mrs. Jenkins, for the time being, and we will be advising her to stay clear of you as well."

"Of course," Seb replied, standing up and extending his wrists towards P.C. Smith. "Can you get these off me please?"

Once he had had the handcuffs removed, Seb made his way from the station and hurried home, trying to work out what he could use to board up the windows.

"Mrs. Jenkins," D.C. Matthews began, as she returned to the room that Ella was waiting in. I have heard Mr. Briggs' version of events, and he has been released pending further investigation."

"You let him go!" Ella exclaimed. "What if he comes to see me? He's dangerous!"

"At the moment we don't have any reason to believe that you are in danger, and he has been advised to stay away from you. If he does approach you, then call us, and we will deal with it. The same applies to you as well though, I do not expect you to be going to his address or contacting him in any way. Mr. Briggs has outlined his intention to press charges against you for criminal damage, which you have admitted to, so this may have to be brought before a court in due course. The chances are that you will have to pay for the damage, and possibly some additional financial costs, but if your allegation of rape is substantiated, your actions may be viewed more leniently. I would suggest seeking some legal advice if you wish to try to dispute culpability for the damage. As things stand at the moment, I will tell you what I have told him, you are free to go, stay nearby and contactable, keep away from each other. When you leave, can you please check with the desk sergeant that we have the correct telephone number for you, as you may hear from the victim support team tomorrow." With that, D.C. Matthews left the room, leaving P.C. Smith to escort Ella through to the front desk.

Behind the station, at the far end of the staff parking area, P.C. Smith found Matthews in the smoking hut, lighting a second menthol from the stub of the first. It was cold out, cold enough to make P.C. Smith's breath look as though he was also smoking, even though it was not a habit that he indulged in.

"So, what do you think boss?" he asked the D.C. "Weird fucking set up, innit? Do you reckon it's some fetish thing they've got going on, trying to get each other in trouble?"

"If that's the case I'll have them both for wasting police time and obstruction of justice. There's nothing clever about making up rape allegations, by either of them. Personally, I would say his version seemed a lot more credible, unless he's a genuine sociopath and, therefore, very convincing. Nevertheless, we can only look at the facts, and if he has photos of her screwing him willingly, she'll have a difficult time convincing anyone she didn't want it the next time. And if he was angry with her for telling his wife, I could almost understand him turning up hammered and giving her a slap but raping her seems a bit much. See what you can find out on both of them, her in particular. Medical files, any previous odd behaviour, find her husband and see what he makes of it. Apparently, he left her not long ago for someone else, and she doesn't know where he's gone, find out where he works." P.C. Smith turned to head back inside, enjoying the police work, looking up to Matthews with great respect.

"Also," she called after him.

"Yes ma'am?"

"I expect there to be a coffee on my desk when I get back in. And not that shit from the vending machine."

"Yes boss," P.C. Smith replied, resisting the urge to give her a Nazi salute and goose-step his way back indoors.

TWENTY

Ella left the station in a terrible mood, disappointed in her own behaviour and the desperation of her actions. Smashing Seb's windows was probably a step too far, she decided, and involving the police was dangerous for everyone, especially herself. She felt, once again, as though she had no control over her actions, almost aware of her obsession for Seb becoming a concern. To begin with, it had seemed like a game, and despite how devious she had been, and how much trouble she had caused for him, she had been convinced that the goal, their future together, was deserving of any initial rocky patches. Now, as she walked home, alone and cold in the middle of the night, she began to doubt whether it was all worth it. But what choice did she really have? She could drop the allegations, but in doing so it would mean any further allegations would, most likely, also be dismissed by the police. She had to take some responsibility for the damage to Seb's house. If she gave up on him now, there was a chance that he would work things out with Natasha, and she would still be alone, all the effort having been for nothing. But were her actions pushing him further away with no foreseeable positive outcome for them? As she got nearer to home, Ella accepted the fact that her choices were now limited. The police told her to stay away from Seb, and so she must lie low and let things take their course.

The intense pain that she felt soon took a hold of her once she was indoors, the emptiness of the house and the overwhelming loneliness hitting home. Once again, she had gotten to the point of needing help to deal with it, the distraction of physical pain over emotional becoming too much to turn down, and she took a Stanley knife from the kitchen drawer. Seven cuts were made in her upper-right arm, all drawing blood but none too deep for any real concern. Once these were made, she lay on the sofa and watched as thin trickles of blood ran down her skin, drying almost immediately, giving the impression of red stripes on her pale flesh. Her eyes were heavy, and she contemplated sleeping where she was but decided against it, dragging herself to bed, collapsing into it, still in trousers and socks, her top half bare. Terrified at the thought of facing another day alone, she drifted off to sleep, fantasies of death creeping into her mind.

Morning came, and Ella struggled to find the strength to pull back the duvet. She had awoken with a sore arm; the fresh cuts had stuck to her sheet, which now featured a few red dots. This had immediately brought the memories of yesterday crashing back, and the thought of doing anything at all was unappealing, to say the least. Hiding under the duvet, however, stuck with a depressing cycle of thoughts, made the time drag, and she didn't think she would survive a whole day like this. Seb was gone. She had blown her chance, and she needed to deal with it. The first thought she had was to drink her way through the day; there was no real reason why she shouldn't drink continuously until she passed out, at least the day would go quicker. This seemed like a logical plan but was hampered by her rapidly diminishing finances. Her tolerance for whiskey had reached the point that, although a bottle would make her rather drunk, she would still be able to manage more. The money she had left would only do a small pouch of tobacco and a cheap blended scotch, but it would be a starting point. She didn't bother changing her socks or underwear, chucked on her bra and top from yesterday, and headed down to the shop, not even bothering to check herself in the mirror before she left. As she was walking out of the house, she realized that she had no idea what the time was and had not picked up her phone. The sun was up though, it wasn't as cold as the last few days had been,

The Broken Doll: Book One

so she was sure that it was late enough for the convenience store to be open by now. Once she had finished in the shop, she toyed with the idea of some food, then decided she would get better value from the whiskey if she didn't eat first. What she couldn't decide on was where to drink, not wanting to speak to anyone, but not wanting to sit alone in the house either. Ella opted for walking and drinking, heading past her house and continuing along the cliff-tops, stopping every mile or so to sit, drink, and smoke. She walked almost as far as the next town and noticed that the whiskey bottle was about half empty, so decided to turn back and drink the rest on her way home, wistfully thinking about falling from the cliff edge to the rocks below. The fantasy of dying dominated her thoughts as she made her way back to the house; a slight disappointment striking her as she got home, alive and well, despite being a little unstable on her feet.

It had been a reasonably pleasant walk and something, under different circumstances, she would have thoroughly enjoyed. However, now she was back it seemed like a huge mistake. She had managed to get drunk, as planned, but was now back at home, still alone, with no alcohol and no money. She was not ready to sleep, and it wasn't even beginning to get dark outside. She felt lost, the solitude being unbearable.

Seb called Natasha once it was a time that he felt was reasonable. He had been after an excuse to make contact with her, despite her requests for him not to, and felt that having the windows smashed in was a good enough reason. Of course, Natasha wasn't happy about the news. Seb had hoped it would help his wife to see the level of madness that he was having to deal with, that his pressing charges against Ella and her outrageous allegations about him would garner some sympathy from Natasha. If she did feel any pity for him, then she managed to keep it well hidden.

"Well, after the whole palaver with the assault accusation, I don't know why you're now surprised to learn that she's mad! And knowing this, you still decided to fuck her. Quite roughly by the sound of it. The insurance will cover the damage, but our premiums might go up so make sure you get something from her for it. And I mean actual money, not just getting her to suck you off a few times as compensation!"

This wasn't the kind of response that Seb had hoped for, but he understood where she was coming from. He changed the subject and, after a brief conversation about the children and asking to come and visit (which was met with a firm 'no'), the call ended, leaving Seb feeling more down than he had beforehand. Seb decided to organize the house, having little option for anything else to do, and not wanting to see anyone at that time. The priority was to board up the windows, which he had neglected to do last night, in favour of sleeping in the living room just in case an intruder came by.

Despite the events of the previous evening, Seb still felt motivated in sorting out his general well-being, intending to wash some clothes, board up the windows, tidy the house a little, and go to the gym or for a swim. He stuck on some music and wrote himself a list, welcoming the distraction as he went about his energetic mission to have a more productive day.

Ella managed less than half an hour of sitting in the living room alone and miserable. *Fuck this!* she thought, searching her bag for any change, before putting her jacket back on and walking out the door. She felt pretty wobbly at this point and had no plan for what she was doing or where she would go but being out of the house felt like a good start. Ella was unsure as to how drunk she appeared, if at all, but didn't particularly care. After scooping up whatever change

The Broken Doll: Book One

she had found at the bottom of her bag and on her bedside cabinet, she was sure it would be enough for a drink of some kind and so decided to wander along towards the beach, knowing that there was a pub on the way. It wasn't possible to tell how busy the pub was from the outside, but only one of the picnic tables was taken so she sat on an empty one and made a cigarette before heading inside. As she smoked, she emptied her pocket of the change that she had collected and added it up, neglecting to include the coins worth less than ten pence. *Almost a fiver,* she thought, feeling unsure about pub prices having not been in one for a while. *It must be enough for a pint of cider or something,* she told herself, wanting whatever drink would last her the longest.

"How much for a pint of cider?" Ella asked the barmaid, trying to sound as sober as possible.

"We only have one on tap. It's £4.05," the barmaid replied, smiling. She looked friendly enough, contrary to Ella's first impression when she was greeted by a girl with half a shaved head and more piercings in her face than she could count.

"That'll be great, thank you," Ella told her, taking a seat at a stall by the bar. Thankfully, the pub was quite quiet, filled mostly by older people eating, so she sipped at her cider in silence, avoiding eye contact with the barmaid.

"Been stood up?" she heard a voice ask. Ella looked up to see a young guy, maybe in his early twenties, standing next to her.

"No," Ella replied. "Just having a quiet drink, is that allowed?"

"Sorry," the man said. "Just making conversation." His eyes then diverted away from Ella, and he ordered two pints of lager, requesting the darts from behind the bar.

"If you're bored, we're playing darts over there, feel free to join us." Ella could feel the barmaid looking at her, maybe wanting to comment about creepy

The Broken Doll: Book One

guys or something of that nature, but Ella stayed quiet. Her cider was almost gone. She felt incredibly drunk now that the cider had topped up the scotch, and it seemed the perfect time to make another bad decision. With a bit of a stagger, she made her way over to the darts' players, asking to join in.

"If I win, will you buy me a drink?" she asked. "I seem to have spent all of my money."

"Sure. If you win," said the guy who had spoken to her earlier. He seemed alright, as though he might actually be nice. His mate, however, was looking at Ella in a way that made her feel uneasy. He wore aviator sunglasses, even indoors, and behind them, Ella could feel his eyes running up and down her body.

"What if you don't win?" aviator guy asked. "I mean, what do we get if you haven't got any money to get us a drink?" Ella knew full well what he was getting at, and that playing with these guys had now become a bit of a gamble, but she was feeling reckless.

"If I win," she repeated, "I get a drink. If one of you wins, you will get a kiss. That's the deal, take it or leave it."

"Sounds good to me. In fact, I'll get you a drink anyway, for while we play," said the creepy guy. Ella accepted the offer and ordered another pint of cider, well aware that it may be enough to finish her off. Worst-case scenario she would have to kiss one of them; it wouldn't be that awful. And so, the evening went on, and Ella lost the first game and gave away a kiss to the nicer guy. The creepy guy bought her another drink anyway, and she knew where things were heading but was past caring. It was almost as if she could see herself from the outside, acting more and more flirtatiously with both guys equally, the creepy one suggesting more and more intimate forfeits if she was to lose. Ella lost every game, unsurprisingly, and told him to keep a tally of what she owed them for later. Her hope was to ditch them before closing time, giving out the odd kiss but

The Broken Doll: Book One

nothing more, in exchange for a free bar. However, closing time came suddenly with the ringing of the bell and the three of them left together, Ella stumbling down the road, an arm around each of the men she had just met.

"So, I guess we need to cash in our prizes," said the one with the glasses.

"Don't worry about it," said the nicer guy. "We've all had fun." Ella was beyond caring by this point and had enjoyed the distraction this evening.

"It's fine guys, come with me," she told them, guiding them up the path which led towards the woods. As soon as they had passed the area which was lit by streetlights, and darkness was surrounding them, Ella placed a hand on each of their groins, rubbing at their genitals. She took turns in kissing them both and, having felt them both grow in their jeans, Ella knelt and undid them. She struggled with her balance, really wanting to get home, but carried on regardless. Everything was a bit of a haze, as she knelt on the concrete path, an erect cock in each hand. She began to suck one of them and heard a moan, moving her head from one dick to another every few moments. The drink had made her feel sick, and she decided that this was going to be a risky procedure, not wanting to embarrass herself any further by vomiting. As she stood, she fell into one of the men who tried to kiss her, but she pulled away.

"I should get home," she slurred.

"Really? You can't leave us like that," she was told, and although she would have preferred to go home, she accepted that she had put herself in this situation. Ella proceeded to pull down her trousers and knickers, facing away from the guys as she grabbed the fence running alongside the path. She bent herself over a little and waited as one of the guys, she didn't know which, put his hand between her legs and then fucked her. It didn't take very long, and she could feel him shudder as he unloaded himself into her.

"Your go," he said. At this point, Ella understood that it was the nicer of the two who had gone first.

"I'm not going there now; it's full of your spunk, mate." Ella felt relieved as she began pulling up her knickers.

"Not so fast," he told her, in a tone she didn't like. "I said I'm not going in *there*. I'll take mouth or arse, your choice." Ella panicked a little, the only time she had taken it in the rear was when Lee had been particularly aggressive, and so she did not associate it with any pleasure, especially without the option of any lubrication. She also felt too sick to use her mouth but out of the two choices it would be more bearable, and she was in no state to fight. Ella closed her eyes as she, once more, knelt on the cold ground, stifling back a tear as she felt his hand take the back of her head, ramming himself into her mouth with enough force and depth that she gagged. This seemed to excite him further and after a few minutes, she felt the warm liquid pouring across her tongue and dribbling out and down her chin.

"Thanks love," he told her as he put himself away. "You should come by next week for a rematch." Ella sat with her back against the fence as she watched them leave, fully regretful about her day, feeling worse than ever. The taste of semen, cider, and cigarettes combined to cause a violent episode of vomiting and Ella's eyes closed, then and there, as she welcomed the black haze of unconsciousness.

TWENTY-ONE

Seb awoke the following morning feeling better than he had done for some time. He had successfully completed his list of tasks the day before, the house now looking, and smelling, much more appealing. He had securely boarded up the windows and had even made it to the gym for an hour in the evening. After almost twelve hours of sleep, he now felt fully re-energised as he stepped out of the shower. He had called the insurance company the day before to make a claim for the broken windows and discovered that he needed a crime number for them to process it. So, this morning his intention was to visit the police station to obtain this information, possibly grab a coffee from Daryl's van, if he was there, and go and assess his stock before deciding about extending his lease on the property.

The trip to the police station was brief and successful. A crime number was acquired, and he also let the desk sergeant know that, if anyone needed to contact him regarding the incidents, he would be at his lock-up, providing them with the address. Seb had noticed a huge change in his mental state and clarity of thought after a day without any alcohol or drama, and intended to keep things that way, for today at least.

Seb was grateful not to see anyone he knew as he passed through the lower half of the high street, and he made his way to the lock-up. Daryl was leaning out of the serving hatch of his trailer, reading a copy of a tabloid newspaper. As Seb approached, he put the paper down, seemingly deliberately, with the bare breasts of page three on show.

"Hello mate, not seen you about for a while. I heard you had a bit of trouble down here?"

"Did I?" Seb asked, a little uncertain about when he last was there.

"Rick, who lives in the flat at the end, said some woman was shouting at you or something? Trouble with the missus?"

"Oh, yeah, right. No, not really, all sorted now. Women eh?" Seb told him, trying to downplay the incident. "You got any bacon on the go?"

"I can stick some on now, won't take long. Anything else?"

"I'll have a large tea as well please, and can you crisp the bacon up a bit, can't stand chewy fat."

"No problem mate," Daryl replied cheerfully as he bent down to take the meat from an under-counter fridge behind him, the top of his butt crack noticeable as he did so. Seb was glancing at the breasts in the newspaper as he heard the bacon begin to sizzle on the grill plate.

"Brown or white bread?" he was asked.

"Brown please. How's business been?"

"Up and down, usual stuff. It's not too bad until we hit New Year then it's hardly worth bothering for a couple of months."

"Yep," Seb agreed. "It's the same everywhere though. I'm just going in to see what I can try to shift before the quiet months. Don't suppose you know anyone who'd be after a couple of Chesterfield sofas, do you? The guy that I got them in for seems to have disappeared." Daryl turned back to face Seb, holding two rashers of bacon in his tongs.

"They done enough for you?" he asked.

"Yeah, that's fine."

"I would love another Chesterfield, got no need for one though," he stated, not really answering the question.

"I've got to get rid of them pretty quickly. The tenancy is up soon, and if it wasn't for those taking up all the room, I could probably not worry about renewing it and store the rest at home. I can deliver them and knock the price down a bit."

The Broken Doll: Book One

"To be honest mate, I wouldn't know anyone, but if you want to make a little ad you can stick something on my counter; someone might be interested. How much you looking for?"

"I was meant to be getting a grand for the two, but I could take a bit less if necessary. The guy who owns the takeaway at the top of town, Sid, was meant to take them, but he's moved away, all a bit out of the blue."

"I heard it had been closed for a while, a few of the guys who work at the car wash down here used to grab breakfast there on the way in, and they mentioned it. Not that I'm complaining, it means they buy from me now instead. I heard something about his wife getting busted having a gang bang or suchlike. Dirty tart!"

"Something like that apparently. I'll print a picture off and drop something over in a bit. Cheers for the food," Seb told him after he had paid, wandering over the road to his premises.

Ella woke up on the cold ground, feeling like shit. There was vomit down her top and her mouth was crusty with a mix of substances that she couldn't even bring herself to think to about. With a lot of effort, she managed to stand up, getting herself awake enough to try to walk the rest of the way home. This was one of the times when she wished she couldn't remember her actions when drunk, but everything about last night came back with a vengeance. She had spent the day drinking, acted like a whore for free drinks, took on two guys, and passed out in the street. *Classy,* she thought. It was only about ten minutes to walk home from there usually, but this morning seemed to take a little longer. It felt early, the sun just appearing, birds making the only noise she could hear. Thankfully, no one passed her on the way, and she hoped that no one had seen her like that whilst unconscious last night but assumed they hadn't, or she would have been woken up.

The Broken Doll: Book One

As she fell through the door, Ella wanted nothing more than to collapse in bed and sleep for the whole day, but she really needed to shower and clean her teeth, remove the man juice which filled her from top to bottom, and try to wash this hangover away. She stripped off and climbed into the shower, the sudden warmth making her dizzy enough to feel as though she would fall. Ella chose to sit in the shower instead, scrubbing herself everywhere and, after brushing her teeth twice and using mouthwash, she climbed under her duvet and fell back into a deep sleep, vowing to never drink, or speak to another man. ever again.

At the lock-up Seb began flicking through the file he kept, which was supposed to be a record of what he had in stock. Essentially, it was a few handwritten pages listing item, description, how much he'd paid for it, how much he hoped to sell it for, and a box to mark if and when it sold. This was the closest thing he had to any accounts to show income and expenditure, never feeling the need to employ an actual accountant. He reckoned that he had about sixty items in stock, the majority being small pieces that could be stored in boxes; some old pocket watches, a collection of postcards from the 1930s, coins, and so on. If he opted to vacate the premises, then he would be able to put these in boxes and keep them at home without much difficulty, focusing on selling these online as they could easily be posted. The items that would cause a problem, aside from the Chesterfields, were a mirrored vanity desk with stool that he had purchased from the tip and refurbished, a set of eight vintage school chairs and four desks, a church pew which must have been fifteen feet long and he had regretted it as soon as he had bought it, as well as a pair of very fragile art-deco lamps in the shapes of peacocks. All these items were listed on his website, so there was no need for any more photographs, and he decided to reduce the price and see what happened as he couldn't justify another twelve-month lease just to store these. Seb made his phone call to the insurance company and was told that someone would be out the following day to replace the windows. He then decided it would be a good time to call his wife, having avoided any unnecessary contact thus far, as per her instructions.

"What now?" was the greeting he received, and he tried to hide his disappointment.

"I wanted to let you know that I've sorted it out with the insurers, and the windows are being done tomorrow. I'm just sorting through my stock. How are you and the kids?"

"We're fine, although I am getting a bit fed up with being here now," Natasha admitted. "It's been a long time since I actually had to live with my parents."

"Yeah, I can imagine it's not great. Maybe you should come home," he suggested, hopefully.

"Maybe I should; I have been thinking about it. I think the children would like to be back in their own beds too." Seb was aware that he was smiling at this, suddenly hopeful that everything would work out.

"But that doesn't mean that I want you there when we get back," she told him, his mood changing in an instant.

"I know," he told her. "And I would expect to be on the sofa for a bit, but I don't have anywhere else to go at the moment. I really miss you. Is there any way we can give it a bit more time and see what happens?"

"You can stay at the lock-up or go back to your crazy bitch. I'm sure she won't mind."

"I can't stay at the lock-up as the tenancy is up soon so I'm trying to find somewhere for the stock, and I told you already, she's fucking nuts and I'm keeping away. I don't want her. I never did. It's you and the kids I want to be with." Seb could hear Natasha sigh, sounding upset.

"Believe it or not, that's what I want too. Even so, I can't trust you anymore. I'm really confused. I think if I worked things out with you, then it's as though I'm condoning your behaviour. I don't want you to think that you can do it again and I'll just take you back each time."

"That isn't what I would think, I know I've done wrong, but despite the way it all looks it was only that one night, after you had told me to get out. I swear to you it won't ever happen again. Please come home. I'll sleep downstairs, just give it time."

Seb could tell that Natasha was crying and trying to hide it. There was a long pause on the line as she thought over her options and, having accepted that she didn't want to be at her parents' for any longer than necessary, she decided to go home and see what could be done.

"I'll come back today. The kids are out at the moment with my dad, but we'll be home this evening. You will be on the sofa, probably for a long time, maybe even forever! You don't touch me, you don't kiss me. When they're asleep we can talk and decide what is best for everyone, not just for you."

Seb's eyes were filling up, and he didn't know what to say except for thank you and that he would see them all that evening, not knowing at that point that, for reasons beyond his control, he would not be there to welcome his family home.

TWENTY-TWO

A little after noon, Seb headed home to make sure everything was ready for his family's arrival, wanting it to be noticeable that he had been there and productive, rather than out all the time or just wallowing in self-pity. Once he was satisfied that everything was in order, that there was food in the fridge, and whiskey in the decanter (just in case Natasha needed a drink), he made a start on updating his website and frantically advertising the larger items. He knocked the prices down almost to what he had paid for them, offered free delivery, and even a further discount for multiple purchases. He began to look for some events that he could have a stall at, planning on selling some of the smaller items from a table. He knew from experience that he would struggle to get a decent price at these kinds of events, but as long as he made a bit of money then he wasn't too worried, plus it would show Natasha that he was being a bit more proactive.

Seb wondered what Ella was doing, glad that he hadn't been contacted by her but, at the same time, a little worried about her. He knew calling her would be extremely foolish, and he did genuinely want her out of his life, but even if the rape allegation led nowhere, he would still have to have some involvement due to the criminal damage charge. After some thought, and trying to guess what Natasha's stance would be, he decided to call the police and drop the charges against Ella. It seemed like the right thing to do as the insurance company would pay for repairs, and he did understand why she had done it.

After being transferred from one department to another, he was finally able to speak directly with D.C. Matthews.

"Mr. Briggs?" she asked, in her croaky, smoker's voice.

The Broken Doll: Book One

"Hello D.C. Matthews. I just wanted to let you know that I have decided not to press charges against Mrs. Jenkins for the windows; it's being sorted out by the insurance company, and I would rather not have anything to do with her."

"I see," Matthews replied. "It is entirely up to you, and I think it's probably a wise idea. I still recommend that you stay away from each other. I can close that case at this end as long as you are sure, as I would rather not have to reopen it again?"

"Yes please, I do think that it's for the best. And, of course, I intend to stay as far away from her as possible. So, will you tell her that I'm not pressing charges? I assume I don't need to tell her myself?"

"No, I will call her and let her know. And how is your situation now? At home, I mean. Are you still living at the family home? I got a message earlier that you could be found at your business premises."

"I am at home now. Things are OK, thank you. My wife went to stay with family for a few days, but she's coming home today, and we're going to work things out, I think."

"I'm glad to hear it Mr. Briggs. Obviously, we are still investigating Mrs. Jenkins allegations against you so you will need to inform us if you have to go out of town for any reason. We'll be in touch if we need anything."

With that, Seb hung up the phone, feeling that D.C. Matthews seemed on side at least, his level of concern about the rape allegation beginning to lessen. *Surely, they can see that Ella's unstable, so there must be a degree of reasonable doubt,* he thought.

Ella had been tossing and turning in bed, waking frequently with an unquenchable thirst. She still felt sick; her head pounded, and the light hurt her eyes. Sleep wasn't happening, and she couldn't manage to read. At a loss for what to do with herself, she went to the kitchen for more water and a couple of painkillers, noticing her phone on the kitchen side. She touched the button on the right to check the time, but it was dead, having been there for all of yesterday. She attached it to its charger and lay on the sofa, unable to think beyond clearing her hangover and generally achy body. Despite having had a shower a few hours earlier, a bath seemed like it might help and, as she had nothing else to do anyway, she ran one, laying in the hot water with her eyes closed until it had turned cold, and she had no choice but to get out.

After slipping on some comfy clothes and blow-drying her hair, she removed her phone from its connection to the wall and turned it on, the bright screen being more bearable now than it would have been prior to her bath and painkillers.

One message came through; a voicemail. She turned down the call volume on the side of the phone to avoid it being too loud for her head to handle and listened to the distinctive voice of D.C. Matthews asking her to return her call. No other information was given, and Ella considered ignoring it but did not want to run the risk of the police coming out to the house. Ella grabbed a pen and paper and played the message again to obtain the correct telephone number and extension, dialling through to the D.C.'s desk.

"D.C. Matthews," came the voice on the other end.

"D.C. Matthews, it's Ella Jenkins. I got your voicemail. What did you want to talk to me about?"

"Ah Mrs. Jenkins, hello. Thanks for calling back. OK, I have had a call from Mr. Briggs, and he has decided to drop the charges for criminal damage. As far as we are concerned that case is now closed. I will remind you, as I did him, that the pair of you need to stay away from each other. This includes contact of *any* sort. This is, of course, only advice, but I don't think either of you would want to have to get a restraining order against the other."

"No, of course not. And I don't want to see him, not after what he did to me," Ella replied, trying to sound convincing.

"I understand," said Matthews kindly. "Mr. Briggs has given me his word that he will not contact you at all. The same advice also applies to Mrs. Briggs. I will be informing her that she should not contact you, and vice versa, when she gets home this evening."

"Oh?" Ella said. "I thought she would have left him after what he did to me."

"That isn't for me to comment on; neither is it any of your concern."

"Right, was there anything else you needed from me?" Ella asked, wondering why Matthews had mentioned Natasha's return home, trying to work out if it had been deliberate.

"Not at the moment, but you are still requested to remain contactable and to let me know if you need to leave town for any reason. I will be in touch shortly regarding the other allegations." And with that, D.C. Matthews ended the call without a goodbye.

She doesn't believe me, Ella thought, a little angrily. *Maybe I shouldn't have asked about Natasha? She brought her up though. Maybe she thinks I want Seb still? Fucking Natasha, why hasn't she left him? What kind of woman would stay with a cheating, violent rapist?? If she was dead, I bet Seb would come running to me.*

Nevertheless, Ella couldn't imagine actually killing anyone herself. It was certainly a step up from just hiding a body. And once again Ella was stuck between the only two courses of action that she could see; moving on alone or destroying Seb's marriage in the hope that he would be hers. *It's too late,* she began to think. *I've pushed him too far. He's starting to hate me, and he's never going to choose me over her.*

The Broken Doll: Book One

Tears began to trickle down Ella's cheeks as she began to realize that her plan wasn't working, her happily-ever-after wasn't coming, at least not with Seb. All she had managed to do was hurt him, hurt his family, and she gained nothing apart from a bit of sex. The thought of being single and available was far less appealing after last night's escapades. For the first time since Lee's death, she began to wonder if she had been better off in her marriage than she was now. At least before she had had company, even if it wasn't pleasant. There had been money and food. She now felt as though she was just waiting for something to happen regarding bills, or the mortgage, that she was on the brink of losing everything. The weight of hiding Lee's body was taking a toll on her, and the burden needed to be relieved. *Maybe I should just confess?* she wondered. *At least in prison there would be people to talk to, I'd be fed, I could read as much as I wanted, maybe get a qualification in something. It's not as if I leave the house often anyway. Although, prisons look quite scary on television, with all the fighting and lesbian rape. I'm sure I could handle it though, if I had the reputation as a man killer, the other women might be frightened of me. Or they might want to fight me to establish a prison hierarchy. Shit.*

Natasha had loaded their belongings into the car and strapped the children in as the day began turning to dusk. After kissing her disapproving parents' goodbye and going through the associated conversation about her making a gargantuan mistake in going back to him, they began the journey home. They hit rush hour, adding half an hour to the total time, but the children were all asleep soon after they left so it was, at least, peaceful in the car. Natasha kept playing over, in her head, the conversation that she wanted to have with her husband. She made a list of demands, things that he would need to change about himself, and his actions,

The Broken Doll: Book One

in order for this to work. She had considered still ending the marriage, wondering how the children would adapt to the change, wondering what other men were about should she feel like dating again. Natasha had always considered herself lucky to have met Seb, especially in such a small town. Most of the men of a suitable age were either unemployed, overweight, seemed to lack anything close to an average IQ, or already had children from multiple partners. In some cases, they fitted all these criteria. She had told this to Seb once before, his reply being that he felt the same, and that that description of the men was even more applicable to the women of the town. It looked as though there weren't going to be many other, if any, options for Natasha, not staying living there anyway. She was past the time for one-night stands, and what was the point if you couldn't hold a conversation with any of them? It had to work out with Seb, for everyone's sake, and maybe, in some perverted way, it could make their relationship stronger.

As she arrived on their road, parking opposite the house, she was a little surprised to see that no lights were on. She could make out the wooden boards across what used to be her living room window, and the large square of chipboard held against the front door with duct tape. The children were still asleep, and so she took the bags from the boot and carried them over to the front door. She had not, until this point, thought about how to explain the damage to the children. If she had told the truth, or blamed an intruder, it might have frightened them, but she could not think of anything else. *Daddy's slut bag girlfriend had a temper tantrum and chucked a brick through them* didn't seem appropriate. Natasha tried the front door to find it locked and went back to the car to retrieve her own keys. She called out for her husband but there was no reply, so she put the bags in the hallway and went back to fetch the children. Sleepily, and reluctantly, they climbed out of the car and made their way to the

The Broken Doll: Book One

living room, staring in confusion at the boarded-up windows.

"What happened mummy?" came one of the little voices.

"Erm, I'll tell you in a minute. Let me just find out where daddy is first." Natasha rummaged through her bag for her phone and saw a missed call from a private number, alongside a voicemail. She made her way down to the kitchen and pressed play. A croaky voice asked her to call the local police station as a matter of urgency, leaving an extension number. Natasha felt something in her stomach, a mix of nervous butterflies and impending sickness. *What the fuck has he done now?!* she wondered, but more worried about what Ella may have accused him of. Her hands trembled as she dialled the number for D.C. Matthews, her stomach in knots. The conversation was a blur, the phone falling from her hands on to the kitchen floor and shattering the screen at the news. Natasha grabbed at the work top, frantically trying to move a mug from the sink just in time as she filled it with vomit. *He can't have done, he can't have done,* repeating in her head as she tried to make sense of the situation.

"Your statement and confession are ready for you to sign," said P.C. Smith as he handed Ella a typed document. Ella sat in the station, eyes glazed and puffy. She looked down at the papers in front of her with a kind of acceptance, as though this was her only option now. She felt a wave of relief sweep across her, knowing that there needed to be no more secrets. She was not afraid as she signed the documents, nor was she regretful. It had to happen; it had always been heading towards this point. Surrendering herself in this way made it less about what she said versus what Seb said, she chose to bear a portion of the guilt and, at the same time, she believed it would enable her to form a new, closer bond with Seb. It meant that they would be apart for a while, with him, unfortunately, getting the worse end of the deal, but eventually they would be able to be together. She would be his only option left when the time came.

"You'll be transferred to custody now," P.C. Smith informed her, picking up the signed statement. He led her along the corridor, past the other interview rooms, and was buzzed through a secure door which opened into the holding area. There, Ella was placed inside a cell and, as the door closed loudly behind her, she took in the magnitude of her situation. This was going to be her home, or a cell like it at least, for some time. As she entered the cell, she saw that the other ones were all open except for one. Someone was banging on the door and shouting, a male voice sounding pretty pissed off about being there.

"What you here for?" she shouted to him, across the room, once the officer had returned through the security door. There was a moment's silence as the other inmate realized he was being spoken to, and by a woman.

"Fucking pigs think I was selling weed by the school, but it's bollocks." *Of course it is,* Ella thought, dismissively.

"What about you? You a hooker?" he asked Ella, sounding hopeful.

"You wish," she replied, trying to assert some dominance. "I doubt that you could afford me, even if I was. I hid a dead body actually." The guy paused for a few seconds, unsure if she was telling the truth or not.

"Fuck off!" he told her doubtfully. "Whose body? You obviously didn't hide it very well!"

"My husband. He was a prick, so I buried him in the garden."

"Shit! You're proper gangster, love." Ella liked this and smiled a little, regardless of how corny it sounded, unused to people *actually* speaking like that.

Yep, don't fuck with me, she thought, trying to get her mindset right in preparation for proper prison.

Seb sat at a desk, hands cuffed, staring at D.C. Matthews. He felt angry beyond words, disappointed that Ella had, yet again, tried to make an accusation about him. However, this one was far worse. The police had arrived at his house earlier that evening, two cars with four officers, including Matthews.

"Sebastian Briggs," she had begun, with the look of someone who had almost been fooled by another person's character and then seen through it.

"I am placing you under arrest for the murder of Mr. Lee Jenkins." Matthews then read him his rights, cuffed him, and he was marched out into the street, embarrassingly in full view of some passers-by, and placed into the back of one of the police cars.

As they sat in silence at the desk, Seb's mind raced. He was told nothing further about the allegation. *Has Ella now decided her husband didn't leave her and accused me of murder?! Surely there's no crime without a body?* The thought never entered his mind that there might actually be one.

"I really don't understand what's going on," Seb began, before Matthews cut him off and informed him that he should not speak until the other officer is present. After a few moments more of the awkward silence, a tall, wiry man came into the room. He was wearing a grey suit with a laminated name badge attached to his tie at an angle.

"Good evening," he began, taking a seat. He played about with the recording machine and, after stating the time, date, and the names of those present, looked directly at Seb.

"Do you understand why you are here Mr. Briggs?" the man, whom Seb now knew was called D.C.I. Watts, asked him.

The Broken Doll: Book One

"I have been arrested for the murder of a man I do not know and have never met."

"I see," Watts continued. "You did not know Mr. Jenkins?"

"That's what I just said," Seb confirmed, a little sarcastically.

"And Mrs. Jenkins?" Watts asked.

"Yes, I know Mrs. Jenkins, as I'm sure you are aware."

"How would you describe your relationship with Mrs. Jenkins? Is it of a sexual nature, is it platonic, do you still have contact with her?"

Seb was scared. He could see where this was leading, and he didn't like it, but he had already told the truth to the police, and to Natasha, and so he just repeated his story so far. He told them how he had met Ella, how she had described her husband, that he had left her, as far as he was aware, for another woman, whose name began with a C, he thought. He told them about Ella's behaviour towards him, the allegations, admitted to the sex yet again, giving them a detailed account of everything up to this point.

D.C.I. Watts then pulled a stack of papers from inside his suit jacket and placed them on the desk.

"We have a team of officers at Mr. and Mrs. Jenkins' property at the moment who have excavated a body, believed to be that of Mr. Jenkins, from the back garden. This is a signed statement and confession from Mrs. Jenkins in which she details your relationship with her and your role in her husband's death."

Seb felt unwell; it was all too much to take in. *There was an actual body! Ella had known it was there the whole time, shit, she must have killed him!*

"And what does she say my involvement is then?" Seb asked, a little angrily. "I never even met the guy, but he used to beat the shit out of her so maybe she fought back and killed him?"

The Broken Doll: Book One

"OK, well, I want to run through her statement with you now that we have heard your side, and we'll see what points you are in agreement on. Before we do that, are you expecting a solicitor at any point?"

"No, I haven't called one. Should I?"

"It might be wise but it's your choice. If you do want to, then obviously you'll need to wait until the morning before we can continue." Seb considered this but hoped to be able to clear his name himself, at least enough to be allowed to go home tonight to see his family. *Natasha!* he thought in a panic.

"I need to call my wife. She was due home by now," Seb said, looking at Matthews this time.

"I have already spoken to her," Matthews told him. "She knows where you are."

"Thanks," Seb replied, wondering if Matthews had mentioned he was there on suspicion of murder. "Right, I'll go ahead without a solicitor. I've told you the truth so it shouldn't be too hard to work out what happened. What does the statement say then?" Between the two of them, Watts and Matthews worked through Ella's statement, almost word-for-word. Some of it was accurate and fitted with Seb's version of events, such as how they had met. Other parts were wildly inaccurate and were a repeat of allegations Ella had made to the police previously. Seb began to wonder if some of it was what Ella believed, or if she was actually psychotic as he went over the main points in his head. They had met, as Seb also had described, when he was walking past and noticed that she had been hurt. However, in Ella's version, Seb had been much more insistent on coming into the house and had begun passing by regularly. Seb struggled to recall the details but accepted that this may have been how Ella had experienced it. According to her, Seb had become angry that Lee was hurting her and refused to leave the house one evening, intending to confront him when he came home from work. The confrontation had become violent, and Seb had stabbed Lee several times in the stomach. Ella had no recollection of where the weapon had ended up, whether it was a knife from her home or if Seb had brought it with him. She then described, in detail, how they had panicked, disposing of the carpet and armchair, and burying the body in her garden. Although Ella had been distressed, she admitted to being pleased Lee was gone after all that he had put her through. She said that she naively felt 'rescued' by Seb and that had been the start of their romantic involvement. Everything from then on was about their relationship, how he kept changing his mind about leaving his wife, how he would visit just for sex. On the night she alleges he assaulted her, Ella explained that it was because she wanted to confess to the murder, that the guilt was too much, and this had caused Seb to lash out. Ella also told the police that on the night that she was raped by Seb, he had arrived just wanting sex, but she had refused, telling him there would be no more until he left his wife, but he would not take no for an answer.

As he listened to it all, he could comprehend how convincing it all sounded. The motivations were believable, and she played the part of the victim incredibly well. He assumed that Ella had killed Lee and began to wonder if she had been setting him up all along, so that if she ever was discovered, she had someone to pin it on.

Seb pointed out which parts of the story were true, and which weren't. He got across his concern that he may have been set up from the beginning, and the police officers listened without making comment.

"So, what happens now?" he asked, nervously.

"You'll be kept in tonight, while we carry out some further investigations. You can call a solicitor in the morning if you change your mind, as you are, currently, being charged with the murder of Mr. Jenkins."

Seb fought back tears as he was led through the secure door and into the cells, wondering which one Ella was being held in. He thought about her, sadly, feeling broken. Behind the door to her cell, however, Ella was smiling, a crafty smile of someone who was winning a particularly devious game.

TWENTY-THREE

After a while, Natasha managed to compose herself enough to get up from the kitchen floor. The children were standing around her, worried expressions on their faces. They knew something was wrong, of course, but they could not have imagined the severity of the situation.

"Sorry guys," Natasha told them. "I was just feeling a bit poorly. I'm alright now." The children seemed less concerned about their mother than the state of the windows, and Natasha did her best to brush off their questions about the damage, saying it had been an accident, without going into specifics. The children were still exhausted, as was Natasha, and she busied herself by going about their bedtime routine and making sure things seemed as normal as possible.

There is no point calling the police, Natasha decided. *They said that they would call when there was any news.* She wondered about asking Dee to come around, but decided against it, choosing to think things over by herself and try to gain some clarity on the events unfolding around her. She regretted coming back now, wishing that she had, at least, stayed with her parents for one more night, long enough to avoid being home right at this moment. Nevertheless, she was here. The children needed the familiarity of home, and they needed her to be strong. She felt as if she needed some help though, someone to watch the children at least, while she tried to figure out what had really happened. There was no doubt in Natasha's mind that her husband was innocent, that this was just the next step of that twisted bitch's game.

Sat at the kitchen table, Natasha gathered a pen and some sheets of blank paper and began, once again, to work through the possible truths of the situation, just as she and Seb had done after Ella had made the assault allegation. At the moment, the time and date of the man's death were not known to her, so she could not, with any certainty, provide an alibi for her husband. She racked her brain, searching for any conversation in which Seb may have mentioned his name. but she could not place it. *Mr. Jenkins* was all that she knew. She had the idea that he was in construction, or some kind of builder, so Seb must have mentioned that at one point. If he was self-employed there may be an on-line presence, and she hoped that, even with the vague details, she would be able to find out something as sleep didn't look very likely.

Seb's laptop was still in the kitchen, so she opened it up and began to investigate. In the search bar she typed his name, the name of the town, the sort of work she thought (and hoped) he did. It appeared that it wasn't too difficult to find out much online and, although he had no website, there were links to his business registration details (unimaginatively called 'Jenkins Building Repairs'), an address (which she recognized as the home address she had visited to confront Ella), a mobile number, and links to his social media business page and personal profile. *Not a bad start,* she thought, now knowing his first name as well.

The business details didn't interest her very much, so she decided to begin with his personal page, nothing having been posted there for a while. *Makes sense,* she thought, *what with him being dead.* She clicked her way through his photographs, most of which were of him in a few different pubs, mostly the King's Head which she recognized largely because of the bar manager being stood behind him in some. There were a few pictures of him and Ella, some of him looking quite happy with other women too. A few faces that she recognized from around the town were also in the photographs, but she very rarely socialized there and didn't know any of them well enough to speak to. One face bugged her though, one she had noticed at the school a few times. Her name was mentioned under the photo; Lotte Dunhill. *Maybe I can ask her about Lee?* she wondered, not sure how to bring up the conversation. She contemplated sending her a message online but thought that it may be better to call Dee first, as she spoke to a lot of the people at the school. *Maybe she knows her?* Natasha didn't want to give Dee the details yet, as she would want to come around, but couldn't think of how to ask about a stranger without raising suspicions. Even though it was quite late to be calling, Natasha knew she would not be able to wait until the morning for answers.

"Hello?" Dee answered, almost immediately.

"Sorry it's late," Natasha apologized.

"That's OK. I'm still up. Are you still at your parents?"

"No, I came back today. Wish I hadn't though." And with that, Natasha filled Dee in on as much as she knew, from the broken windows, to coming home, Seb's arrest, and her online snooping.

"Lotte," Dee said. "That's who I was trying to tell you about; I thought her name was Chantelle. Maybe it's Charlotte then."

"Telling me about when?" Natasha asked, a little confused.

"The girl, from the takeaway. You were asking about who worked there. Seb had something for the guy who owned it?"

"Oh, right, yeah. Hmm, that's odd. Anyway, she's the only one in the photos who looked particularly familiar so I thought I could try to contact her, find out more about Lee."

"OK, that sounds like a good idea. Are the police not doing that though?"

"I don't know," Natasha replied. "Maybe, but they're not telling me anything at the moment."

"I'll go and tell Mr. Grumpy upstairs, and then I'll be over," Dee told her, ending the call before Natasha could say no.

The Broken Doll: Book One

Natasha began writing down her theories on the paper, none of which sat easily with her. She constructed a few different scenarios, but the details of each were bothersome in one way or another. Once she had discarded the ridiculous ones (random home invasion, gangster assassination, etc.), she whittled it down to four plausible ideas;

(i) Ella is telling the truth, and Seb killed him to defend her.

(ii) Ella and Seb were already having an affair, Lee caught them, and they killed him.

(iii) Ella fought back one day and killed him herself.

(iv) Another person killed him, the reason unknown (Someone Ella was seeing? Someone Lee had pissed off? Someone Lee was seeing?).

Natasha tried to ignore the logic of the first two ideas, certain of her husband's innocence. Well, almost certain. The bit that Natasha struggled to explain was how the body had ended up staying at the house. It seemed obvious that he must have died there, so Ella must have been involved with his death somehow. Her third idea made the most sense by far. *If he had been killed by someone, other than Seb, that Ella had been seeing, then that was also quite feasible, but why blame Seb and not the actual killer? If it had been someone Ella had no concern for, then why not report it at the time? Had she been threatened? Was she made to hide the body, thereby incriminating herself along with the perpetrator? It must have been Ella,* Natasha decided. *And an alibi for Seb would clear him. Case (almost) solved!*

The bang on the chipboard attached to the front door startled Natasha as she pondered her next step. She greeted her friend and they made coffee, going over Natasha's theories so far.

"It must have been her, right?" Natasha stated, looking for confirmation that it was the only realistic explanation.

"Probably," Dee replied. "It makes sense, I guess. I got a number for that Lotte girl, think it's the right one anyway. One of the kids went to a party she did a while ago."

"Do you think I should call her? I really don't know. If she was friends with him, then I shouldn't be the one to tell her that he's dead! I don't know if it's public knowledge yet."

"What time does the King's Head close?" Dee asked, looking as though she had come up with a master plan.

"I don't know, twelve, I think. Why? What are you thinking?"

"Just an idea, I'll be back soon," Dee told her as she walked towards the front door. "Just getting a quick drink."

Natasha looked at the clock on her kitchen wall; it was 11.20pm. She couldn't work out what Dee was up to and felt a little trapped that she had to stay home because of the children. She was worried, fearing that Dee would make a scene in the pub about Lee being dead and that Natasha would somehow be in trouble with the police for broadcasting the information. *She'll be back in a minute,* Natasha told herself. *It might be closed anyway.* However, Dee wasn't back for almost an hour, her breath giving away the wine she had been throwing down at the bar.

"It closes at twelve," she informed her friend. "For future reference. And, my God, there are some fatties in there!"

Natasha looked puzzled. Surely Dee didn't just walk out, mid-conversation, to get a bit tipsy on her own?

"Right?" Natasha said, a little impatiently. "And?"

The Broken Doll: Book One

"This detective work is a piece of piss! Especially when everyone around here loves to gossip. I went to the King's Head, told the guy who's always on the bar I was looking for someone called Lee. I'd heard he was a builder or something, and that I had a broken window which needed fixing."

"OK," Natasha mumbled, hoping Dee would get to the point quickly.

"The guy said he knew Lee, used to drink there, but hasn't been in for a while. Gave me a card for a glazer instead who he said could help."

"Is that it?" Natasha asked, looking unimpressed.

"Almost," Dee told her. "I was saving the juiciest info for last so just hang on."

"I'm not really in the mood to play about Dee," said Natasha, not expecting her friend to have actually learned anything very useful and starting to think about heading to bed.

"So, I got my second large glass of Sauvignon Blanc, just as the bell rang for last orders, and sipped at it, looking around the bar. A guy came and started talking to me, not at all good-looking of course, but I smiled anyway. I'm sure he was hoping to pull at the end of the night, but even if I was single, desperate, and blind he wouldn't have stood much chance." *Jesus!* thought Natasha. *Get to the fucking point.*

"So, I told him why I was there, my story about the windows, not the real murder story, and he said he used to play pool with Lee but hadn't seen him for some time. He said that there was gossip he'd left town after getting caught with someone else's wife. Now he thinks it has something to do with the guy who ran the takeaway, which coincidentally closed at about the same time, and guess what?"

"What?!" Natasha snapped, getting a bit fed up with Dee's theatrics.

"Lee was last seen leaving the King's Head with the takeaway guy's wife and some other girl; a girl who worked there too."

"Shit. Lotte?" Natasha asked, now intrigued.

"I don't know for sure, but it seems possible."

"So, what does any of this actually mean though? Was Lee having it off with the guy's wife and that's why he's gone? Fuck! What if he did a runner because *he* killed Lee? Surely that's worth the police looking into?"

"Well, I would have thought so. But we should speak to Lotte first, in case it wasn't anything like that. Shouldn't we?"

"I don't know," Natasha sighed. "I can't think straight. Can we see what the police say in the morning and take it from there?"

Dee took the hint and said her goodbyes, feeling sleepy herself after the wine and headed home, promising to come by again in the morning. Natasha made her way to bed, exhausted from the long day, tired of all the stress and drama, hoping that tomorrow would bring some answers, and that she would be able to bring her husband home.

The children had almost got themselves completely ready for school before Natasha dragged herself out of bed. There were no missed calls from the police, she was disappointed to see, but there was a text from Dee saying she would meet her at the school and come around. The plan, as far as it seemed, was to call this Lotte woman before anything else. Once they had her story, they could then go to the police and find out what was happening to Seb. Natasha was tired, more so than usual, and it felt like an eternity before she was ready to leave the house, aware that the children were close to being late for school. She was unhappy that she had not woken up reinvigorated and prepared for the day's mission, instead favouring the idea of hiding away in the house alone. There was something in her mind that she needed to do today, aside from speaking with the police, but she struggled to place it.

As she hurried the children up the hill to the school, she spotted Dee waiting outside the main gates, leaning against the entry buzzer. She was talking to someone familiar looking, whom Natasha did not fully recognize to begin with.

"Back in a minute," Natasha told her as she ushered the children past Dee and towards their classrooms. Returning towards the gate it dawned on her who the woman was with Dee, her hair now a different colour to that in the photos online. Natasha felt a rush of nerves sweep across her, wondering what Dee had said already. Dee wasn't one to keep quiet about anything and, as much as she loved her, she, therefore, found it hard to trust her to keep any secrets.

"Nat," Dee began. "This is Lotte. I've invited her around for a coffee."

Natasha managed a smile, suddenly feeling a little awkward with a stranger coming into her house. If she didn't already know why she had been invited, then it would look as though she had been tricked into coming around. Dee and Lotte walked along, chatting about the children, whilst Natasha walked ahead of them, not saying a word. She tried to think of what to say and how to approach the subject of Lee's death, how not to sound as though they were making accusations. *This isn't going to be very pleasant.*

"Oh my God!" Lotte exclaimed when she saw the boarded-up house. "What happened?"

"Long story," Natasha replied, wanting to get sat down with a coffee before they started that tale of terror.

After a bit more general chat about the children, Dee, quite smoothly, changed the subject to work.

"You were working in the takeaway at the top of town, weren't you?" she asked Lotte.

"Yeah," was the reply. "That was until Sid disappeared anyway. Well, not disappeared, moved away to live with family." Lotte sounded annoyed by the situation, understandably as she had lost her job, at least temporarily, but she also seemed almost regretful about something.

"Why did he do that?" Dee pressed. "Just out of the blue?"

"I think there were some issues he had. I don't really know," Lotte told them, looking at the ground.

She's fucking hiding something, Natasha guessed, not in the mood for skating around the subject.

"You know Lee Jenkins?" Natasha asked outright. The look on Lotte's face was enough to show she knew him, and that there was something about their relationship that she was keeping to herself.

"Why? I mean, yeah I know who he is, do you know him then?"

"You mean you know who he *was*, not who he *is*," Natasha told her, seeing that the change in tense hadn't registered. "You do know he's dead, right?"

"Jesus, Nat," Dee began. "If she didn't know, that wasn't the best way to put it!"

Lotte began to sob. Natasha felt a little sorry for her, finding out the way she had. Nevertheless, it needed to be said, and it would be public knowledge soon enough.

"The police have Lee's crazy wife and my husband in custody for his murder," Natasha told her.

Lotte looked up through red eyes, a confused expression on her face.

"Murder?" she repeated. "Someone killed him?"

The Broken Doll: Book One

"At the moment, the police think my husband killed him and his wife buried him in the garden! It's fucking ridiculous. So, I need to know what the deal was with you and him?"

"There was no deal," Lotte tried to explain. "We had drinks together if we saw each other at the pub. That was it really. You don't think I killed him, do you?" she asked, looking horrified.

"No, of course not" Dee said, trying to console Lotte. Natasha did not say anything more, silently gazing out of the kitchen window. Slowly, she turned back to face Lotte.

"The last time Lee was seen, as far as we know, was leaving the King's Head with you and the takeaway guy's wife. Anything we should know about that night?" Natasha asked forcefully, trying to walk the line between demanding answers and not scaring her enough for her to try to leave. Lotte appeared frightened now, just quietly sobbing and looking at the floor. Dee fetched some tissues, realizing that they were playing a version of good cop / bad cop as she handed them over.

"No one thinks that you were involved," Dee said, gently. "We just need to find out what we can as my friend's husband could be in a lot of trouble for something he didn't do."

"If you don't want to tell us," Natasha said, "then I'm certain the police would be interested to know you may have been the last person who saw him alive. I'm sure you know how suspicious that makes things look."

"Fine!" Lotte snapped. "We fucked him. Is that what you want to know about? We left that night and went back to mine."

"We?" Dee asked, a little puzzled.

"Me and Maggie, from work. We'd go for drinks a few nights a week She had fucked him a few times before, they were getting a bit frisky at the bar that night. I was hammered. He asked me to join them, so I said yes. I'm not a slag!" Lotte protested, understanding the disapproving look on Natasha's face.

"My boyfriend was being a dick that day," she continued. "Well, he usually is. Talks to me like shit, can't be bothered to help with the kids. I suppose I was trying to get back at him in a way, so we went to mine as he was working nights."

Natasha couldn't hide the disapproval on her face. *What's wrong with everyone in this town?* she wondered. *Fucking inbreeds.* She could tell Lotte was embarrassed, ashamed maybe.

"Sorry," Natasha told her. "It's not really my business, and I don't want you to think I'm judging you but having a threesome with your kids in the house seems a bit inappropriate. Did they have a babysitter?"

"My eldest is twelve; she sorts the younger ones out if I'm not there. And they were asleep when we got back."

"So, was it good?" Dee couldn't help herself. Natasha gave her a dirty look, trying to convey her dismay at the question. Dee pretended not to notice. "I just wondered," she continued. "I've thought about a threesome before, but I've never had one. I just don't think I could eat a fanny to be honest. I'm sure him indoors wouldn't mind though, and I bet Lee couldn't believe his luck!"

Lotte was in no mood to discuss the intimate details, especially as the news was out that Lee was deceased, and this Natasha woman clearly did not approve of their sexual exploits. It would have only added to the shame Lotte felt if she then went on to tell them how both her and Maggie had played with each other for Lee's viewing pleasure, how they had both sat on him, one on his cock and one on his face, kissing each other passionately. It also would not help the situation for Lotte to disclose any further details of that night, of being discovered on the sofa face down, ass up, Lee behind her, Maggie's pussy on her mouth.

The Broken Doll: Book One

"I have to go," Lotte said, trying to stand up with Natasha blocking her way.

"OK, but if you think of anything else, then make sure you let us know please," she told her.

"Please don't mention it to the police," Lotte pleaded. "I don't know anything that can help, and I don't need the aggro at home if it gets out what I did."

Without replying, Natasha stepped aside and followed Lotte to the front door, closing it behind her. No sooner had she turned to walk back to the kitchen than there was a bang at the door. Impatiently, Natasha opened it expecting to see Lotte again, ready to confess to something else that the rough slag had done. However, she was greeted by pair of young men, maybe in their mid-twenties, in matching polo shirts.

"Mrs. Briggs?" the shorter one asked.

"Yes," she replied, trying to work out the logo on their tops.

"We're here to fit your windows." *That's what was happening today!* she thought, slightly relieved that she now knew.

"Ah yes, come in. I'll put the kettle on," she told them, leaving the front door open and returning to the kitchen.

"Well, there are a couple of new suspects then," Natasha said to Dee as they waited for the water to boil.

"Hmm," was the only response that she got, Dee dreamily watching the two muscular, tattooed bodies carrying tools in and out of the house.

"You listening?" Natasha asked, curtly.

"Sorry," Dee apologized, looking back at her friend and then up towards the front door again. "You know, we could almost certainly have an orgy with those guys right now and no one would ever know," she said, half-jokingly.

"Yes, we probably could. Even so, we aren't going to because we have some fucking standards and aren't slutty skanks like everyone else around here seems to be."

"Fine. I bet it would be great though," Dee said with a smile, and Natasha couldn't help smiling back.

"I'm sure it would. Now can I trust you to take their drinks to them without dropping your knickers?" she teased.

"I'll try my best," Dee promised, turning to head up to the living room, deliberately shaking her arse a little.

TWENTY-FOUR

It was a rough night for Seb, by all accounts. The cell was cold, the bed was hard, and he had tried his best to ignore Ella calling out to him. It seemed strange to Seb that they would be placed in such close proximity to one another, the doors to the cells not being what he expected, therefore conversation between them could have taken place through them if Seb had been willing to do so. He presumed that the holding area must at least be monitored, otherwise there was nothing to stop actual criminals from discussing their stories with each other.

Ella sounded as though she was going a little crazy in the cell, Seb had thought. He had glanced over at the locked door a few times, imagining her pacing around, beautiful, yet dangerous. Whenever he had looked in the direction of her cell, it was as if she knew, and she would start trying to talk to him. He found it unsettling, his feelings towards her changing from wanting to help her to wanting to fuck her to, now, wanting to get as far away from her as possible. If her plan had been to trap him, somewhere near to her, then it had, at that very moment, worked. It was amazing how, once you started to know someone, they could become so ugly to you. Sleep had been difficult, despite the late hour, and it had not been helped by Ella's attempts to talk to him. She seemed to think that slutty comments were appropriate, even in their current predicament, but it looked as though she had regretted making them when the guy in the other cell had shown an interest.

"I bet you look fucking hot in there, Mr. Criminal," she had called across to Seb as he sat on the metal bed. "You know, if I could get to you, then I'd be sucking that big dick by now!"

Seb moved away from the door, trying to resist talking to her, fearful he might lose his temper.

The Broken Doll: Book One

The other guy in holding, however, was quite happy to talk to Ella, a little optimistic about his chances for some action.

"Yo, murderer chick. When we get outta here I'm quite happy to give you a seeing to. I'm sure you'd fucking like it."

"Not gonna happen, I'm afraid," Ella had replied. "I'm a one-man girl and that guy there, my murdering accomplice, is the only dick for me."

"He doesn't sound all that interested you know, maybe I'll come visit you when they move you on? See how you're feeling then after being stuck with just skin-head dykes to play with."

Ella ignored the guy after that, wanting Seb to speak to her and trying hard to hide the fact that he was upsetting her by not doing so. As far as she could see it, they were both going to prison, possibly for quite a long time. It was important to her that they made plans for after their sentences had been served so that they could start their new life together.

"Seb," she called, getting no response. "Seb, talk to me!" Slowly turning towards the door, Seb mustered the energy to tell her, once again, that he was done with her. His mouth ran away with him a little as he called her some unpleasant names and vowed to never have any contact with her again. Once he had got that out of his system, he managed to drift into a light sleep, consoled by the quiet rhythm of Ella's sobbing, which could just about be heard, her misery making him smile a little.

Seb jumped at the sound of the buzzer on the security door, followed by the clanging metal as it swung open and made contact with the wall behind.

"Briggs," called the officer standing by the door to his cell. Seb stood up, still a little dazed from the sudden awakening, and looked at the officer standing before him. He was not someone whom Seb had met so

The Broken Doll: Book One

far, and he didn't like the way that he stared him straight in the eye. He looked menacing, one of the sort of police officers that were just in the job for the power, probably quite happy beating suspects up for fun. Seb didn't say anything but just waited there for the officer to do something.

"Time to go," Seb was told as P.C. Thug unlocked the cell and began to lead him towards the interview rooms. Seb didn't even glance towards the other cells but could envisage the cold glare of Ella's beautiful eyes stabbing into his back as he passed. From what Seb could remember from the last time that he had been held overnight, breakfast had been brought round at about 8am and this had not happened today. He wondered if that was because it was still too early, or whether he just wasn't getting any this time around. As he entered the room, he was greeted by D.C. Matthews alone at the desk, the officer who had brought him there assuming his position at the door like a bouncer.

"I just wanted to touch base, see if there was anything else you wanted to tell us before we process you," Matthews told him.

"Process me? Er, no, nothing has changed since last night has it?"

"It's just routine Mr. Briggs, a final opportunity to volunteer any more information if you've thought of anything?"

"No, I think I told you everything last night. You said that I'm being charged?"

"Not at this moment in time," Matthews explained, much to Seb's relief. "You are being released pending further investigations. You are, however, still a prime suspect in a murder investigation and are not, under any circumstances, to leave town. Is that clear? We don't want to have to come looking for you, otherwise you'll have to stay in the cell."

"That's clear enough," Seb confirmed, eager to leave the building. *Guess that means there isn't sufficient evidence to charge me.*

After a little paperwork, and the collection of his belongings, Seb walked out of the police station, and into the bright sunshine of the morning. His stomach rumbled, and his mouth was dry. He turned towards home and paused, unsure of whether Natasha would be there or not. *Had she even come home last night? Had she found out about the arrest and left again? Or was she waiting there for him to return?* Seb decided that it was more likely that she was not there and, in an attempt to avoid going home just yet, went to the bottom of town and into the bakery where he could get a coffee and a breakfast baguette.

As Seb sat, wiping the brown sauce from his chin with a paper napkin, he fought to hold back tears. It felt as though everything was falling apart around him, and he had no idea how to clear his name. He sipped his way through a third coffee, unaware that he had been there for almost two hours already, when he suddenly remembered the window fitters were coming.

Shit, he thought, hoping Natasha had been home to let them in. He gathered himself together and began to walk home, excited about the possibility of seeing his wife, terrified that she now thought that he was capable of murder. As he turned into his road, he was relieved to see the glazers van parked across the street. Most of the boards he had installed had now been removed, and two men were visible in his living room, holding mugs, whilst Dee giggled like a schoolgirl between them.

Of course she's here, Seb muttered to himself as he pushed open the front door. With the gaping hole in the front of his house, it was too cold to take off his coat. Three sets of eyes looked up at him from the living room without speaking and Seb only

The Broken Doll: Book One

managed a barely audible 'hi' before rushing down to the kitchen in search of Natasha.

Their reunion was emotional, hugging each other tightly, both shedding a few silent tears. Seb explained everything from his end, including the details of Ella's statement, which was met with a look of shock and despair from Natasha. The only thing he neglected to mention was Ella's desire to suck him off as that seemed like something Natasha may not need to hear. Seb then took a seat while he caught up with the results of the women's spy efforts, including the information that Lotte had provided not long before he had arrived.

"Sid?" Seb uttered in disbelief. "Do you really think it was him? And, if it was, why would Ella hide the body and blame me? We need to tell the police what you found out."

"I don't know who did what, but the police will want to talk to Sid, and it takes the attention off you for a bit. The fact that he's done a runner makes him look pretty guilty. I was going to go to the station once the guys have finished the windows."

"Well, they seem more interested in Dee at the moment so they may be a while. Do you think she'll be alright here with them if we go and find D.C. Matthews now? She's the one who released me earlier so she could still be on duty."

"How much earlier?" Natasha asked him, confused as to where he had been. "Did you not come straight home?"

"I needed to get my head clear. I wasn't sure if you would even be here, so I grabbed a coffee first, sorry."

Natasha looked suspicious but let the subject drop, opting for a visit to the police rather than interrogating her husband. Dee seemed happy to be left alone with the men, taking a seat in the living room to admire their work skills. Seb and Natasha headed back to the police station with some notes that she had

The Broken Doll: Book One

scribbled down before Seb had arrived. They held each other's hands as they entered the station, portraying a unified front, attempting to demonstrate that Natasha had no doubts over her husband's innocence.

After a repeat of the procedures, D.C. Matthews came out to greet them from the waiting area and led them, once again, to an interview room. P.C. Smith had just arrived for work and took the seat next to Matthews as she played about with the recording device and officially began the interview.

"So, what do you have for me?" Matthews asked, looking at Natasha.

"I did some digging into Mr. Jenkins. I thought you should know a few things that I have found out."

"What sort of digging?" Matthews asked, looking as though she was feeling put out by a civilian trying to do her job.

"Just talking to some people who knew him," Natasha explained.

"Gossip, you mean?" Matthews stated, bluntly. "Just hearsay. And, as far as I am aware, Mr. Jenkins' death has not been made public yet."

"Some is just hearsay. Some is information from someone who knew him well. A woman called Lotte Dunhill. I found out that Lee was a regular at the King's Head, in town. No one there has seen him for a while, obviously, but the last night he was there he left with two women; Lotte Dunhill and Maggie something. When they left, Lee had a threesome with the two women. The interesting bit is that Maggie has a husband, Sid. Sid owns the food place up the road, which has been closed for a while now, about the same amount of time that Lee had been off the grid actually."

"Why has it been closed?" Matthews asked, now a little more interested.

"Because Sid has done a runner. Well, Maggie said he had gone to stay with family, didn't

The Broken Doll: Book One

know when he'd be back. It sounds a lot like he's lying low to me."

"So," Matthews began. "Your assumption, based on these rumours, is that Mr. Jenkins had sex with this Maggie person, her husband found out and killed him, then abandoned his business and went into hiding?"

"Pretty much, yeah," Natasha replied. "Surely it looks a bit suspicious. I just thought it might be a line of enquiry worth pursuing."

"We'll look into it!" Natasha said to Seb as they headed home, repeating D.C. Matthews' last words. "Jesus, she couldn't have looked less interested."

"I'm sure she knows what she's doing," Seb said, hopefully. "They'll find out what they need to know, we just have to wait now."

"Did they let that bitch out or is she still there?" Natasha asked, hoping that Ella would be locked away for the rest of time.

"She was still there when I left," Seb told her. "I don't know about now, but she wouldn't be stupid enough to come near us." *I hope not, anyway,* he thought.

"So, if they've finished the windows in time, what do you want to do before we pick the children up?" Natasha asked. Seb, as usual, took this to be an offer of sex, but he was mistaken. Recognizing the look he was giving her, Natasha suggested going out for coffee or some lunch. Seb smiled, pleased that she wanted to spend time with him, hoping it was a sign that their relationship was not completely broken.

"Lunch would be nice, maybe a few tapas at the pub by the river? Let's check on the windows, get rid of Dee, and head out for a bit."

'Call me as soon as you can. We need to talk; it's urgent!' Maggie read the text as she sat on her

leather sofa, leaning against the leopard-print cushions. Her phone was on silent, as it always was, in an attempt to avoid any contact with the outside world. Since Sid had gone, she had lost the motivation to do much, opting to drink alone at home rather than in the pub where she may have to answer questions about the sudden closure of the takeaway. She lived almost solely on nicotine and cheap vodka, the consumption of alcohol creeping earlier and earlier into each day. She had chosen to ignore the first three missed calls from Lotte, but something wasn't sitting right now. She had hardly spoken to Lotte since the night they took Lee back to hers, not wanting to be involved in the fallout. Yes, of course, she was to blame for Sid leaving her, something which made her feel like shit. She'd cheated on more occasions than she could remember and not felt particularly bad about it, but this seemed different, perhaps because he was actually gone. Deep down, she had always assumed he knew she wasn't one for monogamy and had thought that he was probably not entirely faithful himself. Maggie just presumed that, if she ever did get caught, they would have a fight and then things would be fine again. Even so, there was quite a difference between a drunken kiss at the pub and a filthy threesome. She replayed the events of that night over and over, for days. She wondered if she would still feel this bad about it if she hadn't been caught out, if they had not been interrupted by Lotte's other half. *Poor guy,* she thought, envisaging the look on his face as he walked into the living room, seeing the three of them naked, his wife getting slammed from behind whilst she ate pussy. *And yet he didn't leave her. Maybe he loved Lotte more than Sid loved her, or perhaps it meant he loved her less;* she couldn't decide. Reluctantly, Maggie returned the calls that she had missed, unsure what to expect to hear.

"We need to talk," Lotte began, sounding upset. "Are you home?"

"I'm always home, what's happened?" she replied.

"I'll tell you when I get there." And the call ended. Maggie let out a long sigh, not excited at the prospect of having a visitor and not wanting to deal with someone else's emotional shit. She stayed rooted to her spot on the sofa, waiting for Lotte to arrive, wondering what she had to tell her and, more importantly, how long she would end up staying for.

"We're in trouble," Lotte told Maggie as soon as the door opened, her voice full of panic. "That Lee guy, he's dead. Someone fucking killed him." Maggie was sure there must have been a mix up, but Lotte certainly seemed sure about it. She hadn't seen him since that night, but she hadn't been back to the pub since either so that was no surprise.

"I haven't heard anything," said Maggie, not entirely convinced it was true. "How do you know?"

Lotte went on to explain the conversation she had had with the two mums from the school, explaining that one of their husbands was with the police because of it. Maggie looked angry, betrayed. She began to wonder if Sid was responsible.

"Why the hell did you tell them what we did that night? That was fucking stupid. We may not have killed him, but it's going to raise some questions, don't you think?"

"Sorry," Lotte mumbled, tears welling up. "I didn't know what to say, it isn't right that someone is being blamed for it."

"So, what do you suggest? Do you want to go to the police and tell them everything? Or maybe it's too late and those nosy bitches have done it already!"

Lotte just cried, an annoyingly loud sound, her head in her hands which were wet with tears and snot. Maggie was worried about Lotte not being trustworthy enough, but, ultimately, she knew it didn't particularly matter anymore. Neither of them had known Lee was dead and neither of them had killed him, but if they were the last ones to see him alive, and if the altercation with Lotte's partner, Jim, came to light, it would warrant a police investigation. *Even so, it was only circumstantial, purely coincidence. Jim may have roughed him up a bit, and who could blame him under the circumstances, but not enough to kill him, surely? And if he had, then how did the body end up in a garden?*

"Pull yourself together!" Maggie scolded. "Stop bloody crying. What actually happened after Jim came in? I didn't see anything after he dragged Lee outside." Through sniffles, Lotte managed to string together a few sentences, breathing heavily between each word.

"He took him outside. He was still naked, punched him a few times. I ran out after them with Lee's clothes and threw them onto the grass. I grabbed Jim, managed to pull him back indoors. That was about it, I think. Do you remember anything else?" Lotte's eyes were wide with panic, trying to gather all the details of that night, trying to reassure Maggie of their innocence before the police inevitably became involved.

"Jim walked in, grabbed Lee. I panicked, didn't want Sid to find out so I grabbed my clothes and tried to get away as quickly as possible. I remember you coming back in with Jim. He looked furious, calling us 'fucking whores'. I left as soon as I had some clothes on, Lee was still getting dressed out in your garden. He didn't seem in any hurry; he almost looked like he wanted to stay."

"We didn't see him again," Lotte said, a little too quickly. "I thought he must have just gone home after that. Maybe he did go home, and his wife guessed what he'd been up to? Surely she's a prime suspect if she put him in the fucking garden?!"

The Broken Doll: Book One

Maggie thought this over; it certainly seemed possible. A thud at the front door interrupted her thoughts. *For fuck's sake!* she thought. *One visitor is plenty today!*

"You must be Maggie," came the croaky voice of a female in a suit, standing on the doorstep accompanied by a uniformed officer. "May we come in?"

Maggie didn't answer, but turned to head back to the living room, resuming her position on the sofa. Without the offer of a seat, D.C. Matthews and P.C. Smith sat down anyway, watching Lotte as she continued to cry.

"And you are?" Matthews asked her.

"Charlotte Dunhill," she sobbed.

"Can I ask what's wrong?" Matthews asked, trying her best to sound sympathetic over the irritating sobs.

"You're here about Lee, aren't you?" Maggie stated. "She's just upset because we heard he was dead."

"I'm sorry for your loss," Matthews began, without any real empathy. "I won't keep you any longer than necessary; we just have a few questions. No one seems to have seen Mr. Jenkins since the night he left the King's Head with the pair of you, according to our information. When you took him back to Ms Dunhill's home and had sex?" Maggie glared at Lotte, a little embarrassed to be discussing these details with a stranger.

"We were just talking about that actually. Yes, we left together, had sex then Lee went home. That's it."

"So, no one else was there? No one else knew about it?"

"Nope," Maggie continued, glancing at Lotte.

"And your husband, Sid, isn't it? He didn't know? Or still doesn't? I only ask as he moved away around the same time, didn't he?" Maggie's face

The Broken Doll: Book One

dropped, realizing where the questions were leading. There was no way Sid would do anything like this. He had been upset and left, that was all. Maggie stammered a little as she tried to straighten out her story.

"Sid knows. That's why he left me," she told the police officers, feeling ashamed.

"And how did he come to know?" Matthews asked, jotting things in pencil on her tiny notepad.

"I told him," Maggie lied. "I felt guilty and owned up to it. I thought we'd just fight about it, but he left."

"I see. Do you know where we can find your husband now?" Matthews asked, looking up from her pad.

"He said he was going to stay with some cousins he has, north London somewhere. His phone has been off since he went, I haven't heard from him at all."

"If you could give me any names or addresses that could help us locate your husband it would be very useful," Matthews asked. Turning towards Lotte, she went to speak but decided that it could wait until another time, the woman's hysteria suggesting that questioning her right now might be a waste of everyone's time.

"You can't think Sid killed Lee?" Maggie asked, as she handed over an address for Sid's cousins. "He wouldn't do that."

"Nobody is suggesting that. We have to look into every possibility, of course, but don't worry. It's just routine, so that we can rule him out as a suspect." *Isn't that exactly what they say about someone that they think is guilty?* Maggie wondered.

D.C. Matthews and P.C. Smith spent a few minutes sat inside the police car, talking over their notes.

The Broken Doll: Book One

"So boss," Smith began. "Who did it? I mean, as far as I can see, this threesome is too much of a coincidence to not be relevant, don't you think? We've got an angry wife in the cells already, her bit on the side, now two more pissed-off husbands. It's a bit of a mess really."

Smith's cheerful tone was constant, and Matthews liked it. It didn't matter what he was talking about, his voice was filled with joviality. The tone would be the same if he was telling a child about Santa's magical elves, or if he was giving evidence in court about a room full of dead children.

"So, you think we have four suspects?" Matthews asked, teasing a little. "Do you not think those two tarts in there are capable of murder?"

"Tarts isn't very professional boss, they made a mistake one night when under the influence of alcohol. There's no law against threesomes as far as I know."

"Oh, I don't think they're tarts for having a threesome, Smith. I think they are tarts because they were both in relationships and did it behind their partner's backs. There isn't anything wrong with consensual group sex; in fact, it can be rather pleasant!" she told him with a little smile and a knowing wink, causing the P.C. to blush a little.

TWENTY-FIVE

The day dragged on, even with the help of most of a bottle of vodka. It had taken almost an hour to get the sobbing Lotte out of her house and as soon as Maggie was alone again, she had started drinking. Sid's phone was dead, 'number no longer available' was the message that she now received when trying to call it. After a couple of attempts, she had managed to speak to someone at the house that he was staying in. Sid wasn't there, apparently, and they didn't seem to want to chat to Maggie, so she had to try to get across the urgency of the situation. Although she couldn't be one hundred percent sure that Sid was innocent, she didn't want him to be in trouble because of her behaviour. Maggie managed to get the severity of the situation across to the woman on the phone, who wouldn't say her name, and told her to warn Sid that the police would be coming to talk to him. She only gave a slight indication as to the reason, trying her best to spare too much detail. It was all she could do, and now she just sat, waited, and drank.

It was only a few hours later when the call came that Sid had been arrested for Lee's murder, and it was Maggie's turn to cry. The woman whom she had spoken to earlier, when trying to warn Sid, had had the decency to call back. Maggie heard how her message had not even got to Sid, the police seemingly waiting outside for him to return to the address at which had been staying. They swept him up, with the speed and efficiency of the Metropolitan Police, and bundled him into the back of the car and off to the nearest police station. Sid had looked terrified, she was told. The caller made it clear who was to blame and ended the call. Maggie was devastated, hardly believing that it was real, unsure if he was guilty. Whether he had done it or not, her husband now sat in a cell, having lost his business and his wife, all because she couldn't keep her knickers on. It was unfair and she was ultimately responsible, her and that fucking Lotte. Maggie decided, in her drunken state, to call Lotte and get some of her anger out. *If she hadn't taken us back to her house, then this wouldn't have happened,* she reasoned. *If Jim hadn't come home when he did, no one would have ever known.*

Lotte wasn't answering her phone or replying to text messages. *Fucking bitch!* Maggie thought, getting angrier with each swallow of alcohol. She was barely in any state to walk, let alone drive, but she was past caring, grabbing her car keys from the coffee table. She knew she was too drunk but, at that moment, with the guilt weighing down on her, she wouldn't have minded if she had crashed and died. Fortunately, it wasn't far to Lotte's house, and after driving suspiciously slowly, she had arrived without incident. She hammered on the door, leaning against it for support. The door swung open suddenly, and she was greeted by an angry Jim.

"What the fuck are you doing here?" he shouted.

"I need to talk to you and Lotte," Maggie slurred, suddenly feeling a little sick.

"No one wants to talk to you. My kids are still up, and you're not welcome. Dirty old tramp," he said menacingly, beginning to shut the door.

"Fuck you! It's important. Was it you that told my husband what happened that night? The police have him, and they think that he killed Lee!"

Jim's face registered genuine surprise. Yes, he had told Sid what they had done, he had the right to know.

"Keep your fucking voice down," he told her.

"Lotte!" he shouted into the house. "Tell the kids to go play upstairs." From the doorstep, Maggie heard Lotte shout to the children, and then she appeared in the doorway.

"What's going on?" she asked, nervously.

The Broken Doll: Book One

"Sid's been arrested," Maggie told her, much more loudly than she had intended.

"Jesus fucking Christ, woman," Jim muttered. "Stop shouting! Come inside and keep your voice down." The three of them sat on the sofa, Lotte feeling particularly uncomfortable as Jim sat between the two women, bringing back memories of the last time three people were on that sofa. Lotte made a round of black coffees, mostly for Maggie's benefit, and sat to listen to what Maggie had come to say.

"So, what's happened?" she asked.

"The police have got Sid; they have arrested him for murder. I don't know if he did it, I haven't seen him since he left." Lotte and Jim exchanged glances, something Maggie would have clocked as suspicious if she hadn't been so inebriated.

"I can't let him take the fall for this; even if he did it, which I can't imagine, it still should fall on us Lotte!" Maggie couldn't hold it together any longer; tears of rage beginning to fall from her face. She blamed herself for being unfaithful. She blamed Lotte for being involved. She blamed Jim for telling Sid what she'd done. Everyone had some degree of blame to accept, all except Sid, and he was the one in a cell.

"I'm going to tell the police," Maggie said firmly. "I'm going to tell them that Jim caught us. That he then had a fight with Lee, that we killed him. It's the only way to make this right. I just wanted to warn you first." Lotte looked horrified; Jim's eyes flickered with rage. It was a ridiculous idea, of course; they did not even know if Sid had been charged yet. Nevertheless, Maggie was beyond being reasoned with, determined to try to atone for her mistake.

"But you can't say that!" Lotte pleaded. "They'll take our kids away. If you want to pretend that it was you then go ahead, but don't drag us into it!"

"I don't know what else to do!" screamed Maggie. "This is on us. How the fuck do we make it right?" Jim looked at her coldly, a calm, chilling gaze in his eyes.

"You're right," he told her. "It's not Sid's fault. It's yours. And you should take responsibility for it." With that, he pushed Maggie to the floor, putting a hand over her mouth. She was not strong enough, or sober enough, to wriggle free, her eyes wide with terror. Lotte jumped up from the sofa and grabbed at Jim's shoulders, trying to pull him off her friend.

"Do you want to go to prison?" Jim asked his girlfriend. "Do you? If she goes to the police, we're fucked. Go upstairs and make sure the kids don't come down." Lotte didn't know what to do. Jim was right in a way, and her family meant the world to her. Yes, she'd misbehaved before, but right here and now, this appeared to be the only way to protect them. She went upstairs to join her children who were engrossed in a film, cuddling up to them as she turned the volume a little higher. She tried to hold back the tears as she stared at the television, turning a blind eye to the violence taking place downstairs as Jim pressed a cushion over Maggie's face. He leaned toward her ear and whispered his confession, that she was now his second kill, that he was starting to enjoy it. He pressed down hard, trying not to leave any unnecessary marks on her body, waiting for it to go limp. When Maggie had drawn her last breath, he picked up her body and moved it to the back seat of her car and drove out of town.

Lotte didn't move from her children's bedroom until she heard the front door opening. Jim had been gone for almost two hours and the entire time she had clung on to her offspring, petrified that she may never have the chance to hold them again. She was uncertain what had taken place downstairs but had a good idea. As she cautiously made her way back to the living room, it was as if nothing had happened. Everything was in its usual place, and Jim was sat on

The Broken Doll: Book One

the sofa again, looking deep in thought but not particularly worried.

"What did you do?" Lotte asked him, fearful of his answer, knowing, deep down, what had taken place.

"She wanted to take the blame, and now she will. I don't want to talk about it anymore."

D.C.I. Watts was on duty when the call came in. Two elderly hikers had been wandering along the river bank, just outside a neighbouring village, when they had spotted something floating down the river. The current was strong in this part, and it had moved past them quite quickly but, despite their increasingly poor eyesight, there was no mistaking the woman's body which bobbed along, face down. Forensic teams, an ambulance, and even a police helicopter were dispatched to check the validity of the report. The tide had been on its way out and, fortunately, the body was recovered before being dragged away by the current, into the depths of the English Channel. Police divers managed to pull Maggie's bloated corpse to shore where she was photographed and examined briefly before being moved on to the morgue at the nearest hospital. It didn't take long for the police to come across Maggie's car, which remained unlocked, her bag and purse still inside. There was also a note on the passenger seat, a combination of confession and suicide, along with an almost empty bottle of vodka. With no concerning marks or injuries on Maggie's body, and her lungs completely full of river water, there was no reason to ascertain the cause of death as being anything other than drowning.

"Is that case closed?" P.C. Smith asked his superior.

"It looks that way," Matthews replied, a little distractedly. "I guess it makes sense. Mostly. So," she began, running over the events aloud for clarity as well as for P.C. Smith's benefit, "Maggie sleeps with Lee, they fight about Lee's threat to tell Sid, she stabs him with the, so far, undiscovered knife. He manages to get home, Ella is relieved that he's dead or dying, panics and buries the body. Sid becomes a suspect, causing Maggie to feel guilty and, after a bottle of vodka, she decides to confess and drown herself."

"Sounds viable to me, boss," Smith told her. "I mean, it's a bit fucked up, and I feel sorry for Mr. Briggs, getting the blame for a while. Is there something you don't believe then?"

"Not really, it's solid enough I guess," Matthews replied, choosing not to voice her nagging concern, the one thing that doesn't feel quite right. *If Maggie just thought that she would end up in an argument with Sid if he found out, as she had said when talking with the police previously, then why go to the extreme of trying to silence Lee so violently?* Matthews knew better than to dig any deeper into a case which appeared straight-forward, however, and she was aware that her superiors would not want it sitting unresolved for any length of time. After all, the only other two suspects were Seb and Ella, both having alibis for the night that Maggie went for her final swim. The possibility of another killer on the loose seemed unlikely and she was almost certain that the powers that be would not waste police resources on her chasing a ghost.

It was barely a few days since Maggie's corpse had been discovered before the media got wind of the story, printing every sordid detail of the crime. Seb sat with his coffee, reading the sensationalized tale, wondering how close to the truth it actually was. Sid had been released after a confession was found in his wife's car, admitting to Lee's murder. She claimed to have killed him in a rage after he had threatened to tell her husband what they had been doing. Unwilling to let the innocent Sid go to prison for a crime he did not commit, and also reluctant to face prison herself, her body was found floating down the river just outside of town. The newspaper goes on to talk about Ella, how she had admitted to hiding the body, fearing she would be in trouble for letting him die, freely stating that she could have saved him, but that she chose not to. She was charged with perverting the course of justice, not just for the corpse burying but also for trying to frame Seb, whom the papers refer to as 'one of the many unfaithful people caught up in this shocking tale of lust and murder'.

There was little mention of Lotte and her partner, the only mention being that she had been the other part of the threesome which had set the whole series of events into motion. Seb's mind wandered over the past weeks, thinking over the interactions he had had with Ella, wondering how much difference it would have made if he had not spoken to her on that first night. He recalled the change to Ella's garden and accepted that must have been the time of burial, meaning that he could have still avoided this whole situation by simply keeping away. Seb wondered how things would have played out for Ella if he had not met her, doubting that she would have ever had any reason to confess to the body in the garden unless the police decided that Lee was officially missing. He regretted a lot, of course, some things more than others. He wanted to regret the sex with Ella, but that was difficult. He felt bad for doing it, but that was only because of the hurt that he had caused Natasha; he couldn't deny how good it had been.

The press coverage had been too much for Natasha to stand, with reporters calling and coming by the house in the hope for an interview with her, and she had returned to her parents' house, temporarily. They had been speaking daily on the phone, and Seb felt confident that they would work things out. They spoke about a fresh start in a different part of the country, chatting each evening, as though they were teenagers that had just started dating one another. The conversations became shorter though, as time went on. A couple of hours of chatting became an hour, which in turn became a lot less. It went from daily calls, to weekly ones very quickly, with Natasha being gone for much longer than either of them had anticipated at the beginning. Weeks turned to months, and Seb still sat alone each morning with his coffee and his newspaper, wondering where his life had gone. He didn't chase her. He didn't beg her to come home. It felt like the end, and as much as it hurt, he knew that they had had their time. He accepted the blame, cried on occasion (more than he would have liked to have admitted), tried to keep his head up. She was happier away from him; he knew it would be selfish to try to make her come back. From what she had told him, the children were doing well, having had to start at a new school. She had found a place near her parents to rent and was working part-time in a clothes shop, which she loved. Seb got the impression that her parents were helping her to make ends meet as they were keen to keep her nearby and safely away from him, as they saw it. He also had a feeling that she was seeing someone new, but this had not been confirmed. Seb did not want to think about it too much as it hurt, and he worried that it could just be him being paranoid. Regardless of other people, he now was certain that his marriage had run its course, the only contact he would have with Natasha would be his monthly visits to see the children and the odd text to confirm that he had sent his maintenance payments, which were usually smaller than Natasha expected as he was rapidly running low on money.

    Seb had, by a miracle of sorts, managed to sell one of the Chesterfields, the green one, to a lady who lived near to his lock-up. It transpired that she had seen his advertisement on Daryl's trailer, and he had delivered it on the same day that she had called to

The Broken Doll: Book One

enquire. The amount of profit on the item ended up being virtually nothing, but it was, at least, gone. This prompted Seb to move a selection of items outside to the driveway of his lock-up on a sunny day in the hope of attracting some sales from passers-by. This proved more successful than he had hoped, and despite having to haggle over the prices more than he wanted to, the bulkier items were mostly gone by the early evening. This meant two things; firstly, he would be able to surrender the tenancy on the lock-up, saving him a bit of money each month. Secondly, he still had one sofa but decided that he would take it home for now, making use of it for a bit and dumping the one that he had chosen with Natasha. With the lock-up keys handed back to the owner, and boxes of random items littering the now spare rooms in his house, he had stood staring at the burgundy coloured Chesterfield with a kind of awe. *That bloody thing,* he thought, *that thing had been at the centre of everything.* And Seb was right, in a way. Without the Chesterfields then he would not have been chasing Sid. He would not have discovered so much about Maggie and in turn, learned how everything had fitted together.

"Looks like it's just you and me now," Seb stated, aloud, to the worn, leather-upholstered beast in front of him. "Sorry I was so desperate to get rid of you."

TWENTY-SIX

Ella sat in her cell, pen and paper in hand, wondering how to begin yet another letter to Seb. When it had come around to the trial, when the truth had been revealed about Maggie's involvement, she had broken down in court. Her court-appointed barrister had tried his best, but there was no way out of a custodial sentence. Her confession was signed and was no longer retractable, all the details of her hiding her husband's body being true anyway. Her accusation against Seb had been defended by her barrister, who thought the best way to proceed was to suggest Ella hadn't *actually* seen Seb kill Lee, just assumed it was him. It was a weak defence but seemed worth a shot, at least as a better option than admitting that she had tried to frame him. Ella's case did benefit a little from the truth though, with the defence being able to portray Lee in an exceptionally bad light, reducing the amount of sympathy that the jury had felt for him. Ella was deemed to be unstable, a result of her abusive marriage, which led her to obsess over Sebastian Briggs. This was a persuasive argument, backed up by Ella's admission that Seb had not, in fact, assaulted her or raped her. With no murder charge applying to Ella, she pleaded guilty to obstructing a police investigation, evidence tampering (in the form of a dead body), and a minor fraud charge, relating to her use of Lee's bank cards.

The Judge had been a woman, which had possibly helped. A quite senior Judge, it turned out, who had a lot of experience with cases in which women have been the victim, and perhaps that was how she saw Ella. Ella's barrister told her that they were in luck getting her as the Judge, even before the sentencing. After weeks of going over and over every detail, the day of the hearing finally arrived, and Ella was convinced that she would be going away for a long time. In the beginning, this had not bothered her, expecting that Seb would be gone for longer, confident that they could start over when they both had been released. Now it was different; Seb was free already and Ella didn't want to face prison knowing that the man she loved was out there doing whatever, and whoever, he wanted.

"How long do you think I'll get?" Ella had asked her barrister, almost as soon as they had met each other. He was a large man, overweight, sweaty, but seemed to know what he was doing. He ran through the various options, convincing her to be as honest as possible, to really play on the emotional damage Lee had caused her.

"Your main issue is the body, and we'll have to chalk that up as a moment of panic. They already know you didn't do the deed, and you would be right to think that you would have been the prime suspect. You could probably get the accusation against Mr. Briggs dropped as he's not said that he wishes it to be pursued, and we can argue that you only accessed your husband's finances as a necessity to survive. With him being deceased at the time then, technically speaking, the money belonged to you anyway. At a guess, and with a fair Judge, somewhere between three and five years, time off for good behaviour and, at a push, you could be out in eighteen months. It's only an educated guess, of course, but I'd be surprised if it's any more than that."

Ella was relieved. *Eighteen months wouldn't be too bad, a year and a half.* And so, with this in mind, she accepted all of her barrister's advice, admitted to everything that he told her to, cried in court at the right times, and the sentence was handed to her. The Judge had read each charge out and then looked over to the foreman of the jury for a verdict.

"For the charge of fraud, relating to monies in the account of the accused's late husband, how do you find the defendant?"

"Not guilty, Your Honour."

"For the charge of perverting the course of justice pertaining to inaccurate allegations of crimes committed by Mr. Sebastian Briggs?"

"Guilty, Your Honour."

"For the crime of tampering with evidence and perverting the course of justice pertaining to the concealment of a body?"

"Guilty, Your Honour."

As the verdicts were read out, Ella felt a little sick, her nerves getting the better of her. She had not expected the guilty verdict relating to Seb as her barrister had been clear that Seb did not wish to pursue it. The police, however, did wish to pursue it and she was now frightened that this would add more time to her sentence.

"The jury have read out their verdicts," the Judge continued. "But before I hand down the sentence of this court, I wish to say a few things." She looked directly at Ella at this point, giving away a hint of sadness, or possibly regret for having to send her to prison.

"I am sorry for what you have been through at the hands of your husband, it must have been truly awful, and I strongly believe that he is to blame, in no small part, for the way that you have behaved since. That said, you have your own free will and have been found guilty of a rather serious offence. It is the decision of this court, therefore, to sentence you to a total of thirty-four months in prison, serving no less than eighteen months before any consideration for early release can be made."

With a slam of the gavel, court was dismissed, and prison life was to start. As it turned out, her barrister had been very accurate with his predictions, and they discussed what Ella needed to do to ensure that she would be eligible for early release once the first year and a half had passed. An hour and a half later, Ella stepped out of the van in handcuffs and entered her new home, hoping to God that there was a decent library in there.

Seb was aware of Ella's custodial sentence from the newspapers. *A year and a half minimum, hopefully longer,* he thought. *She's five months in, still plenty of time.* Seb dreaded Ella's release, fearful that time would make him forget what she had put him through. If he was still alone when she got out would she still be after him? Despite the absurdity of it, he was frightened that he would still be tempted, even after everything that had happened. He thought about her a lot, and it annoyed him. Most of the time it was angry thoughts, hatred almost for the woman who had cost him his family. The letters didn't help, coming through the door weekly to begin with. He had read the first few; they were just general chat really, descriptions of the prison and its facilities, what she'd been reading, and so on. They were all ended with 'love always' which gave him the creeps though. Seb was tempted to go to the police, to ask them to make her stop writing to him, but he knew that she had no one else and, in the end, what harm was it really doing. So, he put them in a shoe box, mostly unopened, and never replied.

It wasn't even that he didn't want to write to her, he just couldn't bring himself to do it. He was lonely but determined to stay strong. He wanted to have someone to talk to, but Ella would, undoubtedly, misread it as a sign of his affection for her. He would have liked to tell her how he felt, that he was alone, that Natasha was now seeing someone new. Someone whom his kids seemed to like, presumably more than their own father as they had refused to see him for the last two months due to 'other plans'. And instead of insisting on seeing them, Seb had just accepted it, wallowing in his self-pity as he sat alone most days wondering what to do with his life. He did the minimum amount of work to get by and pay the bills. His diet consisted largely of beer and whiskey. He cancelled his gym membership to save money (at least, that was what he told himself when, in fact, he had lost all interest in going). He'd had friends around to check on him to start with, but they had soon stopped bothering with him, busy with their own lives, and his days had all started to blur into one. The house reminded him of his family, and he struggled to face the outside world, not wanting to go on living in this town any longer.

The status quo had to change, he knew that, and as far as he could see there were only two options, both of which were terrifying and exciting in equal measures. It was impossible to choose between them, even after writing out a list of pros and cons and spending days deliberating. And that's when, after most of a bottle of bourbon, he decided to leave it to fate, despite not believing in such a thing. Chance, perhaps being a better word. The toss of a coin. He wrote on a piece of paper, to not have the option to alter the outcome; heads for suicide, tails for moving on. Standing in his living room, looking run down, with a bottle in one hand, he grabbed a two pence coin from the mantelpiece. *Time for a change,* he told himself as he flipped the coin into the air and closed his eyes.

Ella struggled to pen the latest letter to Seb, not really knowing how to word things. She needed him now more than ever, and she was confident that he would have no choice but to reply this time. She was frightened that he had moved and wasn't receiving her mail but, of course, she had no way to know if this was the case. So, she did her best to get her message across without frightening him, trying to convey that this was good news. *Surely, he wouldn't want his child to be put in a children's home?* she reasoned. *Regardless of how he feels about me, he should be willing to look after it until I'm out.* Ella was happy to be pregnant; it made prison life a little easier too as most of the other inmates kept out of her way. Of course, there were moments of sadness when she thought about missing her child's first year of life, but she hoped that Seb would come and visit once it was born. In an ideal world, Ella hoped Seb would bond enough with the baby that he would want to try to make things work, for them to become a normal family, whatever that actually meant. The thought that he might want to keep the baby and not see her didn't enter her head. Neither had any doubts over who the father actually was, her recollection of the night with the darts players being hazy at best.

Ella re-read the letter, satisfied that it was reasonable. It explained clearly that she was expecting a child, that it was his, when it was due, and what she needed him to do, for the sake of their baby. She deliberately made no suggestion about any future relationship between the two of them, fearful that it would make him hesitant. From what she knew of him, Seb had been a good father, and she was certain that he would step up and take responsibility now. Ella inserted the letter into the envelope, along with an image from the ultrasound scan, and handed it to the guard. Inmates were forbidden to seal the envelopes themselves as all mail had to be vetted for any sensitive information. She felt hopeful as she sat on her bunk, confident that Seb would contact her soon. However, the confidence she felt during that time was in error; she would soon realize that not only was she not going to receive any reply to her letters, but she would not see Seb again, and she would not be getting her happy ending at any time soon.

With some hesitation, Seb opened his eyes and scanned the carpet for the coin. Relief flooded over him as he embraced the fresh start which awaited him, suddenly filling him with motivation. It struck him as odd that the flip of a coin would have this effect, but it had. If the coin had landed on the other side, he had

The Broken Doll: Book One

been prepared to end things, but he was extremely grateful that this had not been the case. Reaching his limit with the life he was living, and knowing full well that something had to change, now spurred him on to make that change, fully accepting this was something he had to do for himself, alone. He frantically moved through the house, turning on lights, trying to put a plan together. It had to be now; he had to make arrangements immediately. The priorities, so far as he could tell, were what to do with the house and, in direct relation to this, his financial situation.

"Seb?" Natasha asked, as she picked up the phone.

"Hi, sorry, need to talk to you."

"It's fine," she replied, sounding friendly enough.

"I'm going to go away for a bit, haven't really figured it all out, but we need to talk about the house. I don't know what you want me to do with it?"

"Away where? Why?"

"I'm lost here on my own," Seb began, hearing Natasha sigh as though he were about to start begging her for some kind of reconciliation. "Work is slow. I'm bored more than anything. I need to do this, for me. A fresh start somewhere."

Natasha understood and, despite all that he had done, she did not wish for Seb to be miserable. He had lost his family already. So, after a fairly amicable conversation, the two of them made a decision to rent out their home, thereby providing an income for them both as well as maintaining somewhere for either of them to return to, should the need arise. Natasha offered to make the arrangements with a letting agency and to let Seb know how much he would be getting and when. It was decided that Natasha should take the maintenance payments from the rental profit and just transfer him the rest each month, giving him a little to live on. Seb liked this arrangement as he no longer felt ashamed that he could not make full payments towards the care of his children. He planned to travel about, taking temporary jobs to keep him fed and with a roof over him. The idea sounded fantastic at the time, roaming freely until something, somewhere, made him want to stay longer. *If I'm destined to be on my own, then I may as well try to make it an adventure,* he decided.

Fearful that he would talk himself out of it, or some change in his circumstances would occur and scupper his plans, Seb decided that he would leave the following day. He struggled to get to sleep that night, excited about the morning, like a child on Christmas Eve. He had no idea where he would go or what to do with everything in his house. He didn't have very much money. Even so, it would be an adventure, at least, and there was nothing to stay there for.

Most of the items from the house had gone with Natasha and so, when morning came, Seb got showered and arranged a storage facility for the belongings that he did not wish to take with him. The bigger items, such as the bed, the Chesterfield that he had grown strangely attached to, white goods, and so on, he left for use by the new tenants when they arrived. He had hoped that this would make the property more appealing, as well as saving him a job. Storage was quite expensive but there weren't any other options available that quickly, so he decided that it would be something to look at again if money became an issue later. Once he had deposited as much as he could in the storage room, Seb called one of his friends to let him know that he was going away for a while and would be selling his car. In exchange for a small percentage of the sale price, his friend agreed to deal with any potential buyers and transfer Seb the money once it sold.

All set! Seb told himself, as he sat in his kitchen for the last time, a black hold all by his feet. He had no intention of returning, he knew that, and therefore, had not changed address with anyone. He fought back tears that started to form as he chose a couple of photographs to take with him, accepting that he may well not see his children for a painfully long time. He had cancelled all payments from his account, intending to bail out on clearing off the credit cards he had, but first there was one more transaction to put through. Taking the card with most available funds, Seb searched the comparison sites for flights leaving London Gatwick that evening, with no preference on the destination. Seb found some genuine bargains, with one-way tickets being much lower in price than he had expected. He opted for Faro, one outbound flight for under forty pounds leaving in four hours' time, all booked. From there he could travel about, he thought. He knew little about obtaining visas and had presumed that, so long as he didn't remain in one destination for too long, and stayed within Europe, it would not become an issue. Seb used his credit card again to pay for the train ticket to the airport and then grabbed his bag and walked out of the front door, pushing his keys through the letterbox. *No going back now.* As he turned towards the street, the postwoman tried to stuff a pile of envelopes in his hand. Recognizing the top one as being from the prison, he directed the letters through the front door, not wanting to know what any of them said. *Wrong address,* he thought. *There is no Mr. Briggs here.* When he got to town, he, rather craftily, chose to withdraw the available funds from all three credit cards and exchange them for Euros. It wasn't a huge amount, but it would see him through the first few weeks, by which point he should, hopefully, have had the money from selling his car and at least one of the rental payments may have come in. Everything seemed to be going smoothly, and Seb couldn't stop smiling as he sipped his coffee on the train, on his way to a new life in the sunshine, with no idea of the chain of events he was about to set in motion.

The Broken Doll: Book One

THE END

The Broken Doll Book 2: Shattered Pieces

ONE

It wasn't really like being in another country; more like a sunnier version of some town in northern England. There were just as many English ex-pats on the Algarve as there were actual Portuguese, if not more. What the area lacked in authenticity, it made up for with an average daily temperature much higher than he had been used to; grey skies now a rarity rather than the norm. Six weeks had passed since Sebastian had arrived in Portugal, his worldly goods amounting to one large backpack and a few hundred euros that he had withdrawn from his credit cards before binning them. The first few weeks were a great adventure; much as he had hoped for. He spent days at the beach, wandered around various towns, hopping on and off buses without any plan as to where he would end up. On particularly warm evenings, he had slept on the beach, but this had only been on a couple of occasions, conscious that he did not want to become some kind of hobo and accepting that there was a risk of this happening.

Seb had moved around continuously, staying in various B&Bs along the coast (of which there were plenty, with varying degrees of comfort). He had not stayed in one town for more than four nights and, perhaps due to the laid-back feel of being somewhere full of holiday-makers and sunshine, he had not been remotely interested in finding any work. A night's accommodation was rarely more than twenty euros, and food and drinks were cheap enough, as was travel. He had got by for over two weeks on the money he had brought with him, feeding himself from supermarkets rather than eating out, drinking a lot of inexpensive, local wine. By some remarkable good fortune, it was on the day he was down to his last couple of notes, possibly enough for a bed for one more night, that he received the news that his car had sold. A friend of his had been dealing with the sale and, at the moment of having the customer face to face, he had had to reduce the price a little without talking to Seb. It was slightly disappointing, but at his current rate of spending, he expected that the funds would see him through for the next two months. *I'll give it another month and then start looking for work,* he thought, trying to decide whether to travel north, further into Portugal, or to head east and work his way across southern Spain.

Travelling through a number of countries held much more appeal to Seb, certainly making the adventure sound grander if he was ever to return home, and so he spent the next few weeks crossing into Spain and working his way along the south coast. It seemed warmer still as he took several buses through the tourist towns that dotted the Spanish coastline. The days had begun blurring into one, consisting of a look around whichever town or village he had slept in the night before, a bit of lunch, and as long a bus journey as he could take before getting off and finding another bed to sleep in. He rarely spoke to anyone, preferring to not have to explain what he was doing there, as he did not really know himself. Ultimately, he was enjoying the adventure but there was still a feeling of incompleteness, as if it was going to have to end soon, and reality would come back to hit him hard.

Natasha had not been happy about him leaving the country, and Seb had the impression that she was worried about him. It wasn't exactly out of character for him to be spontaneous, but this had all the marks of someone running away or suffering a mid-life crisis. Or, most likely, both. All he had told her was that he was going to travel about for a bit and to put their house up for rent. The estate agent whom Natasha had employed to deal with the house only just found suitable tenants, so there was no income from that yet. As soon as the money from the sale of his car had come through, Seb had sent some to Natasha to cover his maintenance payments for their three children. The idea had been for it to be taken directly out of the money they would make from the tenants, and this was money that Seb, perhaps foolishly, had assumed would have started coming in sooner. Ironically, he had more contact with his children now that he was fifteen hundred miles away. After their separation, Seb was due to have monthly visits with the children but these soon faded out as they began to make other plans and lose interest in seeing their father. This may, as far as Seb could determine, have been a result of his replacement in their lives by Martin, Natasha's new partner. The children really liked him, and he could throw money at them to keep them on side while he worked his charms on Seb's wife. And that is what she is, to this day, neither of them having filed for divorce.

Seb had contact with the children weekly now via video calls and would find an Internet cafe each Friday to contact them. They seemed far more willing to talk to him than they had in a while, showing an interest in their father's travels, seeming a little jealous they had not been able to go with him. This had taken place each week since he had arrived and, after talking with the children for a while, Natasha would provide him with an update on their schooling, clubs they attended, and so on. She never hurried the children, allowing them as long as they wanted to speak to Seb. However, this time, whilst sat in a rather dingy cafe in Malaga, things felt different. Seb had been talking for less than ten minutes when Natasha ushered the children from their living room, taking a seat opposite her laptop.

"Is everything OK?" Seb asked her, sensing that something was definitely amiss.

"I think the estate agents have started taking payments. The tenants sound nice; a young family."

The Broken Doll: Book One

"That's great," Seb replied, relieved that there would be some money coming in but still waiting for Natasha to say what she really wanted.

"I went by the house, just to check it over. There have been more letters from the prison, quite a lot more actually. I saw you hadn't been opening them, just sticking them in that box."

"I didn't want to read them; I told you I didn't want anything to do with her."

"I opened the last one, sorry; I just wanted to know who to write to so I could let her know that you'd moved away. I don't want prison letters to keep turning up for the new tenants to see," Natasha explained.

"OK," Seb said, dreading to think what the letter had said. However, he was pleased that Natasha could see that he hadn't been bothering to open them.

"Do you have an address there that I can send them to? The one I opened didn't make a lot of sense, so I opened a few more. You should read them. It's important." Natasha looked upset, her eyes welling up.

"I'm moving around every day pretty much, there isn't anywhere to send them really. Why? What did they say?"

Seb and Natasha talked for almost another hour. They were both emotional with the news, frightened a little, unsure of what it would mean for them and what was left of their family. Seb's initial reaction to the news was that it was a lie; being pregnant would be far too convenient for Ella. Nevertheless, there was a scan picture and, above the alien-like image of the foetus, Ella's name and date of birth.

"You'll have to get a paternity test," Natasha pointed out. "After all, it could be anyone's. Please tell me you had the sense to take precautions with her?" Seb thought back to that night with Ella, now months behind him. He'd been drunk. It had been a lust-filled

The Broken Doll: Book One

frenzy and although he had thought of it at the time, he never got as far as using any method of contraception.

"It could be mine, in theory. But like you said, it could be anyone's," Seb told her, fairly certain that Ella had not had time for anyone else during their nightmarish relationship, if it could even be called that.

"You know you have to come back, right?" Natasha pointed out. "I know you don't want anything to do with her, and I most certainly don't want her involved with my children, even if that thing ends up being their half whatever. But you need to know for sure, and it's got to be best to come and deal with it whilst she's still locked up." She had a good point, she usually did, and Seb told her that he would think it over. Even if he chose to ignore the situation, once Ella was released, she could start making trouble again. If they were to keep tenants in the house, then they couldn't risk a crazy lady coming by to smash windows and shout 'rapist'.

"Are you about tomorrow? Same kind of time. I'll call you back and let you know what I want to do," Seb told her, trying to buy some time, utterly confused about what action he should take. It appeared as though his days of wandering about in the sun had been cut short, or at least put on hold temporarily. From his own point of view, he would have opted to stay where he was, far away from Ella. He didn't care in the slightest what Ella wanted and, as much as he struggled to admit it, he didn't particularly care about his unborn child. He did, however, care about the effect this could have on Natasha and his other children if Ella was to track them down. He had caused so much harm and upset to the people he cared the most for that he had to make amends if he could, and at least try to prevent any further heartache for them. Only he could deal with this new nightmare and, after two bottles of Spanish chardonnay, he returned to the Internet cafe to book a flight home.

Ella hated prison. Of course, it was not supposed to be a pleasant experience, but she had plans when she had confessed. Seb was supposed to be locked up as well, away from his wife. In a way, it may have been better that he wasn't incarcerated as they had a baby to think about and someone would need to care for it as Ella would miss the first year or so. However, he did not write to her. She had no way of knowing if her letters were reaching him, if he had moved, if he was back together living with that bitch wife of his. She often thought about him having moved to some lovely country house with his wife, happily reunited, forgetting all about what they had done. If this was the case, it would be hard to track him down and the more she thought about this, the angrier she became. The most recent letters had become more aggressive, and she regretted sending them, but he had to accept some responsibility for his child. Ella's moods became worse, a combination of hormonal fluctuations and the lack of correspondence from Seb. Once the prison had learned of her pregnancy, Ella had been moved to her own room for safety and increased privacy. Although the move had made her lonelier, it had really been quite fortunate as she began to struggle to control her anger and was best left alone. The only way that she could qualify for early release was through good behaviour and, with no one to fight with, there had been no opportunity to misbehave. Nevertheless, the anger had to be released somehow and, with a lack of any dangerous implements, she had to make do with the ballpoint pen which she used to write letters.

The last two or three weeks were the hardest, pregnancy making her uncomfortable, loneliness and rejection taking its toll. Cutting herself used to help; the pen was certainly not mightier than the sword, or kitchen knife. In moments when she felt herself teetering too close to the edge, she would jab at her upper thigh with the pen in rapid succession, as hard as she could bear. The wounds hardly ever bled, causing more bruising and redness than anything else. Eventually, the marks had been spotted by the nursing staff during a routine check-up, and they had offered her counselling, which she had declined. Prisons take self-injuring very seriously, not wanting the backlash of a dead inmate, and so this fairly minor act then led Ella to be placed on suicide watch. She didn't care about this but did very much care about no longer being trusted with a pen. The pen had been her outlet, both in the harm she caused herself, and in being able to write things down. When this was taken from her, a dark cloud of hopelessness overwhelmed her, and she snapped. Two hours after having the pen removed, Ella was restrained to a bed in the infirmary. A rage had enveloped her, and unable to control her actions, she had begun hitting her head against the wall of her cell. If she hadn't been on suicide watch, then this may have been her last moments. After three hard strikes, her forehead starting to bruise, two guards had grabbed an arm each and pulled her to the centre of the room. Ella fought wildly, not wanting to go on without hearing from Seb, the future being too uncertain to dare think about.

The next few seconds were hazy for all concerned, but Ella had sunk her teeth into the guard who held her right arm. As her arm was released, she swung for the other guard, catching him unawares. As both guards reached out to regain their grip on Ella, she stumbled, falling forward towards the metal corner of her bed. There was a gut-wrenching crunch as her forehead, already bruised, came into contact with the metal. The force of the blow was enough split the skin deeply, rendering her unconscious. Thankfully, for the sake of the baby at least, Ella's head had taken the entire impact, and she barely bumped the part of her which carried new life. Once the guards had radioed through to the medical staff, Ella was quickly taken to a ward where they examined her and the baby determining that it was nothing a few stitches wouldn't take care of. The same number of stitches, in fact, that the guard required for his freshly bitten hand.

The prison warden had been to visit Ella the day after she was admitted into the infirmary, concerned about her safety as well as, more pressingly, the reputation of the facility. The woman was clearly unstable and, even without any potentially dangerous implements to hand and the added benefit of a guard keeping watch twenty-four seven, if she genuinely wanted to harm herself or the baby, then she would find a way. He had gone over Ella's file before visiting her, reading the transcripts from her court hearing. There were concerns raised at the time about her stability; possible questions over her grasp of reality. Nevertheless, as so often happened without any further evaluation taking place, she had been thrown into a regular prison as she would be less of a financial burden than if she had been institutionalized.

Over the next few days, and whilst under a degree of sedation, Ella met with a psychiatrist. This was not something that Ella wanted, and hence she rarely spoke. Her sessions with Dr Eaves were therefore largely one-sided, but he was a professional and well-practiced at 'reading between the lines'. He also happened to be under an unwelcome amount of pressure from the warden who wanted this 'disaster waiting to happen', as he'd once referred to Ella, out of his prison as soon as possible. It was decided fairly quickly, without any dispute from the experts or Ella herself, that she should leave prison and be admitted to an institute. The length of her stay would be determined once she had been properly assessed but, from what she could understand, as long as she appeared sane and cut out all the self-harming, it could mean being free a lot earlier than expected.

After a total of four days in the infirmary, Ella was escorted out of the prison gates to a white van. It was a little beat up on the outside, the prison logo fading from sun exposure. Two guards sat up front while she was placed in the back, handcuffed but reasonably comfortable. Everyone at the prison had treated her much more humanely since the pregnancy had been confirmed, and Ella was aware that her situation could be vastly different if she had remained on the open block with the other women. The journey was short, only a little over thirty minutes, and she was unloaded from the van by two unfamiliar male faces. They were not dressed like prison guards but more like medical staff. The taller of the two men did not speak as he led her towards the main entrance of the Marlow Centre for processing. The other man was the complete opposite, chatting non-stop, asking her about her journey, commenting on the weather, asking how the pregnancy was treating her. Ella did not answer anything the man said, managing only a smile. He seemed pleasant, and she liked the sound of his voice; it made her feel safe and that, perhaps, her new home may not be too bad.

Concentrate on being sane, she told herself as they made their way to the reception desk inside the clinical entrance hall. Now Ella did not consider herself to be anything other than sane, and this was the dilemma that she was stuck with. She was aware that some of her behaviours had been enough to raise concerns, but she dismissed them as a result of feeling particularly low. *Everyone goes through bad times,* she thought. *I just need to appear happier and not hurt myself. If there's a chance of getting released early, maybe even in time to have the baby, then I'll be able to find out why Seb hasn't written to me.* Ella was fairly confident that she could pull this off; after all, she wasn't hearing voices or going on about aliens or government conspiracies, so how mad could she really be?

The Broken Doll: Book One

The Marlow Centre was actually quite nice and, still handcuffed, Ella was given a brief tour of the necessary areas. There was a communal room, along with a large security presence, which featured a television and some board games. It reminded her of an old people's home in appearance; the cosy furnishings in contrast to the minimalist design of the hallways and reception area. There was a canteen area, very similar to the one at the prison, and the chatty guard went on to explain to her that she would be eating in her room to begin with, until she has been assessed.

"We can't let just any old crazy person mix with the others until we know you won't hurt anybody," he told her with a wink, an attempt at humour Ella assumed. Once they had seen the medical room, the ladies shower room, and the offices in which she would have her sessions, Ella was shown to her room.

"Not a padded cell?" Ella asked her escorts, rather cheerfully.

"You have to work up to that," she was told. "We call the padded rooms the luxury suites. You have to do something pretty nuts to get ones of those!" The room looked almost identical to her cell at the prison, only more nicely decorated. It contained the regulation bed, toilet, and hand basin; all in white. The walls, floor, and ceiling were white too. Everything was spotless, as one would expect from a medical facility.

"What do I do now?" Ella asked, as the tall, silent guard removed her handcuffs. "Can I get a book? Or a pen and paper?"

"Sorry, you can't have anything just yet. You'll need an initial assessment first. You'll just have to wait, and hopefully you'll get seen today." With that, the door closed, and Ella lay on the bed, her head sore from the cut and bruising still, closed her eyes, and focused on the bizarre feeling of the new life moving around inside of her.

The Broken Doll: Book One

THE END

ALSO FROM THE AUTHOR

Collection I: Embrace the Darkness & Other Stories

Step into the mind of the unstable, where nightmares become reality and reality is not always as it seems. Embrace the Darkness is a collection of six terrifying tales, exploring the darker side of human nature and the blurred line between dreams and actuality.

Collection II: Tunnels & Other Stories

From the author of Embrace the Darkness, Tunnels takes you on six terrifying journeys full of terror and suspense. Join a group of ghost-hunters, dare to visit the Monroe house on Halloween, peek inside the marble box, and feel the fear as you meet the creatures of the night.

Collection III: The Artist & Other Stories

The nightmares continue in this third instalment of short horrors from P.J. Blakey-Novis. The Artist and Other Stories contains a terrifying mix of serial killers, sirens, ghosts, claustrophobia, supernatural powers, and revenge guaranteed to get your heart racing and set your nerves on edge.

Collection IV: Karma & Other Stories

Karma & Other Stories is a collection of six terrifying stories, with tales of vengeance, the occult, a deadly competition, a weekend trip which turns violent, witchcraft, and things which go bump in the night. These short stories pack a punch, with endings that will haunt your dreams.

Short Horror Stories Collections I - III: A Box Set

Available in e-book and paperback, Short Horror Stories contains all 18 stories from Embrace the Darkness, Tunnels, and The Artist.

Four: A Novella

Four friends spend a night away camping in the English countryside, each taking a turn to tell a horror story that will terrify the others. But the group soon discover that there is more to be afraid of than just some campfire tales, and that no one is as innocent as they seem.

The Broken Doll: Book One

In a small town in southern England, a chance encounter triggers a catastrophic series of events from which no one will emerge unchanged. When Sebastian Briggs meets Ella, she needs his help. The type of help required, however, is far from what he had expected, dragging him down a path of lust and violence. As a married father of three, Sebastian must fight between his loyalty to his family and the desire he feels for another woman, a woman full of secrets and with sinister intentions. What begins as a simple conversation between two strangers soon escalates beyond any expectations, tearing apart Sebastian's home life, and leaving death in its wake. The debut novel from P.J. Blakey-Novis is a fast-paced tale, full of twists, crime, and steamy passion.

The Broken Doll Book Two: Shattered Pieces

The Broken Doll: Book One

After trying to outrun his problems, Sebastian Briggs is pulled back to his home town to confront his past, with devastating consequences. Having to deal with his estranged wife, and the unstable woman who tore his life apart, Seb discovers that he is now a wanted man, the net quickly closing in with the threat of violence around every corner. Shattered Pieces is the nail-biting follow-up to The Broken Doll, and the second book in the Broken Doll Trilogy.

Printed in Poland
by Amazon Fulfillment
Poland Sp. z o.o., Wrocław